Praise for

Sense of Touch

"An enchanting historical romance about a young woman who is determined to marry her one true love, despite the many obstacles in her path. The heroine's quest for self-determination defies the rigid social structure of Medieval Europe as it gives way to the Renaissance. Set in the court of Anne of Brittany, we also learn much about the woman who was twice Queen consort of France and her struggle to produce a living heir for the throne . . . Well-paced with period detail."

—*The Westchester Guardian*

"Readers who love their romantic fiction intertwined with real-life figures from history will find *Sense of Touch* a compelling read. The touching love story gives an interested glimpse into court life in France in the late 15th century. The fictional heroine is well drawn and a formidable counterpart to Anne of Brittany."

—*RT*

"An exquisitely written piece that eloquently describes Queen Anne as the gracious, kind, yet shrewd monarch that she is, a woman before her time."

—*InD'tale Magazine*

"*The Horse Whisperer* meets costume drama based on true events. Rozsa Gaston weaves fact and fiction, made-up characters and historical figures as effortlessly as the artist of the unicorn tapestry she describes in *Sense of Touch*."

—Hilde van den Bergh, author of *Hemmahoshilde Blog*

ALSO BY ROZSA GASTON

Paris Adieu: Part I of The Ava Series
Black is Not a Color: Part II of The Ava Series
Budapest Romance
Running from Love
Dog Sitters
Lyric

Sense of Touch

LOVE AND DUTY AT ANNE OF BRITTANY'S COURT

ROZSA GASTON

Renaissance Editions

New York

Cover painting of Anne of Brittany by Jean Bourdichon, c.1503,
from *The Grandes Heures of Anne of Brittany*, courtesy of Bibliothèque
Nationale de France, Paris

Back cover photo by Rozsa Gaston of 15th century tapestry design,
courtesy of METRAX-CRAYE, Belgium

Back cover and interior images of coat of arms of Anne of Brittany,
courtesy of wikipedia.org

Published by

Renaissance Editions
New York
www.renaissanceeditions.com

Printed in the United States of America

Library of Congress Control Number: 2016901252

ISBN-13: 978-0-9847-9062-3 (pbk)

ISBN-10: 0-9847-9062-4 (pbk)

ISBN-13: 978-0-9847-9063-0 (ebook)

ISBN-10: 0-9847-9063-2 (ebook)

CONTENTS

PART I: 1497-1498

PART II: 1499-1500

She is the spectacle of us; new tunes of joy and a mighty love

For Rachel and Celeste
who touch my heart

and for Anne of Brittany
may you rest in heaven, your babes at your side

15th century tapestry design, courtesy METRAX-CRAYE, Belgium

Author's Note

Fiction

Nicole St. Sylvain serves at the court of Anne of Brittany, Queen of France, in 1497, at age fifteen. Working with horse trainer Philippe de Bois to heal the queen's stallion, she shows an aptitude for diagnosing horses' ailments through her sense of touch. Soon she has fallen in love, but not with the man her father has chosen for her. Duty pulls Nicole and Philippe in different directions and Nicole becomes a wife, mother, then widow while immersing herself in the healing arts. When Anne of Brittany begs her to save her infant daughter, Nicole works alongside a physician from the South whose reputation for healing began with his work with horses. Will Nicole succeed in saving the queen's only child? And if she does, will the queen reward her with the greatest desire of her heart—marriage to the only man she has ever loved?

Anne of Brittany inherited the Duchy of Brittany at age eleven, upon her father's death in 1488. Three years later, she married Charles VIII and became Queen consort of France. Instrumental in introducing new techniques of architecture and craftsmanship from Milan to France, Anne of Brittany ushered in the Italian Renaissance to France. By age twenty-one, she had buried her husband and all four of her children. Within nine months, she became wife of the new king, Louis XII. Pregnant fourteen times, seven times by each king, she raised two children to adulthood. Both were daughters.

Anne of Brittany by Jean Bourdichon, c. 1503, courtesy gallica.bnf.fr

She is known as the first female ruler of France to bring together young women of noble birth at court, where she educated and trained them, then arranged appropriate marriage matches. A ruler of influence, refinement, and resources, she rose above personal loss with dignity and grace, while espousing the cause of women's advancement. Her story is for women everywhere.

The coat of arms of Anne of Brittany was devised of two parts: one representing the fleur-de-lis arms of the French crown; the second representing the ermine tails arms of the Duchy of Brittany, courtesy of wikipedia.org

PART I

1497-1498

CHAPTER ONE

The Court of Anne of Brittany

"What do men know of what we endure?" Nicole raged as she hurried down the hallway from the queen's bedchamber. Better to be angry than sad. The latest was beyond unbearable.

She slipped into the outer room of the king's quarters, catching the eye of Hubert de St. Bonnet, the king's head chamber valet. Quickly she shook her head and glanced away.

He would understand. Silence spoke volumes. It always did at these moments.

Hubert hurried to Charles VIII at the far end of the room. Nicole watched as the men conferred, their backs to her. By the time her monarch turned to her she told herself he would be ready to receive whatever fortune had to deliver.

"The queen?"

"Fine, Sire. She is resting." Nicole couldn't bear to go on.

"And the dauphin Francis?" King Charles' posture held erect. His fourth son had been born three hours earlier. He had briefly seen him and given him the name Francis for his wife's father, Francis II, Duke of Brittany.

Nicole opened her mouth but nothing came out. The thought came to her that if she didn't say the words, they wouldn't be true. Finally, she spoke.

"The doctors would like a word with you if you can come."

"Does my son live?" the king thundered.

Perhaps he was less ready for the answer than she had thought. He had had plenty of practice receiving similar news in times past, but who could be prepared to hear it yet again?

"He—I cannot say, Sire. The doctor has asked only that you come," Nicole stammered. Better to let those more senior than she deliver the blow.

A tinge of gray passed over the young king's face before he turned from Nicole to his valet. At the age of twenty-seven he had already sired four sons and two daughters. All rested under the Earth save the one who had just arrived.

Hubert de St. Bonnet nodded, almost imperceptibly. "I'm sure they are doing everything they can for—"

"Silence!" The king smashed both hands down on the wood table next to him. Then he overturned it. Courtiers scattered out of the way, the youngest running toward Nicole.

"Go now. The king will come when he is—when he is ready," he whispered, giving her a small push toward the door. The contact was comforting.

"Of course." She bowed her head but looked up through her eyelashes. For the briefest moment before Charles covered his long angular face with one large hand, she saw abject anguish there, a look of misery that made her heart drop. No such expression should cross the face of a man so hale, so fit and full of life as her monarch.

She backed out of the room, then turned and ran down the hallway to the queen's rooms. She could only imagine how the queen felt if the king's grief was that evident. Pray God Anne of Brittany was asleep, drugged with the sleeping draught the doctor had been preparing when Nicole had left. What comfort would the queen have when she woke up and found no small warm being snuggling at her side?

Oh God, how could You be so cruel? Nicole crossed herself.

Who knew what was in the mind of the Master Creator? What point for a woman to hope, to suffer, then finally to labor in unbearable pain at the end of the better part of a year only to deliver a child to die just hours after being born? No doubt God was a man with such faulty designs for womankind. She hoped one day she would get a chance to ask Him why he'd come up with this particular one. Catching herself, she crossed herself again and told herself to stop questioning what was beyond her ken.

⚜

The stallion had arrived the week before from one of the royal estates near Toulouse, in the region of Aquitaine in southwestern France. The queen was due to see the stunning new horse the king had gifted her with after the loss of their latest child. Six weeks had passed since the dauphin Francis had died and Anne of Brittany, Queen of France, had seemed on the road to recovery.

But over the past week the queen had been out of sorts. Nicole hoped the combination of the glorious early September weather and the arrival the day before of the groomsman from Agen who would train the new horse would put her in better spirits.

"I am not in the mood today. Someone must go in my place," the queen said, looking sourly toward the cluster of maids of honor at her side. Her expression looked out of place on her young, fair face. Heart-shaped, with a charmingly pointed chin and rosy cheeks, such a face seemed ill-suited to wear such a world-weary expression. Losing six children by the age of twenty had had its effect.

Nicole discreetly scrutinized her royal employer. Her broad forehead glowed with health despite the downward curve of her mouth. Either all was not well or perhaps it was the best of all possible news. Whichever it was, she couldn't bear sitting around trying to coax the queen out of her doldrums any longer.

"Your Majesty, I will go," Nicole and Marie de Volonté offered simultaneously. Nicole looked at the younger girl next to her. The newest addition to the queen's ladies, Marie's head of lush, dark brown curls was beginning to be matched by the promise of an equally lush figure. At age fourteen, she would soon be a candidate for the queen's considerable matchmaking skills, if she showed promise at court.

"Whoever." The queen raised a limp hand, and let it drop again in her lap. She breathed deeply, then leaned back in her chair, closing her eyes. One of her attending ladies stepped forward and held a vial of violet musk perfume under her delicately upturned nose. It was the queen's favorite scent.

Nicole's heart leapt. She had seen that bone-tired attitude before. She would wager it heralded the first weeks of a pregnancy; a time when no one dared breathe a word but when all of the court ladies included the queen in their evening prayers and petitioned God for the child to grasp hold of its mother's womb and refuse to let go until the full time had come to enter the world. Later, the even harder work of keeping the newborn infant alive would begin.

Only once had the queen succeeded: she had given birth to Charles Orland almost five years earlier. The following year, Charles Orland's brother Francis had been delivered prematurely, stillborn. Twice since, the queen had been pregnant, but delivered stillborn daughters. Then the worst had happened.

Just after his third birthday, the young dauphin, Charles Orland, had succumbed to measles. Almost nine months to the day after that terrible event, the queen had delivered a new dauphin, again named Charles. The boy lasted several weeks before a sudden high fever sent him back to Heaven. After that, the latest delivery; again a son, again named Francis like his stillborn brother. The new Francis lived a mere three hours.

Some wondered if perhaps the queen had begun breeding too early, producing Charles Orland just ten months after her marriage at age fourteen to the king. Most didn't though, since it was common practice for royals to marry as soon as they reached puberty; especially if the marriage was one to cement an alliance for reasons of state. In Anne's case, she had agreed to marry Charles VIII in order to retain her country's independence after the Franco-Breton war of 1491. The best way for her to secure her position was to produce a dauphin for France. If only one of them had lived.

Nicole glanced at Marie, who glanced back. She was feisty, much the way Nicole had been when she first came to court to serve as one of Queen Anne's maids of honor. Nicole was still feisty, but she had learned to hide it. Marie would learn, too. Nicole wasn't the only older colleague of the court who would be all too happy to coach Marie on the essential qualities of demureness, submissive obedience, and tender concern for the queen's needs above all.

If the younger girl was smart, she'd learn how to exhibit those qualities while getting exactly what she wanted at the same time. It was what all the most seasoned courtiers did, and it was the queen herself who set the example, beginning with her marriage to Charles VIII, King of France.

The king was away most of the time. At that moment, he was fighting a war in Milan. It had been a hardship for the queen not to have seen him for the past month, but perhaps another hardship had just begun that would happily distract her from her husband's absence and make a wonderful present with which to welcome him home, no matter the war's outcome. Most of his Milan campaigns had been undecided; everyone knew the king waged them as an excuse to soak up the latest architectural and artistic wonders there in order to introduce them in France.

"Clotilde, go get two marguerites from the garden. Make sure they're different sizes but with similar heads," Jeanne de Laval commanded. "Whoever draws the longest one will go." Madame de Laval was the queen's confidante and senior lady-in-waiting. She was wise, still beautiful at age thirty-six, and a mentor to them all, foremost among them the queen, who was now twenty.

Anne of Brittany, Queen of France, clapped her hands and rose, drawing Nicole's eyes to the tapestry of her coat of arms on the wall behind her. On one side, the gold fleur-de-lis of France against a blue background depicted the coat of arms of France; on the other, the coat of arms of the Duchy of Brittany was depicted, black ermine tails against a white background. Nicole wondered how the queen managed her loyalties to both at the same time. It couldn't be easy for her to weigh duty to France, as its queen, against her love for her homeland. As the Duchy's hereditary ruler, her interest was to maintain its independence. Yet the Kingdom of France was eager to acquire Brittany's rich lands for its own. From what Nicole had seen at court, being a monarch was a continual balancing act.

"Come, ladies, step up to the circle center and face each other." The queen indicated the beautiful inlaid marble circle set in the center of the Chateau d'Amboise's main receiving room. She had had it made based on a design the king had brought back with him from his last campaign in Milan. All the newest art came from there.

Nicole had heard one of the Milanese craftsmen tell the queen that some of the trim on the design for her new chapel could be done in gold leaf. She had immediately turned to the king and requested him to put in an order should the Genoese return with gold from his next voyage to the mysterious new lands to the west. He had promised the king and queen of Spain that much gold was there, but hadn't brought any back yet.

Nicole's heart swelled as she noted the queen's beautiful but wan face, her expression serene, unflappable. Distraction from whatever might or might not be happening deep inside her body was exactly what she needed. What mysteries women were, even to themselves, Nicole mused. No wonder men seemed afraid of them, at times. She herself was afraid of what lay ahead for her as wife and mother, with the queen's deliveries resulting in tragedy after tragedy. It was a miracle the queen kept on trying. But what choice did she have? It was her duty to produce an heir.

Marie de Volonté came forward, then Nicole. She smiled sweetly at the younger girl. She would win, she knew. Or so she told herself. It was a trick her father had taught her; to have courage and be bold, and always believe that luck was on one's side. It hadn't always been, but she liked believing it was likely to be. It worked more often than not for her father in business, although it hadn't worked so well in his home life.

Marie stared back, looking unsure.

"Here, darlings." Clotilde had wrapped the end of her surplice around the flower stems, to conceal them. She held out two pale yellow marguerites between the two girls. "Who will go first?"

"I will," Marie and Nicole chimed simultaneously.

"My lady?" Clotilde asked, turning her head to the queen.

"Let the little one go. She spoke up first, no?"

Nicole stayed strong inside as the younger girl smirked at her. She had been smirked at before as well as done her share of the smirking. She could withstand a little pressure. "Go ahead," she agreed.

A gracious and unflappable exterior was the name of the game at court. Intrigues and liaisons occurred only beneath the silky-smooth cover of diplomatic correctness. Not only did the courtiers' jobs depend on it, but so did their marriage prospects, and sometimes their lives. Nicole was a fast learner. Without a one-hundred-percent noble background like the other maids of honor, she had to be.

Marie reached out and touched one of the flowers.

As she did, Nicole nodded her head ever so slightly, as if to say, "good." It was a maneuver she had learned at cards to confuse her opponents.

The younger girl hesitated, looking at her uncertainly.

Nicole gave her a wide smile, as if to say, "Go ahead; take it." Inside she told herself she would win. She loved horses, the day was warm and bright, and she itched to be outside, to see and feel the sun on her face and hands and to smell the vital, healthy aroma of a thoroughbred. Would he be spirited? Would he be biddable? Excitement coursed through her at the thought of approaching the new stallion. He would be as unsure of his new surroundings as she had been when she first came to court.

Marie shifted her hand and took the second flower instead. Pulling it out, she smiled at the sight of its long stem.

"Now you," Clotilde instructed, turning to Nicole.

Nicole reached out and slowly pulled the second flower from Clotilde's hand. Its stem was long. Very long indeed. The murmur of the ladies grew louder as it became clear that Nicole's stem was longer than Marie's by over a thumb's length.

"You will go, then, Nicole," Jeanne de Laval said, laying a hand on her shoulder. "The trainer who has been sent should be at the stables already. Go change into your oldest surplice and cover your hair."

"Yes, Madame," she curtseyed.

She turned to Marie to ease the younger girl's disappointment. She knew what it was like not to win, although she never dwelt on it; except when thoughts of her mother stole over her in the night's deepest hours. At those moments, her body ached with sorrow; she had taken comfort from the sight and sound of Marie's sleeping form next to her. "I'm sorry you lost, Marie. You can go next time, all right?" she offered.

"Someone else will decide that. Not you," Jeanne de Laval corrected Nicole. Nevertheless, Marie's face brightened, and she looked less downcast as she inclined her head ever so slightly.

Thirty minutes later, Nicole was outside, on her way to the stables. Happy to be away from the hot-house atmosphere of the court, she breathed in the smell of late summer. All around her, nature was peaking, ripe for harvest. Yellow and orange flowers and fruit-laden trees lined both sides of the path from chateau to stable, a carnival of colors waving and nodding as Nicole skipped down the path. She passed the worksite of the queen's new garden, being laid out at the far end of the castle grounds. Workmen hammered and measured as the sounds of

Italian phrases and oaths rang through the air. The king had brought back a team of skilled workmen, under the direction of a master garden designer from Naples he had found on his last campaign.

The season was portentous for the queen. She had delivered Charles Orland in October. Then Charles, his brother, in September the year after Charles Orland had died. He had lived for three weeks. What heaviness must lie on her heart at this time for her, Nicole thought. She now knew that, no matter how promising the start of a pregnancy seemed, bringing forth a healthy living babe and keeping it alive was not guaranteed. Madame de Laval had told her it was frequently the worst pregnancies that produced the healthiest babies. Nicole prayed for a truly uncomfortable one for her queen so that she might give birth to another dauphin, or, for that matter, to any child who lived to adulthood, male or female.

Nicole crossed herself and prayed that her own time to become a wife and mother be delayed awhile longer while she enjoyed the fresh fruits of being fifteen, healthy, and at the queen's court. Already she had been granted one reprieve, when the suitor chosen for her the year before had unexpectedly died. She hadn't minded in the least. He had been ancient, over fifty years of age, her uncle had told her.

"Down, Petard, down. Stop him. Show him the carrot," a male voice rang out. Youthful authority resonated in its tones. Drawing closer, she spotted a magnificent black horse rear up on hind legs and whinny, then gallop away.

"Go on, brave one," she called to the horse. "Don't come back just for a carrot. He can do better than that."

"Who do you think you are?" the owner of the voice demanded, swinging around and scowling at her. As she watched, a parade of expressions chased themselves across the youth's face. He looked furious, and then his angry stare became simply a stare, and finally, a gaze she couldn't fathom.

"I am the queen's lady, sent down to help break in her horse. She was to come herself, but she is engaged, so she sent me instead," Nicole replied, looking down her nose at the youth.

"She sent you to do what?" The youth wiped his hands down the sides of his leggings.

"To help the man from Agen who is to break in the horse." The queen hadn't really specified "to help," but Nicole loved horses, and she wanted to be a part of taming this one.

"I am he." His gaze was level, his expression assessing, as his eyes locked onto her. Were they green? Blue? She couldn't tell.

"You? You are a boy." She drew herself up to her full height of just over five feet. Who was this youth? She had expected a man.

"I am nineteen, Mademoiselle." The youth blushed. "Do you take me for a boy?"

She studied him. Perhaps he wasn't a boy any longer. His voice was deep and his forearms broad, with downy hair on them.

"They sent you to break in this horse? I am surprised they sent someone so young," she said cheekily, although she was younger than the youth before her by four years.

Taking the counteroffensive to hide vulnerability was a game she had picked up at court. Her queen played it best of all. Nicole had seen the spark in the king's eye when the queen needed something from him. She had been at Charles VIII's mercy when they had first met, but she had soon enough turned around the situation so that it was the king who endeavored to give Anne whatever she desired when she fixed him with that certain glance that rattled his composure and set his loins on fire. Nicole didn't know exactly what that meant, but the moue of

Madame de Laval's mouth when she spoke of such things to the older ladies of the court informed Nicole that this was business between a lord and his lady, and if the lady had her wits about her, she made sure the transaction held an outcome favorable to her interests. Anne of Brittany was one such woman. Nicole wanted to be, too.

"It was the king's trainer who was supposed to come. But he had an accident and was unable to, so he sent me in his place."

"An accident? What happened?"

"Lady, it was nothing too serious. A horse he was training took it to mind to step on his toe. The horse was heavy and would not get off."

Nicole laughed then clapped a hand to her mouth. She could just see a large animal staring down a man trying to break it, with its hoof firmly upon the man's foot just to let him know it wouldn't be wearing a saddle anytime soon.

"I am sorry. I do not mean to laugh, but it sounds so funny."

"It was funny, my lady." The youth's grin took her by surprise. It was wide, stretching almost ear to ear, indicating perhaps a broad capacity to be amused. Or to be happy. "I was there when it happened. I had to push the horse off of Jeannot. He will be alright, but he is hobbling now. He will not forget his new mare anytime soon." The youth smoothed the side of one thigh with his hand, as if to protect himself from encroaching horses.

"Perhaps she was putting him in his place." She crossed her arms in front of her chest to let the youth know that she would be capable of such a job, should the occasion arise.

"Do you think so?" he replied, his eyes scanning her face. They were grayish green, she decided, like the moss under certain trees in a thick forest. The stable-hand had disappeared into the barn.

She blushed, ashamed of herself for staring at the youth so directly. He was handsome, with shaggy, blondish-brown hair that fell into his face.

"I am Philippe de Bois, Mademoiselle." He bowed slightly then swept his hand toward the paddock. "Why don't you sit in the staging area so Petard cannot hurt you?"

"I am Nicole St. Sylvain. And Petard will not hurt me. I want to get to know him. I will stand here and be fine." Ignoring his suggestion, she leaned against the fence and hooked one foot onto its lower rail. It felt good to move the muscles of her body under the golden September sun. Court life was constrained, behavior circumscribed by rules and protocol. There were times she craved the outdoors, the wind in her hair, the grass beneath her bare feet. So rarely did she get a chance to run and play the way she had as a child. She was fifteen already, but childhood years were not so far behind that they did not beckon still.

"Petard. Come here! Come meet the lady," Philippe called out to the stallion on the far side of the enclosed paddock. The horse snorted and dug the ground with both forefeet in response.

"Petard has a lively name. Is it apt?" she asked, referring to the explosive firecrackers that were used to breach doors or walls, mostly during sieges.

"Very. His hobby is to come at anyone who tries to tell him what to do."

"A sound policy. Sounds like your Jeannot's mare followed it. I wish the rest of us could do the same."

The queen, along with Nicole's father and uncle, had been looking for a suitable husband for her since the year earlier, when she had matured. After the first candidate had died, Nicole had been given a few months' reprieve. Now a second candidate loomed on the horizon, but she did not know any details. She shuddered, thinking of what might lay ahead for her, as surely as one season followed another.

The husband part wasn't so bad; it was the childbearing part that terrified her. What the queen had endured already as a young mother was more than Nicole could bear to imagine. Yet who was she to not follow Her Majesty's example into marriage and motherhood? The queen had invited her to court as a maid of honor in order to groom her for a suitable marriage to a man of rank. There was no way around her duty to serve and follow her, acquiescing to whatever choice of husband the queen approved for her.

She touched the indent at the base of her throat, noticing how intently the youth gazed upon her.

If she did manage to have children successfully, and keep them alive, she would feel so terribly for her queen, who had failed time and again. Her happiness would be at her sovereign's expense. That is, unless Anne of Brittany, Queen of France, managed to bear a child and keep it alive. Nicole would do whatever she could to resist embarking on marriage and motherhood until the woman she admired most had her own child to raise. If only there was some way she could help her to keep one—just one—alive.

She sidled closer to the beautiful black horse, but didn't attempt to attract its attention.

"Be careful, my lady. He does not take kindly to those who try to force him to do their will," Philippe warned.

"Then I will not." Did he take her for a man? She was grown enough to know that a woman's path to getting her way never involved force. Wit was more suitable.

"Excuse me?"

"I will not play into his hands. So to speak."

"Then what will you do?" The youth studied her curiously, whether because he truly sought her answer or simply liked what his eyes rested upon, she wasn't sure.

"The opposite of what he expects." Another technique she had learned at court. When in doubt, confuse the opposition. In this case, not just the horse, but the youth in front of her, too. The way his eye color changed but his expression didn't when he looked at her intrigued her. Her insides tumbled like acrobats warming up the crowd at a jousting tourney.

Philippe de Bois's eyebrows rose as his eyes widened in surprise. "I already tried the carrot. Will you try another food?"

"No, silly boy; food is what he expects. I'll give him food for his soul," she brashly remarked.

"A horse does not have a soul," he protested, his eyes now greenish-blue in the golden September sun.

"Who knows which of God's creatures have souls and which do not? Do you?" She tried to look haughty as she stared him down.

Philippe's gaze turned faraway, as he considered her question. "Not really. But it is what the church teaches."

"The church is created by men to serve men's idea of God. That tells you how limited it is, does it not?" Nicole tipped her chin and slit her eyes, the better to study the color of the youth's eyes without being obvious about it. Now they shone gray, almost transparent.

"I would not dare to say." As he spoke, his eyes lingered on her. A warm breeze lifted the edges of her headdress, matching the restlessness she felt inside.

"Do you think a creature as beautiful as this one lacks a soul?" Nicole pressed him.

"I do not know, my lady."

"So since we do not know, I will appeal to his ears," she declared.

"His ears?" Philippe studied her doubtfully.

"Ladaa Ladiii ladaa," Nicole began to sing. She hummed as if to herself, privately, neither making eye contact with the horse nor Philippe. She hummed as if she were one of the Earth's tiny creatures basking in the late summer sun. She hummed as if she were the speck of a hidden babe clinging to the side of the queen's womb.

Then, she began to walk slowly down the length of the fence, sliding the fingers of her left hand over the top of the rough-hewn railing as she went.

Petard stopped pawing the ground and pricked up his ears. She noticed immediately out of the corner of her eye, but didn't respond. Why should she? Petard was a male animal which would come to her sooner or later, as invariably as fall followed summer. It was simple. Since spring of the year before, she was no longer a girl. Nature had informed her, but also the glances of the men at court. She was a fully grown woman, a force of nature with which to be reckoned.

Moving her shoulders ever so slightly from side to side, she felt the warm sun bore into her shoulder blades. Just as Philippe's eyes were doing, she sensed.

"You've calmed him down, my lady," the youth remarked.

"Shhhh." She incorporated the "Shhhh" sound into her tune, singing a shushing sound until it became a whistle.

At the sound of the whistling noise, Petard took a few tentative steps in her direction.

Idly, she moved away and went over to the feed stall, where she bundled together a stack of hay and brought it back to the fence. She laid it gently on the ground and pushed it under the lower rail toward where the horse stood. At no time did she make eye contact with the stallion. Why should she? She had better things to do: enjoy the warmth of the morning sun on her skin and the knowledge that the half-man/half-boy's gaze was glued on her. It was power of some sort; power she had only recently acquired. She didn't quite know what to do with it, but she would learn. Perhaps this youth in front of her would help her figure out how to wield it.

Continuing on her way, she rounded the corner of the fence and trailed her hand along its top rail. By the time she had gotten to its end, Petard was at the hay pile, chewing her gift to him thoughtfully, ears still perked to hear her song.

"That is the way to do it, until we make friends," she sang, eyeing Philippe. The shadow of a beard dusted his jaw line; tightly coiled muscles under his leggings announced he was well on his way to manhood.

"And it is working," Philippe said, eyeing her back. His voice was low.

"And it cannot be rushed if you know what I mean," she continued in song form.

"It is hard not to rush when you are nineteen," Philippe admitted, sounding rueful.

"It is hard not to rush when you are fifteen, too," Nicole sang out.

The horse stopped eating and picked up his head to watch them. He appeared to be trying to figure out what they were saying. Nicole was trying to figure it out, too. Philippe de Bois seemed to be saying something to her without words, and, unable to stop herself, she was saying something back to him, equally wordlessly. As much as she had felt her power over the youth a moment before, she now felt herself being powerlessly drawn to him.

"My lady!" One of the houseboys ran down the path toward her. "My lady, you're needed at the keep."

"What is it? Is the queen alright?" Nicole cried, thinking immediately of her queen's possibly delicate condition.

"No. I mean, yes. Not that. It's Lady Jeanne. She said you must come back and change your clothes for something. Someone is coming; I forget who she said."

"Something? Someone? Are you daft?" she scoffed at the houseboy.

"I think it is a craftsman, my lady. The one who is to deliver designs for the tapestries the queen is having made. A courier came a short time ago and told us he is due midday."

"What business do I have with this?" Nicole asked crossly.

"Lady Jeanne says all the demoiselles are to gather in the main hall so the artist can choose who he will sketch for the designs. Whoever he picks will be the lady of the tapestry and will end up with a fine husband."

Behind her, Nicole heard Petard snort, as if with laughter. Whirling around, she addressed the horse.

"Shut your snorter, you brute. I will be back soon enough, and you will miss my songs in the meantime." Out of the corner of her eye, she saw Philippe de Bois stifle a laugh.

"Tell Lady Jeanne I will be there shortly. Go!" She waved the boy away with an imperious hand. Court life had taught her much. She could act docilely when the occasion required, and, when it didn't, she acted with authority. She was being trained to become a noblewoman, after all; her queen was her example. Once her father and uncle had succeeded in marrying her well, she would be noble in title and duty-bound to be in behavior as well. Until then, she had some time.

"Duty calls, my lady?" He looked at her slyly. This time his eyes flashed silver, mirroring the scattered clouds overhead, one now passing in front of the sun.

"I suppose it does." She didn't doubt she would be evaluated carefully for the role. Both her father and uncle were anxious to see her married well, soon. On her mother's side, Nicole had inherited noble blood, but her mother was dead and her father came from the merchant class. Michel St. Sylvain was intent on rising further as quickly as possible, most immediately through marriage of his daughter to a titled man well-allied to the king and queen.

"The life of a woman differs from the life of a man, does it not?" Philippe asked, his mobile mouth looking as mischievous as his eyes looked grave.

"But our lives are similar, in that we are both young, yet neither of us know how many more days we have, although it is likely we have fewer than we think," she countered. "Do you know that, too?"

"I know, and I do not care. Do you?"

"I know I care about living fully while I am alive." She wasn't sure why she said that, but the breeze lifted up the edges of her headpiece as if in agreement.

"I'd guess you do that well." Again, that broad smile; a merry slash across his handsome face.

"And you?" Cheeky youth.

"I care about doing a good job for the king's household so I can keep my position."

"And if the king were to switch you to the queen's court for awhile?' She wouldn't mind helping Philippe to continue training Petard, if he were to remain at Amboise.

"I would gladly go where the king places me."

"Ahh." A thin plan began to hatch in Nicole's mind, much like the tiny living being she hoped was hatching at that moment in the innermost chamber room of the queen.

"Will you come again when you are free?" Philippe looked uncertain, just a bit downcast.

"I might. As the queen bids, of course," she loftily replied. A shiver ran down her spine.

"I will let the stable manager know how well you calmed Petard," he mentioned as he stroked the horse's jet-black mane.

"I am not always so good at calming creatures," she confessed.

"No, I imagine you are better at rousing other types of creatures."

"Yes. I am," she agreed, then caught herself. What did he mean? Like rousing the ire of little Marie de Volonté? Or some other type of rousing? The downy hair on her arms stood up as she contemplated the unknown. "How would you know?"

"Only a guess, my lady," Philippe replied, his face inscrutable, as if he were holding back something, she knew not what.

"A curious one, then." Her head spun in confusion. She had no idea what was being said or how to respond. Best to exit quickly. "Goodbye!" she called then turned and ran lightly up the path toward the chateau. Behind her she heard Petard whinny in protest at her departure. Was it the late summer breeze that had tickled her as Philippe spoke or had it been the teasing words coming from the youth's mouth?

Feeling ten times lighter than she had on her way down to the stable-grounds, she vowed to return as soon as she could escape royal and household duties. Before she thought to stop herself, she turned one last time.

Philippe de Bois stood rooted to the ground, staring at her.

She giggled and fled up the path.

⚜

"We are traveling to Paris tomorrow. Go and prepare your things."

"Madame, how long are we staying?" Nicole twisted her hands before her. She had rarely ventured beyond the castle walls since arriving at the queen's court three years earlier.

"Several weeks, *ma chère*. Your uncle has arranged for you and a few others to have your likenesses sketched in preparation for the tapestries he is having made for the queen."

"Will Her Majesty accompany us?"

"No, my dear. She will stay here for now." Jeanne de Laval raised her eyebrows. "Perhaps if she feels well enough, she will accompany the king to Grenoble when he leaves for Milan, and then stay in Lyon for awhile."

"Paris, Madame! I have never been!"

"It is a big, dirty city. You must stay very close and not think to explore it," Jeanne de Laval scolded.

"I cannot wait!" Nicole's thoughts raced. She would see Paris . . . France's most glorious city, many said. The queen did not, but she had a horror of dirt. Exacting and orderly, noise, confusion, and bad smells did not appeal to her. She had enjoyed being crowned Queen of France in the basilica of St. Denis outside Paris, but had been relieved to return to Chateau d'Amboise to oversee the renovation plans on the king's childhood home that Charles VIII had begun to please his new bride.

Madame de Laval frowned. "I believe your father has arranged for you to meet someone there. You must pack your best gown."

"My favorite one? The dusty rose one?" Whoever this some-one was, she hoped he wouldn't be a doddering old man, like the last one had been. Fortunately he had doddered into his grave before the marriage contract had been fully hammered out. She shuddered, thinking of being in bed next to a body covered with wrinkly, paper-thin skin. It was loathsome to contemplate. She would make sure such a thing did not come to pass.

"No, *ma chère;* this is not about your favorites anymore. This is about your future. It is important to represent yourself and your family well. You will pack the blue one with the gold braiding and red insets."

"But that one is so uncomfortable!" Her formal gown was heavy, weighing her down when she wore it. She shifted from one foot to the other, remembering how light she had felt just moments earlier under the gaze of the shaggy-haired youth back at the stables.

"Get used to it. It will prepare you for married life." Madame de Laval motioned to the staircase. "Now, go and pack."

"Madame, if married life is so tedious, why should I desire it?" Nicole asked petulantly.

"There are hidden compensations." Madame de Laval's mouth gave a twitch as if some secret thought had just pulled at it from the inside.

Nicole's eyes widened. "What do you mean, Madame?"

"There is only one way to find out." Her eyes formed into narrow slits as she assessed her.

"Do you mean what goes on between a man and a woman?" Nicole's mind wandered back to the stable-yards and the broad shoulders of Philippe de Bois. Her insides contracted as she thought of their sturdy suppleness, their probable power. She had never noticed a youth's shoulders before.

"Shhh. Just know that married life is not altogether unpleasant." Madame de Laval had been widowed for several years. It was whispered at court that she was pursued by the much younger Duke d'Agincourt who came to Chateau d'Amboise every few months. It had been noted that Madame de Laval and the duke frequently rode horses together, disappearing for hours at a time whenever he visited.

"So that *is* what you mean!" Nicole cried.

"This is not a topic to speak of here and now." Madame de Laval's mouth formed itself into a prim line.

"Madame, just give me a sign that that was what you meant. A secret sign."

"Enough. You will do as I say." The older woman looked stern, but Nicole knew better. Madame de Laval had many sides to her, some of which perhaps only the Duke d'Agincourt was able to fully appreciate.

"Of course, Madame." Nicole curtsied then leaned toward Madame de Laval's beautiful, dignified face. "Just touch the key on the chain at your waist, and I will know you mean the private world of husband and wife," she whispered into the older woman's ear as she straightened herself up again.

"Cheeky girl, get upstairs and start packing. Now." Madame de Laval pointed imperiously to the stairway.

Nicole scuttled up the stairs, then paused at the top and looked back.

Madame de Laval gazed up at her, a small smile playing on her lips. Her right hand dangled at her side then slowly slid to the key that hung from the chain at her waist. As Nicole watched, the older woman closed her fingers firmly around it.

CHAPTER TWO

Negotiations

"Do not move your head, Mademoiselle. Please stay as you are," the artist ordered.

As Nicole tried to sit still for the man sketching a few paces away from her, the door to the room opened. Her father and Uncle Benoit entered with a third man, standing near the doorway.

Swiveling her head back to where it had been, she moved only her eyes to take in the men at the door. Her uncle and father framed the stranger, who wore traveling clothes and a hat with a crest she didn't recognize—a nobleman then. Knowing her father, no one less than a wealthy, titled candidate would be considered as a possible husband for her. Her father's family was ambitious, but not yet arrived at the social station to which they aspired. Michel and Benoit St. Sylvain had made considerable money in the cloth-weaving business, but they were merchants, lacking in titles. Nicole herself was a noblewoman in her own right, but only on her mother's side. Her beautiful and loving mother was no longer alive, unable to lobby for a good match on her daughter's behalf. Nicole's father and uncle had both married well; they intended for their children to do the same.

Swiveling her eyes back to the men, she saw the stranger with them glance at her.

Electricity streaked ran up her torso, closing her throat as the image of Philippe de Bois's arms, taut and slimly rippled with muscles above the elbows, flashed before her. Were the arms of all men much the same? Even if they were, there were other parts that were not; those were the parts that most interested her.

The brain, for example. She swayed the tiniest bit, saddened at the thought of not being able to explore further what might be in Philippe de Bois's brain. With his eyes changing color with every new thought that came to him, she imagined there was quite a lot in there she'd like to know about.

"Be still, Mademoiselle," the artist interjected sharply. "That is, if you can, just for a minute longer," he followed more gently as the three men in the corner stirred.

Nicole glanced toward them again. Was this the man now under discussion to be her husband? If so, did she have any say in the matter?

She knew the answer. Even the queen herself had had no say in her marriage to Charles VIII. All she had been able to influence was its outcome, which she had done masterfully at the tender age of fourteen. Not only had she succeeded in not losing control of Brittany, but in having the crown of Queen of France placed on her head within two months of her marriage to the king. Charles VIII had not been required by law to do so, but had crowned her

Queen consort of France with alacrity and pride. Why? Because, already, he loved her so. His captive bride Anne had turned the tables on him and captured his heart.

From late summer to the fall of 1491, Charles VIII and his army had laid siege to Rennes, Brittany's second most important city, after Anne's birthplace of Nantes. With the intent to annex Brittany to France, the siege had gone on for three months until the people of Rennes began to starve as the Treasury of Brittany emptied out.

At age fourteen, Anne was Duchess of Brittany; she had inherited the title from her father, Duke Francis II, who had died three years earlier. Anne had a small number of loyal Breton troops to defend the besieged city, to which she added mercenary troops.

But after a month, funds ran out with which to pay them and the mercenaries began to loot and misbehave. Faced with enemies both inside and outside the city walls, Anne of Brittany had no choice but to come to terms with her besieger.

The young king, camped on the outside of Rennes's city walls knew this as well as Anne did within. To soften her hard stance against him, he sent for his older French cousin, Louis, Duke d'Orléans, to come to Rennes to parlay with the duchess. Preferring not to humiliate the young, but unbowed and anything but humble, ruler of Brittany, Charles asked his cousin to find a way to come to terms that preserved the honor of both sides.

The twenty-one-year-old king had heard much about Anne of Brittany over the years. He had received diplomatic missives from her more than once categorically refusing to hand over her Breton lands to him, although it was evident that such a small country with a young girl at its head was going to have to ally itself, if not cede hegemony, to one of its larger neighbors, either France, Spain, England, or the Holy Roman Empire on France's eastern border.

Louis d'Orléans was only too happy to assist. Since siding with Anne's father, Duke Francis, against French troops that had invaded Brittany in the Battle of St. Aubin of July 1488, he had been imprisoned by the king's older sister and regent, Anne de Beaujeu, at a castle in Montils-les-Tours in France, three days' ride to the east of Rennes.

Overjoyed to be sprung from prison after three long years by the king himself, who was now of an age to take control of his own kingdom from his older sister, Louis entered the city gate of Rennes alone and unarmed to accomplish his delicate diplomatic mission. He had been a long-time admirer of the young duchess within, whom he had met when she was seven years of age and he twenty-two and married. Now, seven years later, Louis suggested to Anne a way out of her predicament that would transform her from captive to queen: marry Charles VIII of France. It was a brilliant idea, but only Anne could seal the deal by agreeing to it, then ensuring that Charles VIII was willing too. Both were already betrothed, a minor obstacle frequently overcome by royals when a more politically advantageous match arose. Louis d'Orléans remonstrated with Anne and her counselors for several days, until, finally, she agreed to meet with the young French king. Already she knew that marriage with no one less than a head of state or the son of a head of state was her future. She needed to see for herself whether this particular head of state would do.

It had been Anne herself who had noted the gleam in Charles's eyes at their first fateful meeting. With a savvy borne of three years of playing her Breton advisors against one another, in order to maintain her leadership over them all, she had quickly realized her powers of attraction over the not-terribly-handsome twenty-one-year-old monarch with an imposingly royal aquiline nose and short, squat stature. Anne was short, too; petite and graceful, with a limp she had kept secret from all but a handful in her royal Breton household. Endowed with beauty, brains, and courage, and an unusually thorough education, she agreed to begin negotiations to become Charles VIII's wife, not prisoner, ensuring that Brittany would be allied, but not annexed, to its larger, more powerful neighbor France, on favorable terms. There was no other way out.

With no sons, Anne's father, Francis II, Duke of Brittany, had raised his eldest daughter to rule. The Duchy of Brittany was not bound by Salic Law, as was the kingdom of France. Females could inherit in Brittany if the male line died out. In Anne's case, she was the eldest of two sisters; at age eleven she had inherited the Duchy of Brittany upon her father's death.

By the time Charles VIII laid siege to Rennes, Anne had ruled over Brittany for three years. She already thought like a statesman. Surrender of her beloved land to France was unthinkable to her. Fortunately, Charles VIII thought not only like a statesman but also like a man. Instead of being angered, he found himself impressed with Anne's refusal to hand over her city and her country to France. By the end of their first meeting, he had fallen for the regal and authoritative fourteen-year-old duchess, who offered herself in place of her country in order to save it.

Marriage terms had been hammered out, led by Louis d'Orléans, with a team of notaries and lawyers. They included the complete withdrawal of French troops from Breton soil, the succession of Brittany to whichever of the two outlived each other, and, if it were Anne, her subsequent remarriage to no one of less stature than the king, meaning another king. Interestingly, that king would be Louis d'Orléans himself, should he be free to marry, and if Anne and Charles produced no sons.

All these terms were brokered in a matter of days in utmost secrecy. Speed was of the essence, before word got out that Anne and Charles were both about to break their betrothal contracts: Anne to Maximilian of Austria, and Charles to Maximilian's daughter, Marguerite. Such a double insult to both father and daughter would enrage the emperor-elect to the Holy Roman

Empire. It would be talked about all over Europe with much shaking of heads and more than a few sniggers over the folly of Maximilian leaving his betrothed alone to defend her lands from invaders. Many would say he had gotten his just deserts.

After an all-night session of painstakingly preparing the marriage documents with their extensive stipulations, shortly after sunrise on December 6, 1491, Anne, Duchess of Brittany, and Charles VIII, King of France, were joined in marriage at the Castle of Langeais, a half-day's ride to the west of Amboise where Charles made his home.

It had not been a marriage of love, but soon it became one. Within weeks, Anne was pregnant. Charles Orland, heir to the throne of France, was born October 11, 1492, one day before the Genoese Christophe Colomb arrived in the mysterious new lands on the other side of the great ocean. Anne was young, but no one could say that she was naive. She was energetic, clever, and courageous; instead of allowing the king of France to capture one of Brittany's most important cities, she had saved her lands by capturing the heart of the king.

As Nicole pretended not to notice the man watching her from the doorway, the shadow of a black horse galloped across her heart, a youth with gray-green eyes riding on its back.

"Smile, please," the artist instructed her.

Nicole tried, but didn't succeed. How could she smile when her future was being decided at this very moment? Had Anne of Brittany smiled at Charles in that fateful first glance? Nicole doubted it. Anne had been born to rule, first as a duchess, then because of her skill in statesmanship and the careful handling of her own charms and beauty, as queen. A smile would not do to capture a man's heart. It was only after capturing it, with terms clearly defined, that a betrothed woman might venture a tiny smile; at most, perhaps a small show of affection, quickly withdrawn . . . if the man pleased her, that is.

It was important for the smile to disappear soon so a man might labor to restore it to his lady, Nicole mused. She had grown up in her father's household, her older, ambitious uncle a frequent presence. Men were born to strive, from what she had seen. Why not give them something to strive for?

"Like this, Mademoiselle." The artist stood alongside her now, taking her chin in his hands and turning it up a tad. He smiled faintly to show her what he meant.

She imitated him, feeling self-conscious.

Cocking his head, he studied her. "That isn't what I meant, but it will do," he finally said, then grunted.

It will more than do. This is what you get, so be happy with it. She was no ninny to be directed like a servant; especially in the presence of the man she might one day direct herself. Inside, her heart fell at the thought of it. She would so much more like to direct the likes of Philippe de Bois, with his taut young muscles and changeable eyes. Could she direct the colors of his eyes to change as she pleased?

She smiled at the thought . . . Gray for stormy moments, green for desire, then blue for reconciliation, whatever form that might take. A shiver ran up the back of her neck.

"Hmm. Yes. That will do nicely. Hold your position, Mademoiselle." The artist had gone back to his sketching board a few paces away.

Hold your orders, servant to my uncle. Yet they were all servants. Even the king and queen were servants to duty. The queen had yet to fulfill hers: to provide an heir. Still, Nicole felt like Petard, wanting to chafe and whinny under the saddle of her heavy gown, however gorgeous it might be. She could hardly wait to get back to the horse and see what progress Philippe was making with him. Her knees twitched as her mind wandered over the brownish-blond-haired youth with undecided eyes.

Then her heart sank. Would she be allowed to go to the stables once she was betrothed? And what about when she was married? Would she even have time?

The men in the doorway had begun to talk amongst themselves, too low for Nicole to hear. If ever a woman was on inspection, she was. Holding her chin in exactly the position the artist had indicated, she told herself to ignore them, especially the one in the middle.

Still, she couldn't help taking a peek. Out of the corner of her eye, she noted the man's long, angular face with deep vertical furrows down each of his cheeks. She couldn't make out the color of his eyes from across the room.

Focusing on her queen, she thought of how Anne must have held herself at that first meeting with Charles, her captor and future husband. The young duchess of Brittany had known how to play the cards she had been dealt. Nicole vowed she would do the same.

She stole another glance at the stranger at the door. He wasn't young, but neither was he horribly old, as the last one had been. His posture was erect, his height medium, with a medium to slim build. His face wasn't young and handsome like Philippe's, but it wasn't loathsome either. She wished she could get closer to see what kind of smell hung about him, but whatever it was, she had no choice in the matter. Perhaps it was better, since whatever scent he had would not be the bracingly fresh one of Philippe de Bois.

With a silent sigh, she willed her raging thoughts to be as still as her body was. Soon her life would change. She would comply with the changes, following the example of her queen, the woman she admired above all others.

The image of Madame de Laval came to her, her hand lightly touching the key at her waist. Perhaps there were pleasures to look forward to shortly. She hoped the man with whom she would one day share her marriage bed knew how to provide them. She stamped one foot, as if to blot out the image of Philippe that stubbornly refused to leave her head.

"That will be all for today, Mademoiselle," the sketch artist said. Relieved, Nicole turned to join her father and uncle and to catch a closer glimpse of the man with them.

But the doorway stood empty. She rushed toward it to find them. Instead, she bumped into Madame de Laval coming down the corridor.

"Madame, where is my father? Who was that man with him?" Nicole cried.

"Your father has just left with his guest, Monsieur de St. Bonnet. He said you did a very good job posing today."

"Who said that; my father or his guest?"

Madame de Laval cleared her throat. "You are too old sometimes, for someone so young. Do not rush your youth, *ma chère;* it flees from us all too soon as it is."

"So it was the guest. What did he say?" She tried to remember the features of the long-faced man but they blurred into generalities best described as old-ish and uninteresting. Instead, greenish-gray eyes flashed before her, along with a slashing, broad smile that lit up her heart.

"As I passed, I heard him say to your father that you had done a noble job posing and that the expression on your face that you wore before the artist corrected you had been far more interesting than the one he forced you to wear."

"Really?" Nicole felt confused. "Who is this man?"

"He is the cousin to Hubert de St. Bonnet, the king's close advisor, *ma petite.*"

"What does he do? Where is he from?" If he was from the family of one of the king's closest advisors, she knew her Uncle Benoit meant business. Uncle Benoit didn't choose his friends for good company alone. He was a man with a mission; one that her father shared. The mission was to get the St. Sylvain family onto the rolls of France's noble families. Nicole understood it well; it was a worthy goal, and one of which her mother also would have approved, had she lived. Sighing, she buttoned up her feelings inside. There was no escape, either within or without.

"You will find out all in good time," Madame de Laval told her. "Your father will dine with him this evening. You may ask him about him tomorrow."

"My lady, you know men do not say anything, just the bare bones. I want to know something about this man. What is his first name?" Nicole wished madly that her mother were still alive at that moment. She had died giving birth to Nicole's younger brother, who had followed their *chère maman* to Heaven a day later. The thought of that time made Nicole's blood turn to ice. She didn't know what she wanted out of life exactly, but she knew what she didn't want: neither to die in childbirth, nor for any child of hers to die.

There was only one way to ensure that didn't happen. Yet, the path of never bearing a child wasn't open to her; not if her father and uncle had their way. What more was she on this Earth than a pawn to advance the social standing of her family? And who was she to think she might be anything more?

Angrily, she pulled at the bejeweled neckline of her bodice. It was tight; she was uncomfortable. How in the world did the queen manage to dress in such cumbersome clothing every day, no matter how magnificent?

"Let your father talk with you first. Then, when whatever is to be decided is done, I will tell you what I know," Madame de Laval said.

"Madame—tell me this, then," Nicole put her hand on her arm and sought her eyes with her own.

"Yes, dear?" The older woman's eyes twinkled, despite her stern expression.

"Do I have a choice?"

"Yes. Your choice is to choose."

"But what if I don't?" She knew the answer already.

Madame de Laval shook her head gently. "Your father will decide for you." She straightened the bejeweled circlet on Nicole's head. "Think, *ma chère,*" she continued in a lower voice. "Did our queen have a choice? Did our king's cousin Duke Louis?"

Nicole remained silent a moment, trying to calm the raging waves of her rebellious will. She wasn't sure what she wanted, other than more time with Philippe de Bois; to train Petard together and to feel the mystery of new sensations sprouting inside as he worked alongside her. Finally, she spoke.

"Then tell me, Madame, will I be happy?"

Jeanne de Laval laughed; a tender, reassuring sound that warmed Nicole. "You yourself decide whether you will be happy or not."

"Because of him or because of me?" Nicole implored the elegant older woman. She made a good role model for the daughters from noble families invited to Queen Anne's court. Following the queen's and Madame de Laval's example, they would all end up as married noblewomen, running their own households and lands one day.

"Because of you, darling; you will be the one to decide. And like your queen, if I know you at all, you will choose to be happy." Madame de Laval gave Nicole a playful pinch on her chin, and then smoothed her long golden hair.

CHAPTER THREE

Treating the Stallion

"What's wrong with him?" Nicole cried. Petard stood with his head down, his right hoof off the ground, tightly bound with a bedraggled cloth. He looked miserable, so unlike the noble horse she had grown to love.

"He has a gash in his right hoof," Philippe told her, his brows knit together. "I found blood on the floor of his stall this morning." He shook his head, looking worried.

"What did he step on?" she asked as she gently approached the horse.

"This, I think." Philippe held up a rusty hook used in the barns for hanging tools. The tip was sharp, rusted.

"It's dirty!" Nicole wailed. Like her queen, she had a distaste for dirty things. It was a wonder she ever wandered down to the stables at all, but her love of horses trumped her loathing for dirt. Plus, Philippe was there. That final autumn of freedom, before winter closed in along with her father's and uncle's plans for her, she wanted to feel her oats. The stables seemed a fitting choice.

"Not a surprise," Philippe remarked, "but not good for our boy."

"He'll get a fever if the dirt works its way inside," she observed.

"I have cleaned it out, but he keeps getting the cloth dirty." Philippe looked worried. He squatted and tried to brush some dirt from the bandage covering Petard's hoof. The stallion nervously moved away, whinnying in pain.

"We need to put something on the cloth to heal the wound," Nicole said. Gently, she laid her hand on Petard's flank, feeling the stallion quiver beneath her touch. She stroked his warm side firmly to reassure him. The horse continued to tremble, but didn't move away.

"What do you mean?" Philippe asked. He scratched his head, looking puzzled.

"A poultice," she specified.

"What kind of poultice?" he pressed.

"There is one I watched my mother make before she—she left us." As a young girl, she had watched her mother prepare poultices for sick people in their household. Nicole had sometimes accompanied her to the woods to gather herbs and seeds with which to make them. There had been one in particular her mother had used that had seemed to have powerful properties.

Nicole wished Blanche St. Sylvain was alive now to help them, but she had died in childbirth under the hands of a physician. No wonder the queen didn't trust doctors. Best to rely on wise women who knew their way around forests and herb gardens, as well as sick, frightened patients.

She closed her eyes and saw the image of her graceful, practical mother in the kitchen, mixing ingredients and stirring them in a pot over the fire. *What ingredients should I use on Petard, chère Maman?* Blinking rapidly, she fought back the tears that welled up at the thought of her beautiful mother, so serene and dignified, yet so aware of the needs of her household. Her nature had been as noble as her lineage, manifesting itself in her concern for the needs of those under her charge.

"Do you remember what it had in it?" he asked.

"Spider webs to stop the bleeding."

"There're plenty of them around here. The barn is full of them," he observed. "What else?"

"The blue and green part of old bread when it's been left somewhere damp," she described. Vaguely, she remembered her mother using moldy bread in potions for household members who had been feverish, either from illness or from a wound.

"Ugh," Philippe wrinkled his nose. "Isn't that something like poison?"

"Do you think I know what I am talking about or not?" It was important to her that he trusted her. Why, she didn't know.

He studied her for a moment, his gray-green eyes a lush impenetrable forest. "I do," he finally said.

"Then gather some spider webs and I will go look for old bread." She spoke briskly, hoping he hadn't noticed the roses that sprang into her cheeks at his gaze. She turned from him, trying to hide her thoughts. The moss of a forest floor had come

into her mind. His face was over hers, and she was falling back-
ward onto its velvet carpet.

⚜

Throughout the day, Philippe and Nicole took turns checking
on the horse and changing his bandage. Nicole had been called
back to the house, but, in the early afternoon, when the household
rested after the midday meal, she stole back down to the stables.

The day was hot and the fields hummed with the low summer song of the tiny creatures that lived there. Petard rested
under the shade of a large plane tree in his paddock. Philippe
was nowhere to be found.

Nicole tucked her gown up under her knees and swung her
legs over the fence. Before the men of the stable-grounds came
along and disturbed her time alone with Petard, she would try
a few other techniques on the stallion her mother had used on
injured workers on their lands.

Slowly, she approached the horse. He stood on three legs
only, the injured hoof lifted slightly off the ground. Putting
her hand on the upper joint of his injured leg, she held it there,
accustoming him to her touch. After a moment, she smoothed
back his sleek coat. When he didn't move, she worked her hand
further down his leg, stroking then grasping his fine forelocks,
until her fingers found their way to his ankle, the tips touching
the dirty edge of his bandage.

Petard snorted and reflexively moved his leg, shaking off
Nicole's hand. She waited a moment, and then placed it back
in the same spot.

"Good boy. Good boy. Let me hold you. *Chère maman* will
hold your leg and make you better. Let *maman* hold you," she
whispered. Channeling her own mother, she felt a wistful comfort by imitating her. Blanche St. Sylvain had been as fine of

manner as she had been of feature. Nobly born, but to parents who lost much of their fortune after her father died when she was a young girl, she had married Michel St. Sylvain, a wealthy merchant interested in obtaining a title for his family.

Blanche St. Sylvain had known how to manage and grow everything Michel had brought to their marriage: a small fortune and a small household staff. Everything she had touched had flourished under her hand. Nicole told herself part of her mother was inside her, living on through memories of her comforting, competent touch.

The horse started again, trying to shake off Nicole's hand. Nicole released him, then put her hand in place again, encircling Petard's ankle just above the wound. After a moment, the stallion calmed down and allowed her to keep her hand there.

Slowly, she probed; first with feathery strokes of her small fingers, then with gentle squeezes. She wasn't sure what she was looking for, but she had felt her mother touch her in a similar way when she had fallen and hurt herself. Whatever she had been looking for, her mother's touch had comforted her, no doubt speeding her healing. She would try to do the same for Petard.

She moved her hand down slightly lower, closer to the horse's wounded hoof. Immediately, the horse started, almost kicking Nicole in the face.

She turned her head, feeling the horse brush her headpiece. As she did, a movement on the other side of the fence caught her eye. She watched as Philippe de Bois lifted a tightly curved leg and vaulted over the railing as easily as a young boy skipping. Would that she was a man, to move so freely in space. Her senses sharpened, she watched him approach, his body moving gracefully with long-limbed musculature. As he got closer, his greenish eyes flashed blue at her in the bright mid-afternoon sunlight.

"My lady, he almost kicked you. Have a care; he is a wild thing after all," Philippe reproached her.

"He is no such thing; he is simply skittish because of his wound," she answered sharply.

"How does it feel?" The youth squatted beside Nicole, the blades of his broad shoulders straining through the back of his sun-bleached brown tunic.

"He wouldn't let me touch the wound. I think it's infected. But I feel no throbbing above it, so it hasn't yet spread."

"It will if your remedy doesn't stop it." Philippe looked grave as he tried to touch the same ankle Nicole had just held. Petard snorted and moved away.

"It will," Nicole said with more authority than she felt. Her mother had always used a firm tone with the mothers of the sick children she had tended. It had calmed them, which had calmed their children in turn. "But let's freshen the poultice," she added.

She stood, dusting off the folds of her gown as she squelched an urge to reach out and touch Philippe's shoulder blades with the same firm grip she had used on Petard. The youth's back spread out before her, only half an arm's length away. The scent of him wafted up to her, tickling her senses with the fresh tang of male youth and sweat. It was pungent, something that usually made Nicole hold her breath when men passed nearby.

This time, she breathed in deeply. Suddenly dizzy, she closed her eyes, but the heat and hum of the cicadas only made her dizzier. She stumbled back against the plane tree for support; before she touched it, Philippe grasped her arm.

"My lady. Are you alright? Did Petard hurt you?"

"No! Not at all. I'm fine, it's the heat, that's all," Nicole murmured. She tried not to tremble under Philippe's touch. Was this how Petard had felt a moment before, under her own touch?

Philippe's other hand grasped her other arm. Gently, he directed her down, onto the grass at the foot of the plane tree. She complied, holding her breath so as not to breathe in any further scent of him. She would faint if she did. Or worse, reach out and pull him towards her.

Petard stirred restlessly behind Philippe. His nostrils flared as if scenting something new in the air.

"I will bring some water," Philippe said, releasing her arms.

"Good," she agreed, needing a moment to recover herself. A sharp pang caught her heart as she watched him turn and run to the fountain at the entrance to the stable-yards. *Hurry back before I am gone forever; out of your reach and into the arms of a husband I didn't choose.*

Again, she closed her eyes and rested against the tree. Near her she could feel Petard's warm breath. She stretched out her hand, palm up on her knee, neither beckoning nor moving.

In a minute she felt the warm, thick muzzle of the horse nosing her gown then resting on her palm, his velvety lips grazing her skin.

She laughed and opened her eyes. There stood Philippe de Bois, several lengths away, tankard in hand, his eyes rooted on hers. They blazed greenish-blue in the sunlight, moving from her face to her feet. She followed his gaze and sat bolt upright, flinging down her gown over her ankles. With his muzzle, the horse had inadvertently dragged the hem of her robe up over one knee. Nicole flushed to the roots of her hairline then put her hand up to cover her face.

"Do not worry, my lady." Philippe reached her and squatted down. "I will not share such a pretty sight with anyone," he said in a low voice as he handed her the tankard.

Again, his young male smell flooded her senses. If she was going to recover from her dizziness, she needed to get busy making the poultice. But something more than the heat was sapping her will to move. She felt an alert authority in her still-ness, a new way to exercise power; one that appeared to work most effectively on the males around her, horse or man.

She drank deeply and handed the tankard back to Philippe. Then she struggled to her feet, feeling his hand grasp her arm once again. She could have shaken him off, but she didn't.

He might have released her arm once she stood, but he didn't.

Instead, they stood there a moment and gazed at each other. Then slowly, ever so slowly, Nicole lifted her hand and cov-ered Philippe's hand with her own. Neither of them noticed the slight figure that slipped around the side of the barn behind them.

"Thank you," she whispered.

"Thank you, my lady," he murmured back. His eyes shifted to her mouth and rested there.

Finally Nicole broke away, holding her arm where he had grasped it. "I'll be back with the poultice," she told him, a new-found authority in her tone.

"Soon, I hope," he answered.

"Soon," Nicole echoed. Quickly, she walked away, back up to the house. This time the cicadas hummed more loudly, as if in agreement that something more was in the air than had been there the last time she passed their way. Something more was there; a sharp energy that heralded childhood's passing and the arrival of something exciting and new in its place.

⚜

"He's putting weight on his hoof. Look!" Philippe was already at the barn when Nicole arrived early the next day.

In her hand, she carried the remainder of the poultice. She planned to spread it out over three more doses, since she had run out of moldy bread. Indeed, the horse looked better.

"Dom said he slept through the night," Philippe continued, referring to the son of the garden designer from Naples who helped out at the stables. "He is doing better, my lady!"

"That's fine, but let's keep dosing him," she said, motioning to Philippe to remove the bandage now on the stallion's hoof so she could put on a fresh one. "We want Petard back in the tournaments, don't we?" she asked, referring to the jousting tournaments the king and queen held at least twice a year. She didn't understand why men wished to put on heavy armor and ride at each other with lances to try to hurt their opponent, but she understood that men would be men. Their strange sex seemed to have an enormous amount of pent-up energy that needed to be let out one way or another.

Secretly studying Philippe, she wondered how he released his energy. He seemed calm and diligent at his duties, but there were times when they worked with the horses side by side when she felt a sort of crackling energy coming from him. Was it simply because he was male or was he responding to her nearness? Whatever it was, it brought out a newfound stillness in her, something she sensed was inherently womanly, a quality she hadn't known she possessed before meeting Philippe de Bois. It was like discovering a new version of herself.

"There now, we'll get you back to as good as new," Philippe addressed the horse as he carefully unwound his bandage. Once it was off, he leaned in and inspected the wound.

"Bleeding's stopped and it looks less red," he commented.

"Good. But we should put the poultice on till it is all gone," Nicole counseled.

"Then what?"

"We pray the poison is fully drawn out by the bread's poison, or we pray that the bread I put under a damp cloth last night has some mold on it by tomorrow," she reasoned.

By the next day, Petard was looking even better and was able to walk about. Nicole had managed to find another crust of moldy bread, and had made a new batch of medicine.

"Let's treat him for one more day," she told Philippe, remembering that her mother had always used this particular remedy for at least three days, even if the patient seemed better. That day, Nicole continued to paint strips of cloth with the poultice and handed them to Philippe in the morning, and noon to bind the stallion's wound. As she leaned toward Philippe, she noticed his blondish-brown hair was plastered to his head with sweat, separating into strands at the ends. No matter how taken she felt with the youth from Agen, it was undeniable; his hair was filthy.

"You should wash your hair," she blurted out.

He stared at her, his face changing color before her eyes. "What do you mean?"

"I mean your hair is all sweaty and—and, well, smelly." She didn't mention that usually he smelled good. Very good.

"My lady, I will pour a bucket of water on my head this evening after we've put on the final bandage." Philippe's face looked red with embarrassment; something else was there, too. Was it sadness? Suddenly, she regretted her impulsive remark.

"I'm sorry. It's just that your hair usually looks so nice. It doesn't match the rest of you when it's all greasy and dirty." She put a hand to her mouth to stop herself.

"I—it's just that I never really did wash my hair. I mean— I just pour a bucket of water on my head, and that's it," he stammered.

"Silly boy! Do you mean to say you've never had your hair washed? Then why did it look so good when I first met you?" Again, she put a hand to her mouth to stop anymore babble from escaping.

"My lady, it was the lady cook who washed it the day I arrived. I don't know how to do it myself." He looked sheepish, as if he'd just admitted he didn't know how to ride a horse.

"Then who washed your hair before? I mean in Agen?"

"It was the wife of Jeannot, my master."

"But did your mother not teach you how to do it?"

Philippe's face changed. He turned his back to her, and the words that fell from his mouth were barely audible. "She is long gone, my lady."

Nicole's heart ached. "Mine too, Philippe. Mine too." Unthinkingly she reached out and put her hand on his forearm.

He didn't shake it off.

"I have an idea," she said, to get them off the subject of what was unbearable for both of them to think upon.

"You seem to have many, my lady." He kept his eyes averted, busying himself with Petard's leg. "What's that, then?"

"Finish up with the bandage and we'll go wash your hair in the horse trough."

"But—but—" He lifted his eyes to her, a mixture of interest and alarm in them, and she saw his shadows had passed. She knew what those moments were like. They stole upon her at unexpected times, when a certain scent or the sight of a fine lady in a crowd reminded her of her loss. For a brief instant, Nicole would be wild with joy, but then the realization that her mother was gone forever would grab at her heart and squeeze it hard. Unbearable moments. Thankfully, they didn't come too often.

"Don't argue with me. Cook's soap is too rough for your hair and I know her scrubbing style," Nicole declared.

"Aye, 'twas a bit harsh," Philippe agreed. "I've been keeping my distance ever since."

"I'll do it better. Besides—" she wrinkled her nose, "you really need it done if you want anyone to sit next to you at dinnertime."

"No one sits next to me at any time, my lady. I take my meals under the tree there and I sleep in the hayshed."

"Poor you," she blurted out.

"Not so poor me, I'm thinking." He gave her a look that told her he didn't think he was so poor at all.

"Don't think; just meet me at the water trough as soon as you're done." Her advice was more for herself than for him. Everything about time spent with him advised her not to think, just be. She wasn't sure what breeze had blown in such unsound counsel, but it was sweet and fragrant, and set her insides aflutter.

Petard blew air out of his lips at that moment as if to remind them why they were there. Philippe turned to the stallion and put his hand on his mane.

"I'll go fill it with fresh water," Nicole told him.

"My lady, are you—are you sure?" His words were hesitant, but the look in his eyes told her otherwise.

"Of course I am. I can't stand smelling your hair like that any longer."

"Oh." He looked taken aback.

Nicole reached out to touch his forearm again, but this time she pinched it. Mysterious new feelings swelled inside her, urging her to experience something new, something that had nothing to do with reason.

As she moved between the well and the trough, filling it with fresh water, she began to worry. What was she thinking to lay her hands on a strange youth's head? She looked around. It was just past noon, and no one was about. Most likely, the stable-hands were all asleep under a tree after their dinner. She would get the job done quickly, before anyone saw them.

Within a few minutes, Philippe arrived, his face bashful and uncertain like a small boy meeting his tutor for the first time.

"Lie there and put your head over the trough," she ordered him.

Philippe eyed the trough doubtfully. "Is that water fresh?"

"As fresh as you are." She made a face at him.

He returned it in kind. "Fresher, I'd wager. As fresh as you, then."

"Oh, undoubtedly. Now lie down and shut up."

The youth obeyed, his eyes looking up at hers with a wistfulness she hadn't seen in them before. Over the past few minutes, he had confused her with his new expressions more than he had the entire few weeks they had known each other.

"Close your eyes," she ordered.

He complied.

With one hand, she supported his head as she slid a thin plank under it. That done, she lifted the full bucket of water she had drawn and, with both hands holding it, she poured it over his head, careful to avoid his face.

"Ahh, that's cold!" he complained, his body jerking.

"Quiet!" she thundered. It was rather fun bossing him around.

Philippe shut his mouth, closed his eyes again and settled down.

Nicole dipped her hands into the fresh water in the trough, and then lathered them up with the bar of soap she had found in the stable. She prayed it wasn't as harsh as the one Cook used in the kitchen, but it would have to do. Laying her hands in his hair, she began to massage his scalp.

"Ahh . . ." The sigh that escaped Philippe this time was different in tone from the previous one. Underneath her hands, he visibly relaxed, his head surrendering its weight to her.

"Don't open your eyes, I don't want soap going into them," she ordered. *I want to look at your face without you knowing.*

It was such delicious pleasure to study the lines and curves of his well-cut features. As a young unmarried lady, she was supposed to avoid looking into a man's face at all times, unless it was her father, uncle, or the king. But why was it that men were allowed to gaze at women all they liked, yet women were supposed to notice nothing, and never stare back? Meanwhile, they noticed everything, as everyone knew, yet weren't allowed to let the person they'd noticed know. As usual, it was unfair, and, as usual, she would find a way around it.

"Ummm. . ." Philippe expelled, opening his eyes for a second.

"Shut your eyes till I'm done!" she barked, trying to sound stern. Inside, she felt just the opposite. A new sensation was playing within her, humming and vibrating, as if her insides were dancing.

She leaned in closer, and began splashing the water up from the trough onto his head to rinse out the soap. As she did, the fresh, young scent of him stole over her.

She breathed in deeply, and as she did, Philippe opened his eyes again. The tip of his nose touched the fabric of her dress just between her breasts.

"I'm not done yet!" she scolded him.

"Take your time," he replied, closing his eyes.

Harshly, she splashed water onto the silly smile that appeared on his face.

He burst out laughing, infuriating her.

For that, she poured the next bucket of water all over his face. "That's for your rudeness!" she yelled.

He jumped up, and shook his head like a dog after its bath.

Quickly she took cover so that he wouldn't get her all wet. It was bad enough that there was now a wet spot on her bodice, right in the middle of her bosom. She could imagine what

Cook might have to say about that back in the kitchen; or little Marie de Volonté if she caught sight of her before she changed.

Grabbing a cloth off the fencepost, she threw it to Philippe. "There, dry your head and be done with it," she said. She felt guilty as soon as the words left her mouth. He hadn't been particularly rude. And she hadn't particularly minded when he had opened his eyes to find his nose nestled between her breasts. She couldn't really blame him for how it got there.

She watched as Philippe clumsily swiped at his hair with the cloth.

"You're such an oaf. Here let me do that," she bossed, going over to him and grabbing the towel from his hands. Quickly she slapped it onto his head, ruffling his hair in all directions as his arms flailed to either side of her. Giggles welled up inside her, but she stifled them.

After a minute, he stopped flailing and stood in surrender to her efficient maneuvers.

Seeing he had stopped resisting, she took her time fluffing and ruffling his hair, his face hidden from her by the cloth. Finally, she was done.

She flicked the towel from his head. Prepared to offer another cheeky retort to whatever he might say, she was stunned to see his face.

Philippe's expression was sad, his eyes looking somewhere far in the distance. He stood still as stone. But even worse, a single drop of water rested on his cheek, although the rest of his face was thoroughly dried. Was it what she thought it was?

"Have I hurt you?" She was so shocked, she didn't know what to say.

The youth shook his head and looked down.

"Philippe, was I that rough? I'm sorry, I thought we were joking. I—I—"

"My lady, 'tis not that." He shook his head again, his gaze remote, looking toward the ground away from her.

"What is it? What is it, Philippe?"

"My lady, forgive me. It was wonderful. I mean—thank you."

"Then what? What happened?" Without thinking, she put her hand on his arm and looked into his face.

He returned her gaze, his lips pulled in as if he was holding himself in. For a moment they stood there in silence, their eyes locked together. Nicole could see that something deep and private lay in his thoughts. Whatever it was, she knew she should tread delicately.

"You can tell me," Nicole said quietly.

"My lady, it just reminded me of—of another lady who washed my hair when I was young." He looked down again, and this time the tear was unmistakable. It rolled down his cheek and onto the ground.

"Your mother," Nicole breathed out.

"Yes."

Together they stood, each with eyes fixed on a different spot, far away and long ago. Then the stable-manager rounded the corner and the moment was over. As Philippe greeted him, Nicole ran back to the house, her emotions a jumble from all she had learned about the youth from Agen.

"So what was it like?"

"What was what like?" Nicole hugged her arms to her chest so Marie couldn't see the wet spots on her bodice. Noticing some linens on the kitchen table, she picked them up as if to take them somewhere. She would have to put them out in the sun to dry as soon as she escaped to her bedchamber to change.

"Paris, silly. Was it wonderful?" The younger girl looked at her with wide eyes.

"It was—it was noisy and dirty. It was wonderful too, but I hardly got to see any of it." Thank God, Marie had meant Paris and not what she had just been up to with Philippe. Slowly, the pounding of her heart subsided.

"What do you mean?"

"I mean Madame wouldn't let me go anywhere other than straight to the artist's studio. Then I had to stand for hours while he painted," Nicole described, hugging the linens to her chest.

"What was that like?" Marie asked, following Nicole out of the kitchen.

"Like a statue on display, being sold off to the highest bidder." Nicole made a face. "Let me take these upstairs and I'll tell you about it in the garden when I come back down." She turned around on the stairs to block Marie from following.

"You'd better change your bodice while you're at it. It's all wet, and now you've got the linens wet too," the younger girl accurately observed.

Nicole looked down at them to hide her reddening face.

"I was looking after the stallion down at the stables."

"I know," Marie said.

"How did you know?" Nicole tried to sound unconcerned.

"One of the workmen told me."

"Which workman?" She prayed it wasn't Philippe she meant.

This time it was Marie's face that reddened. "How would I know?" she asked.

"You don't know the name of the man you were talking to?"

"I wasn't talking to a man!" Marie sounded indignant. "Just a boy working on the new garden."

"A boy working on the garden?" Nicole knew children were kept away from the worksites, which were dangerous places for them to play.

"A youth, I mean."

Nicole had guessed it might be. Marie was almost as old as she. It stood to reason she would be noticed by the many workers on the castle grounds that the king had brought back from the other side of the Alps, where he had discovered wondrous works of art and craftsmanship on his military campaigns.

"Then what were you doing with him?" *Take the counteroffensive when cornered.* It was something her father had taught her years earlier. She had treasured their time together in the weeks after her mother and infant brother had died. Michel St. Sylvain hadn't had any idea of what to talk to his young daughter about when she had suddenly been thrust into his care. They had taken long walks while he had spoken of what he knew best: his business. Nicole hadn't fully understood, but she had treasured those rare moments alone with her father.

Within weeks, he had arranged a place at court for his daughter then resumed his trips abroad, importing cloth from Flanders with which to supply his wealthy clients. On his infrequent visits to court to see her, they would resume their conversational walks. It had been their special time together. He would be proud to know she was finding ways to apply some of the principles he had taught her.

"I wasn't doing anything with him!" Marie protested. "He was in the kitchen, picking up dinner for the workmen, and mentioned he saw you go down to the stables."

"And that's all?" Nicole kept her tone stern.

"Yes, that was all. Why?" The roses in Marie's cheeks were so vivid that Nicole knew she had stumbled onto something. She would fan the flame of Marie's guilt for whatever it was, to put her further on the defensive. It might come in handy at some point. That had been another of the principles her father had touched upon. *Gather information about those around you. Then, if they accuse you of something, you have something with which to gain their silence.*

"Oh, just because he asked me about you when I was on my way back to the house," Nicole improvised.

"Dom asked you about me?" Marie's pretty face looked shocked.

"Yes. He wanted to know if you are promised to someone." So it was Dom Pacello's son she had been talking to. His father was the gardener the king had brought back from Naples a few years earlier to design the queen's new gardens. His boy, a clever youth of not twenty, bore the same name. Handsome, with a full head of black hair, he divided his time between helping his father and doing odd jobs at the stables. Had he seen her washing Philippe's hair? She hoped not. Whatever he had seen, she would keep Marie quiet about it by focusing on the young woman's apparent interest in him. It was as forbidden as hers was in Philippe, she reminded herself.

"He didn't!" Marie's expression shifted; slightly pleased chased pleasantly surprised across her face.

"Are you?" Nicole kept the pressure on.

"Am I what?"

"Are you promised to someone?"

"No, I am not!" Marie looked indignant.

Nicole leaned down to the younger girl and whispered close to her ear. "Then make the most of it before you are." She turned and ran upstairs.

"What do you mean?" the younger girl called out. Her voice sounded excited. No doubt she was discovering new feelings similar to the ones Nicole was.

"Meet you in a minute," Nicole called over her shoulder.

"I'll be in the garden," Marie called back.

Breathing a sigh of relief, Nicole hurried to her room to change out of her wet things. For the moment, her counter-offensive had worked, throwing Marie into relief and herself into the background. It was delicious to think of having something on the younger girl; almost as delightful as the thought of meeting Philippe later to check on Petard.

Changing her bodice quickly, she went back downstairs and out to the herb garden next to the kitchen.

Marie de Volonté sat on a bench, twirling a purplish-white flower. It didn't look like one from the flower beds.

"Where did you pick that?" Nicole asked.

"I didn't pick it. It was in the basket over there." Marie motioned to the kitchen door. A large basket sat next to it on the ground.

"That's Cook's bunch of wildflowers for her potions," Nicole pointed out.

"So?" Marie put the flower up to her face and inhaled deeply. She seemed to be in a playful mood. Had Dom Pacello the Younger put her there?

"Shouldn't you stay away from those? " Nicole asked. "Cook doesn't like anyone nosing through her things."

As if she had heard, Cook emerged from the kitchen and picked up the basket Marie had pointed to. Scowling, she peered across the garden at the girls.

"What's that you've got there, my lady?" she asked Marie.

"Just a flower from the basket," Marie replied.

"Put that down, my lady." Cook was a large woman, but before Marie could respond, she was at her side. She snatched the wildflower from her hand. "Highly poisonous," she breathed out, panting from exertion.

"What is it, Cook? What kind of flower?" Marie asked curiously.

"'Tis pennyroyal, my lady. Stay away from it."

"What does it do?"

"Never mind what it does. You didn't put any of it in your mouth, did you?" Cook's brows knit together.

"No! I was just holding it." Marie shrank into herself, looking frightened and thoroughly chastised; first by Nicole, then Cook.

"Best go wash your hands, my lady," Cook advised. "Scrub them and rinse three times."

"Three times?" Marie looked alarmed. She stared down at her hands as if afraid of them.

"Wash them thoroughly, my lady; you don't want any trace of the stem's oils left on you."

Marie got up and hurried away.

"I thought I'd taken that basket inside," Cook muttered, looking angry with herself.

"What do you use pennyroyal for?" Nicole asked once Marie was out of earshot.

"My lady, best you don't worry about such things. Leave me to my job and I'll leave you to yours." Cook's mouth set in a tight line, as if nothing further would be pried from it anytime soon.

"But, Cook, I helped my mother with healing the people of our household when I was a girl. She used such herbs and flowers. I think I have seen this one before." She studied the small undistinguished purplish-white flower that peeked out from Cook's apron pocket.

"My lady, when you marry, I will teach you of its uses. Until then, stick to healing horses. And don't go near this flower, either in my storeroom or down by the river where it grows."

"But, Cook, I need to know what it's used for. Maybe it will help with the horses," Nicole pleaded.

"For sure, it won't. You will know its uses soon enough one day," the large woman replied mysteriously. "But, for now, all you need to know is to stay away from it."

Cook turned and walked back to the kitchen, hugging the basket to her. Nicole heard her mumble, "God in Heaven I should have hidden that basket," before she disappeared inside, slamming the door shut behind her.

Nicole stood; she felt restless. She slipped to the end of the garden and into the cool interior of the chateau at the other end from the kitchen. She didn't feel like talking to Marie about Paris, or teasing out any more information from her about what she had been up to with Dom Pacello. He would return to Naples when his father finished his work for the king and queen. It couldn't go anywhere, so what did it matter?

All she wanted was to be left alone with her thoughts. New and delicious sensations flooded through her when she sifted through what had transpired with Philippe that day. She decided to go find some old rags and rip them into bandage strips to use on Petard.

She hummed happily as she found the rag pile in the laundry room and picked out one or two pieces to rip up. She couldn't wait to treat the queen's stallion again with Philippe in a few hours. What would happen, she wondered. And why did she sense so thoroughly that something would?

A deadening thought struck her. The strange, exciting feelings Philippe had awakened in her had nowhere to go either. Just like Marie, she was one of the unmarried maids of honor of the court, being groomed by the queen to marry husbands of rank. Stable-boys and workmen were invisible. Consorting with them was unthinkable.

Briskly, she ripped the cloth in half, as if to rip to shreds the tedious, grown-up thoughts that had come like thieves to steal her pleasure. She wouldn't let them. At least not now. The future was far off. Meanwhile, the weather was warm, Petard was on the mend, and she was in no mood to quash the mystery that had begun between her and the youth with changeable eyes.

⚜

That evening, the horse nuzzled Nicole as Philippe crouched low, examining him. All traces of his sadness of a few hours earlier were gone.

"The wound looks better," he remarked. "No more red around the gash. And look at him. Back to his old self!"

"You tickle me, Petard," Nicole giggled as the horse burrowed his large muzzle under her arm.

Philippe looked up, his expression hard to read. The crackling energy she felt from him at times was back. Suddenly, he no longer seemed like a youth anymore, but a full-grown man.

She watched as his eyes followed where the horse's muzzle was on her body. Philippe's every muscle seemed alert, alive.

Digging into her further, the horse's huge head knocked her off balance; she stumbled back.

Philippe's arm shot up to steady her, hugging her around her lower back. With his other arm, he grabbed her just below the soft curve of her backside. It was a place no one's hands had touched since Nicole had matured the spring before.

The sensation of him holding her so firmly, of his eyes locking onto hers, gripped her as tightly as his arms did. No longer in danger of falling, she felt as if she were. Slithering shards of energy traveled up and down her torso and legs. Petard had moved back, his head turning in the direction of a bird's cry from behind where Philippe crouched.

Returning Philippe's gaze, she placed her hands on his shoulders. Underneath her fingers, she could feel the tautness

of his muscles; even more so, the focused attention at which
they stood, as if waiting to receive direction from her.

Of course they were.

She slipped down to his crouching position. His hands slid
up over either side of her torso until they rested under her arms.
His thumb-tips pressed lightly into her collarbones, then more
firmly.

Staring at him, she sensed a boundary present, a decision underway. It was hers to make, judging by the attentive-
ness with which he held her. Her time to reach for what she
wanted was now, before she disappeared forever into the
confines of married life.

Have courage and be bold slipped into her mind. Her father
would not be pleased to know how she planned to apply
one of his favorite dictums. She vowed he would never find
out.

With one hand, she covered Philippe's and pulled it out
from under her arm, sliding it over her breast.

Philippe's sharp intake of breath told her he was cognizant
of the forbidden territory they now travelled. Would she allow
him to wander farther?

Taking her hand off his, she waited to see what he would
do. Slowly, he moved his hand over her other breast then back
again and, finally, sure of its terrain, it proceeded to the middle
of her chest and upward to the base of her throat, against her
warm, bare skin.

It was as if her heart had slowed down, along with time
itself. Each beat seemed deeper, more resonant. She raised her
head, waiting.

With fingers splayed, Philippe's broad hand traveled up,
twisting as it went to fit the line of her jawbone. There it

rested, his palm cupping her chin, his index and middle fingers on her cheekbone. His thumb rested on the side of her mouth.

She opened it slightly and felt his thumb journey along her lower lip and back. Her entire body quivered.

"Philippe," she whispered.

"My Nicole," he murmured back.

"Am I?" For the moment, she belonged to herself, but by the following summer she would be a married woman.

"I wish you were," he answered, then moved his face toward hers until their noses touched. "And you?" he asked, almost imperceptibly.

"I wish I was," she answered, closing her eyes and letting go of every conscious thought that could come between them. There were many, but at that moment there were none.

His kiss was tender at first, then firm, heady. As it deepened, his hands came around her back, pressing her to him.

When she opened her eyes, she saw that his own were wild, as if starlit, with an expression in them she had never seen before. A hint of danger glinted there, yet she knew him, didn't she? Was he not still her Philippe, the youth whose hair she had washed?

Reaching for him, she pulled him to her. This time, it was her lips that sought his, opening beneath his, feeling his tongue press into her mouth, tasting and probing. Not expecting such an intrusion, she pressed her teeth gently down on his tongue, bidding him stop till she was ready to proceed again.

Soon enough, she was. This time, she put her own tongue into his mouth, dancing and rolling over his. They were like two lambs frolicking in a pasture. His taste was delicious, unlike anything she had savored before—fresh, young, and virile. Perhaps hers was, too, judging by the way he breathed so deeply.

His breathing sped up, and he stood, lifting her to her feet with him. She flung her arms around his neck, receiving his kiss in the pink and purple rays of the setting sun. Never had she felt like this before, never did she want to let go of this moment.

"Nicole! Are you there? Nicole!" a voice called. Great shuddering gasps came over her, whether from awe at what had just taken place, or shock at having it end so suddenly, she knew not.

"I will be right there," she called, quickly breaking away from him and smoothing her hands over her gown.

"Where are you? I don't see you!" Marie de Volonté exclaimed.

Good. Nicole looked up at Philippe and put a finger to her lips.

Catching his stunned expression, she giggled. Inside, her heart stirred, not her loins. But now, for the first time, she knew what it was to have her loins stir, too. She had never known before. It was a powerful sensation, as if an ancient call from the wild was pulling and straining at her, rendering her reason senseless, her senses as tight as the string of a well-tuned lute.

Putting her hands up to her hair, she smoothed it over her shoulder, checking with her fingers that no telltale hay or grass was caught in its long locks. Satisfied, she gave Philippe a small smile.

"Tomorrow?" he murmured.

"Tomorrow morning. Take care of my stallion," she bade him.

"Take care of my heart, and bring it back tomorrow," he replied.

Her own heart leaping for joy, she turned and ran toward Marie de Volonté, still searching for her on the far side of the paddock. "Here I am!" she sang out, finally ready to be discovered. As she caught up to the young noblewoman, she prayed Philippe had hidden himself.

"Happy to be working with Petard again?" Marie asked. Her face was impish.

"He's better today. My poultice is working its magic," Nicole told her.

"Something is working its magic," Marie replied, studying her closely. She reached over and plucked a stray piece of straw from Nicole's hair.

Nicole looked at her guiltily then caught herself. "How did you know I was here?" she asked sharply.

"I didn't. I asked Cook where you were and she said to go ask the stable-boy."

"Oh, you mean Dom." Relief flooded her. She would use what she knew about Marie and him to keep her quiet.

"No, not him," Marie answered.

"Then who?" Alarm rose in Nicole's stomach.

"The one over there." The younger girl pointed toward the barn.

"No one's over there," Nicole said, straining to see in the gloaming.

Marie looked in the direction Nicole did. "Oh. Well, he was there a minute ago. I asked him, and he pointed over there," Marie indicated where Nicole and Philippe had just been.

"Do you know who it was?" Nicole asked, hoping it hadn't been Philippe that Cook had meant. Besides Dom, there was another young stable-hand who mucked out the horses' stalls. Had he seen them? If so, how much had he seen? Her heart thumped wildly at the thought. He was said to be slow-witted, but that didn't mean he was mute. No one was at court.

Marie shrugged. "No."

"What did you see?" Nicole asked, trying to sound unconcerned.

"Nothing, my lady. Your eyes are as full of magic as your healing hands," Marie answered blithely as she sauntered up the path.

"What does that mean, pray tell?" Nicole demanded. Unused to being on the defensive, she didn't like it. She would switch positions as soon as she found a way.

"Lucky the one they touch, that is all," Marie replied mysteriously.

"What one do you speak of?"

"I will not say," the younger girl giggled, then put her finger to her lips in an identical manner to the way Nicole had just done with Philippe.

There was nothing more Nicole could do than swallow the next thing she wished to say. It wouldn't do her any good to blurt it out; it would just incriminate her further. Biting her tongue, she joined Marie in laughter, praying that the younger girl would keep a secret. Besides, Nicole felt like laughing too. Her heart danced for joy at the memory of Philippe's touch.

⚜

"Going to the stables this morning?" Marie asked the following day.

"Yes. I need to check on Petard. He was better yesterday; let us hope he continues to heal," Nicole said.

"Are you using any more of that smelly stuff you were making?" Marie asked curiously.

"I'm all out."

"Used it up last night, did you?"

"Yesterday, three times. That was it. Say a prayer for me for Petard's sake, will you?"

"I will say a prayer for you for your sake, too. And someone else's," Marie added slyly.

Nicole sensed it was time to adjust the balance of power before it shifted against her. She needed to act quickly if she wanted to keep Marie under control. Stepping closer, she took hold of Marie's arms and firmly backed her up against the garden wall. Then, she put her index finger under the tip of Marie's chin, and pushed it up, forcing the girl to look straight into her eyes.

"Stop!" Marie protested.

"Do you know what?" Nicole asked, her voice low.

"No. What?" The younger girl looked startled, but also curious. She squirmed under Nicole's touch.

"I know you know more than you're telling me, and that's fine because so do I." She tightened her grip on Marie's arms, careful not to dig in her nails. She didn't want to hurt the girl, only to scare her a little until she figured out a more effective way to get her to keep quiet about whatever she had seen.

"All right," Marie whispered back.

"What do you mean 'all right'?" Nicole demanded.

"I mean I understand."

"And will you keep it secret?"

"Will I keep what secret?" Marie's eyes slid sideways, indicating that the secret between them had a very short chance of remaining so for long. At court nothing remained a secret forever.

"Whatever it is that you've seen."

"Why should I?" The younger girl grasped Nicole's hand with her own and pushed it off her chin. Her expression was defiant.

"Because I will make it worth your while," Nicole whispered.

"How?" Marie whispered back.

"By not mentioning anything about you and Dom."

"But there isn't anything about me and Dom!" Marie's eyes darted from side to side. Something was there.

"Let me know if you need me to cover," Nicole told her, relying on intuition in place of actual facts.

"Cover what?"

"Whatever it is you're doing with Dom." Nicole didn't know what exactly, but it was enough just to know there was something.

"I'm not doing anything with Dom!" Marie cried.

"Well when you are, you can use me to help you," Nicole said, pressing her fingers into the girl's arm. "That is, if you don't say anything more about whatever it was you thought you saw."

Marie stared at her a moment, her eyes narrowing to slits. Finally, she spoke. "Now that I think of it, I saw nothing."

"Then you may ask me for a favor when you need one, *ma belle*," Nicole offered, releasing her.

"I will remember." Marie smiled a small, secret smile that told Nicole she would be asking for one soon. Then she shoved Nicole back, to even up the score.

Nicole caught herself, then turned and ran down the path toward the stables. Behind her, Marie's laugh trilled through the air.

CHAPTER FOUR

Awakenings

utumn flew by, and Nicole's awakening to womanhood ripened like the harvest. Philippe was her heart's desire, but time was short. Her father was due to visit at Christmastime. With him would come news of whatever plans for her future he and her uncle were negotiating.

She prayed plans had fallen through with the man who had accompanied them at her sitting in Paris, but if they hadn't, she hoped they could be pushed back until the following year. She was not keen to marry at age fifteen. Her queen had done so at fourteen, and had been pregnant every year of her married life thus far. With three stillbirths, the tragic loss of the little dauphin Charles Orland, then two more sons dead within weeks after birth, her queen knew more than her share of loss at age twenty.

Nicole and Philippe exercised Petard, who had fully recovered, and broke in another horse, this one a mare named Fleur, who had been brought to breed with the stallion if all went well.

All went well indeed. It was an inspirational sight to catch moments when Petard frolicked with the mare in the far corners of the pasture on early evenings, as well as early mornings when the dew was fresh upon the grass and instinct welled high in both man and beast.

Nicole's own instincts that autumn were not overly ruled by reason. She felt no urge to resist the new feelings Philippe elicited in her. It appeared they were reciprocated. However, a measure of restraint seemed to season his wild desire for her. It was he, not she, who slowed down at moments, cautiously reminding her that she must not ruin her prospects, although he himself felt ruined because he was not one of them.

"And why can you not be?" Nicole teased one evening as they lay on the gently sloping hill that overlooked the stables. She fingered the laces of his over-shirt, loosening them so she could run her hand inside, over the light down of hair that was beginning to sprout on his chest.

"You have laid it out to me yourself. Your father is a St. Sylvain. You know as well as I that he wants the best for you, to ensure once and for all that you escape the class of merchants he comes from. He wants you fully a noblewoman. If I were him, I would want that for you, too."

"But I am a noblewoman from my mother's side," Nicole protested. "If I was not, I wouldn't be here at court." Queen Anne invited only young ladies from noble families to join her at court as maids of honor. She paid their expenses and arranged their dowries, as well as most of their marriage matches.

"That is even more reason that they will never allow you to marry beneath your class," he whispered, tracing his fingers down the side of her torso as they lay on their backs studying the clouds dotting the brilliant blue sky overhead.

The autumn had been unusually warm. The grass was long and a large rock outcropping below shielded them from the gaze of anyone in the stable-yards. From the outer ramparts of the chateau, Nicole was not so sure. Much could be viewed from there for miles around. Soon enough, her father's retinue would appear on the road leading to the castle, and she would need to rush to prepare herself. Her heart sank to think of it.

"Your father wishes to secure his position. Of his own blood, he has none, other than wealth. Your mother's blood was noble, but she is dead, so it is you alone who can bring to your father's house the titled stamp he seeks. If you marry a nobleman, your children will be titled. If you marry a merchant, your family will go back to middle-class status. It is the way of the world, little one." He stroked the underside of her chin tenderly then traveled down her throat to her breast, circling then cupping it.

"I'm not so little." She shivered, feeling her breast swell beneath his touch. Then she took his wandering hand and guided it over her heart.

"I see," he murmured, leaning over her and grazing her lips with his, his kiss igniting her.

In a flash, her emotions ran from mild arousal to fiery-hot feeling. Nobility and noble alliances be damned.

"I want all of you. All." She traced her hand down to the well where his belly button lay and circled around it. Below that area, she felt his loins spring to life, straining to escape the confines of his leggings. It was impossible to ignore. Slowly, she moved her hand farther down.

"Ahhh," he exhaled, grasping her wrist and pushing her hand hard upon him. He was a swollen raging dam about to break.

"I want to be with you always," Nicole whispered, her lips tasting the salt on his earlobe.

"I as well," he groaned, pushing her hand away after he had practically broken it at the wrist, pressing it into him.

Men were confusing. She knew it had something to do with whatever beast that raged within their bodies once they matured. She wouldn't try to understand Philippe. It was enough just to love him. Strangely, she knew that he loved her, too, because he was pushing her away.

⚜

Two weeks later, a courier burst into the room, shouting that a convoy of men was riding to the castle, a red banner heralding their arrival.

At the news, Nicole ran up the four sets of steps that led to the castle ramparts. Scanning the winding road that led to the Chateau d'Amboise, she strained to make out the design on the red banner fluttering in the breeze on the early December day. Sure enough, a diagonal blue line bisected the banner. It was the banner of the St. Sylvain house that only her uncle bore the right to display.

Not exactly a coat of arms, it was nevertheless a concession the king had granted him in return for his help in financing his last campaign in Milan; it meant Uncle Benoit accompanied her father. She shivered, praying the man from the house of St. Bonnet was not also amongst them.

Whoever was in the party, she knew her future crowded in upon her. Running back down the stairs, she rushed toward the stables to tell Philippe.

"Where are you going, Nicole?" Madame de Laval called out, catching her arm as she passed.

"I—to—to see Petard. I need to make sure he—"

"No, my dear. Your Petard is fine, and your stable-boy is gone."

"What? What do you mean? He's gone? I mean—who's gone? Where?" Nicole burst out.

"You know very well who." Madame de Laval's look was stern. "He was sent back to Agen early this morning."

"What? Madame, why?" She struggled to conceal her shock.

"Do you want to know the real reason or the reason that was given?"

"Both!" Nicole ached to think Philippe was gone before she had had a chance to bid him farewell.

"The reason given was that Jeannot, his old master in Agen, is ill, and asked for him."

"And the real reason?" Nicole's blood quickened, her temper rising. She knew before Madame de Laval's mouth opened what it would be.

"You know the real reason, *ma chère.* Your future arrives now at the castle. The queen was told of your father's and uncle's visit a few weeks ago. Perhaps your future husband is with them."

"Why was I not told of this?" Nicole's heart thumped wildly. She couldn't bear either piece of news, especially that Philippe was gone.

"Because your rash behavior has been noted. We feared it would become even more rash if you knew your final days together were upon you."

"But, Madame, I would have liked to say goodbye." Nicole felt as if the blood had drained from her body. It was impossible to think that never again would she feel Philippe's strong, warm arms around her.

"My dear, you both knew your paths were soon to separate, and you had your goodbyes all fall. The queen allowed you your moment. She was once a girl, too, you know."

"But she married the man chosen for her, not the one she chose with her heart!" Nicole blurted out angrily. She didn't mean to speak out against her sovereign, but her heart was breaking.

"Your queen has made many sacrifices for the good of our country. She asks that you make a sacrifice for the good of your family and the children you will one day bear."

"But was she in love?"

"She has come to love her husband, as we all see." Madame de Laval smiled. It was true that anyone at court could see that the king and the queen were close. When he was home from campaigns, they would spend hours walking over the grounds together, discussing architectural projects fueled by new works and techniques he had seen in Milan and Naples. Luxurious tapestries, paintings, and gold-work pieces arrived constantly at the queen's request. Most glorious of all was the new garden the king was having made for the queen by the Neapolitan garden designer, Dom Pacello.

"But how can I take on the yoke of wife to another man when my heart is wifed to another?" Nicole cried.

"My dear, it was out of the question on all levels." Madame de Laval shook her head. "You had a first love. It was sweet to see, and the queen did not wish to deny you your moments. But those moments, when enjoyed too closely, end in danger for a young woman. You know that, do you not?" Madame de Laval frowned at Nicole as if to say 'you would be a fool if you didn't.'

"Yes, Madame. Of course." Nicole blushed. Who had noted them? Had Marie said something? Had it been the stable-boy or Dom Pacello the Younger? "But the queen cannot possibly know what agony this is."

"Your queen can and does know. She herself was fond of her cousin the Duke d'Orléans as a young girl. But he was married to Jeanne of France, so a match was out of the question. When the time came for her to marry the king, it was the duke himself who brokered the nuptial agreement. He ensured that the queen retained her sovereign rights over her lands and came to the union as ruler of Brittany rather than a hostage."

"A hostage? What do you mean?" Her regal sovereign wasn't the type to be anyone's hostage. It was unthinkable.

"The king wanted Brittany for France. His army laid siege to Rennes until its people were starving, our queen as Duchess of Brittany had no more money to pay her mercenaries, and they were turning on her own people within the city walls, fighting for food. With her father dead, and Maximilian not coming to her aid, she had no choice but to come to terms."

"Do you mean Maximilian of Austria?" She couldn't imagine her queen married to the dumpy Archduke of Austria, emperor-elect to the Holy Roman Empire. She had heard his long nose had not just one but two bumps in it. The rest of his description had been equally unattractive.

"Yes. The very one. He did nothing to save the country of his intended bride. Brittany was at risk of being swallowed up by France."

"Why did he not send troops to save her?"

"Why not, indeed?" The older woman sniffed. "To begin with, he had never met her. They had been betrothed by proxy. Plus, his own army was fighting in Hungary."

"*Mon Dieu.* What did she do, our queen?" She had heard the story before, but never from Madame de Laval's lips.

"Our clever queen allowed the Duke d'Orléans to negotiate on her behalf, when she saw there was no way out. He sized up the situation and realized her greatest defense was her own charms. He set up the meeting between the king and the duchess, where it was King Charles who became hostage to our queen's beauty and wit."

"So the Duke d'Orléans encouraged the union, even though he loved the duchess himself?" Nicole's heart turned over at the thought. She would never encourage Philippe to marry another woman. He was hers already. And she was his. How could she go through with her father's and uncle's plans for her? Yet, how could she not?

"Yes. He was already married, so he looked out for the duchess when he saw that the king was taken with her. Because he loved her, he did his best by her, with no recompense to himself other than admiring her from afar."

"So his love was sacrificial," Nicole observed. She felt like a wild horse about to be saddled.

"Wise words, my dear. True love is indeed sacrifice. The queen knows this kind of love above all: the true love that places duty above pleasure."

"But love must be felt to begin with!" Nicole protested.

"My darling, your queen had not known King Charles for more than two weeks when she married him. Charles Orland was born eleven months after their wedding day. If a match is well made, it does not take long for feelings to grow. You will learn to love your husband, Nicole. Your father and uncle have chosen wisely for you."

"My heart is with Philippe, Madame. What can I do?"

"You must follow the example of your queen, who did what she needed to do. Your Philippe is no longer here, and your future husband is about to arrive. Think of your queen, and do your duty."

"Yes, Madame," Nicole answered quietly, her eyes downcast as she tried to hide her agony.

"Let me share a secret with you," Madame de Laval said, lowering her voice.

"What is it?"

"Doing one's duty can be extremely pleasurable at times," she whispered.

"What do you mean?"

"You will find out soon enough." The older woman's hand shot out and caught Nicole's pointed chin. She winked as she tweaked it, then hurried off.

CHAPTER FIVE

Winter of Worry

"Papa, I am not ready to marry." Even as the words spilled out, she knew they held no weight. Girls were considered ready for marriage from the moment they matured, regardless of their personal feelings.

"Nonsense. Our queen was married at age fourteen," Michel St. Sylvain's voice was curt, but not unkind. He reached out and took Nicole's hand in both of his, trapping it in his grip.

And look what has happened to her, Nicole thought. Six pregnancies in six years of marriage and not a single child alive. The queen was only twenty, yet already she carried more grief in her heart than Nicole ever wished to know.

"But I don't even know this man!"

"Besides, she has offered to host your wedding here at Amboise this summer, the last Saturday in June," he continued. "Gilles' brother, Hubert, arranged with the king to have a word with her."

"But I don't love this Monsieur de St. Bonnet. I don't even know him!" So his name was Gilles. How strange to learn the name of the man she was meant to marry after being told her wedding date. Inside, she burned. She wasn't ready; she never would be. But what did it matter? She had no choice but to follow the path laid out for her. No one did.

"My daughter, you will come to love him. As did your mother and I. As did our king and queen. You will represent your family well and you will do your duty." He pounded the table with his fist, then gruffly stood, towering over her.

She was not afraid of her father; she knew him too well not to know he loved her. But of the future he had laid out for her, she had misgivings. Especially at the thought of children by a man she didn't love. Would she love them? And if she did, then came to lose them, what would she have left?

At least the queen loved the king. And now a royal babe was on the way, due in late spring. The court was guardedly hopeful. It was the queen's seventh pregnancy. With no living child to show for the previous six, one could only hope and pray.

Nicole clasped her hands together and held them out to her father.

"Papa, I have something to speak to you about." Duty called; she had no choice but to submit to it. But she wanted her father to know what was in her heart. Then, she told herself, she would bury it forever.

Michel St. Sylvain's eyebrows raised in alarm.

"You have not brought disgrace upon your family, have you, daughter? Not upon the good name of your mother?"

"No, Papa. I would never. Not that at all." *I would have gladly if only Philippe had consented.* She shuddered to think of the consequences of her own rash moments with him over the past few months. He had pushed her away, valuing her own future more than she herself had. For that, she loved him even more.

"What is it, Nicole? Our guests arrive at any moment."

"I—it's—" How to begin? And how much should she say?

The door to the chamber opened and a courtier entered. "Monsieur?"

"Yes?" Nicole's father turned, his voice short.

"Sir Hubert de St. Bonnet wishes a word with you, Monsieur. He is here with another gentleman—"

"What other man?" Michel St. Sylvain asked sharply.

"I do not know, Monsieur."

Nicole's father looked at her. "You will put foolish thoughts out of your head now." His tone softened as he put his face down to hers. "Your duty, daughter, do your duty." He reached out and twitched her headdress, affection seasoning the sternness of his gaze.

"Send them in," he barked.

How she wished her mother was alive. She needed her so desperately at that moment. Yet she knew what Blanche St. Sylvain would direct her to do. As much as her parents came from different social backgrounds, their interests had been aligned when it came to securing the futures and fortunes of their children. Now she was the only one of them left alive. How could she throw away her parents' hopes for her and their future grandchildren? Even worse, how could she shame her queen?

Taking a deep breath, she willed her heart to be still as she straightened her back, and waited.

The door opened, and the scent of male bodies underneath eau de cologne overpowered her for a second. Looking up, she saw the king's valet, Hubert de St. Bonnet, a tight smile on his face. He looked strained. Behind him, a second man stood, obscured by Hubert.

Nicole lowered her eyes and fixed them on the floor in front of her. The scent of power and maturity filled the room. It wasn't unpleasant, but neither did it ignite her heart the way Philippe's scent did.

When she looked up, she would meet the eyes of a man, not a youth. Was she ready? Taking another deep breath, she thought of Philippe de Bois and wished him Godspeed to fulfill the duties life had given him, as she was about to fulfill hers.

She looked up, ready to meet her future.

Instead, her eyes met the eyes of her uncle, Benoit St. Sylvain. Gilles de St. Bonnet was nowhere to be seen. Her heart flopped, relieved.

Uncle Benoit's eyes flickered over her, then turned to her father.

"Where is he?" Michel St. Sylvain asked, sounding annoyed.

"He couldn't come," Hubert de St. Bonnet began. "He sends his deepest apologies to you both." He turned to Nicole. "And his very best regards to Mademoiselle."

"What do you mean, he couldn't come?" Michel St. Sylvain snapped, his tone as sharp as it had been with Nicole a moment earlier. He addressed Hubert de St. Bonnet, but his eyes sought his brother's as if to ask, "'What is the meaning of this?'"

"He had a transaction to finish in Paris," Hubert de St. Bonnet explained. "There was a delivery delay."

Michel and Benoit St. Sylvain exchanged looks. This was language they spoke. It was not what they had wanted to hear, but at least it was understandable.

"Are we to expect other delays, then? With plans we have discussed?" Nicole's father asked. His fingers drummed the table in front of him. He was not happy.

"Absolutely not, Monsieur. My cousin Gilles anticipates with rapture the summer nuptials with your estimable daughter." Hubert de St. Bonnet had lapsed into courtier language.

It was hard to know what to believe and what not to, but Nicole had spent enough time at court to discount the flowery openings and closings and listen instead for the hard facts in between. The wedding was to take place as planned. Her heart fell.

"This is unexpected, Hubert." Michel's tone was icy. "My daughter is not a horse to be handed over to her new owner on her wedding day. We expected to introduce her to Gilles today so they could get to know each other before the ceremony."

Thank you, Papa. You do love me after all. Nicole's heart warmed at her father's defense of her feelings. But she knew him too well to think that was all it was. Michel St. Sylvain would use this breach of etiquette as a bargaining tool, should he need one. It was yet another business maneuver he had touched upon with Nicole on their long walks together: *Always insert an opt-out clause. You may need it in the event of an unexpected turn.* From what Nicole had experienced of life, there were many unexpected turns. How she longed for another leisurely walk and talk with him.

"Understood, Michel. But you know how it is. Business calls, and the Baron de St. Bonnet's business is very successful. He will provide well for your daughter, especially with the successful conclusion of this particular transaction." Hubert de St. Bonnet ably defended his cousin's absence, reminding the brothers of his wealth and rank in a single deft statement.

"Hmph." Michel St. Sylvain's eyes sought his brother's. Displeasure flickered in them.

Nicole watched as Benoit St. Sylvain's eyes lit up with curiosity. She knew what lay there. He was bursting to learn the details of whatever business had prevented Gilles de St. Bonnet from meeting his future bride. Perhaps he himself could get a piece of it as a soon-to-be in-law.

"I have an idea," Nicole broke in to ease the strained silence.

All three men gazed at her with dismayed expressions. Fifteen-year-old maidens were not encouraged to have ideas; certainly not to voice them to their elders.

"Uncle, I would like to spend some time alone with my father before he leaves. Why don't you have Monsieur de St. Bonnet tell you about my future husband's business in Paris while I catch up with my dear papa?"

She looked at her father. His sour expression had disappeared and a small smile had broken out on his face.

"What do you need from me, daughter?" he asked, his words harsher than his gaze. He looked relieved that she was suggesting a way for him to escape present company so he could regroup after the unexpected change in plans.

"A small favor." She prayed he would be receptive.

"And that is?" Michel St. Sylvain's face lit up as she reached up on tiptoe and put her mouth to his ear.

"A walk, Papa. Let's take one of our walks," she whispered, so that neither of the two other men could hear. She knew her father. Careful and methodical, he sought immediate retreat when confronted with unexpected events. He was not a rash man, but a considered one.

He nodded and straightened up, turning to the men. "Gentlemen, my daughter and I have business together. I will join you at dinner."

Taking Nicole's arm, he led her from the room. Behind them, she did not see the amused smiles exchanged between her uncle and Hubert de St. Bonnet. Cordial relations had been saved, everyone had gotten what they wanted, and a woman had arranged it all. What could be more natural?

The herb garden was empty, a perfect place to speak quietly. Father and daughter strolled in silence for a companionable moment. They walked to the gate at the end; there they paused, looking out over the hills beyond. She sensed her father's equanimity restored after his tense conversation with Hubert de St. Bonnet. It was time to speak before she lost her courage.

"I have thoughts of another, Papa." She squeezed his arm lovingly. "What should I do?" *Always toss the ball into the other court* was one of her father's dictums. It bought her time, and her father was a natural problem solver. As a merchant, it was his specialty.

"Daughter, your uncle and I have worked long months on this proposal. What other man can a fifteen-year-old girl know of who could bring our family more fortune?"

"I—he is—we are . . ." Philippe de Bois was in no position to bring more fortune to the St. Sylvain family. Of that, Nicole was sure.

"Is this man of noble birth?" her father demanded, his back straightening, as if he could will himself to ascend a few notches on the social scale. By straighter posture, he could not; by his daughter's good marriage, he could.

"He—"She fingered the ends of the corded belt she wore. The queen had given it to her after Nicole had been at court for a year to formally recognize her as a member of the Order of the Cord she had created for her maids of honor. Nicole's heart sank. How could she dishonor her queen by marrying beneath her rank?

"Who introduced you? Who is this man?" her father pressed.

She thought fast. Philippe was a horse-trainer. If she disclosed his name to her father, she could count on never seeing him again. Michel St. Sylvain would make sure of that.

"He is not of noble birth," she confessed.

"Then why speak of him?" her father thundered. "Have you lost your mind, child?"

"No, Papa! Not my mind, but my heart," she spoke, her voice barely above a whisper.

"Don't speak to me of your heart, daughter. You are too young to give your heart away. Your duty is to guard your heart until the day of your marriage to the man I have chosen for you." He did not mention Gilles de St. Bonnet by name. Had his absence that day given Michel St. Sylvain pause for thought?

"Yes, Papa." Her hands pulled at the knot of her corded belt. If she undid it, it would fall off and no longer serve its purpose. There was nothing else to be done but to keep it knotted, serving its purpose, as all things and creatures were made to do; just as she must remain in her designated place in the design of her life chosen for her by others. Who chose their own design? No one.

"Who is this man? Give me his name," her father's voice was a knife slicing her thoughts into bits, as well as her dreams.

She froze. Whatever name she gave him, he would make sure she never laid eyes on him again. It was no use. She wouldn't disclose Philippe's name. It must remain sacred and secret, hidden away in her heart.

"Papa, it is as you said. My heart must go where duty directs it. You are right," she answered. She batted her eyelashes then focused on a spot on the wall behind her father's gray head. Perhaps if she acted dutiful, her heart would follow. Perhaps not.

"The name of the man. Give it to me," Michel St. Sylvain demanded.

"I cannot, Papa. It would serve no purpose."

"Then why did you speak of this?"

"Because my heart is full," she blurted out, throwing herself at him.

Her father's arms closed around her, holding her tight. The sigh that escaped him, over her head, was deep.

"My daughter, what do you want me to do?" he asked, his voice more tender than it had been a moment before.

"I want you to know that my heart is already occupied. And I want no other man there."

"Daughter, let's sit down." Carefully, Michel St. Sylvain directed Nicole to a stone bench.

They sat, and Nicole felt her father's arm come around her back. He hugged her to him.

"You are your mother's daughter, no question," he remarked.

"Why do you say that?"

"Because of your heart, as well as your beauty."

"My heart?"

"You hold someone in high regard in your heart."

"I do." She warmed at the thought of the one she held in high regard. She had held him in her arms, too. Of that she would not speak.

"So did your mother."

"So did my mother?" She looked at him, startled. "It was you, no?"

"No." He shook his head gently, not without love and admiration in his eyes.

"What?" It was unimaginable to her that her mother had loved another man, one who was not her father.

"I loved her on first sight, and she came to love me." Michel St. Sylvain let out a sigh and looked into the distance.

"Not at first?" Nicole was shocked. "What do you mean?"

"I mean, your mother was a mystery to me. And part of that mystery was what she held in her heart when she came to our marriage."

"Do you mean she loved another?" She couldn't believe it.

"She never spoke of it. But I heard."

"And what did you do?" Nicole stared into her father's eyes. Instead of anger, she saw nothing but love and forgiveness there.

"I loved her. That's all I could do," he replied quietly.

"But she loved you, too, didn't she?" She had to. Nicole couldn't bear it to be any other way.

"I became her husband; I gave her my heart, and, when you were born, she gave me hers." He smiled faintly, his thoughts far away.

"She didn't love you until after I was born?" Nicole asked, having trouble imagining her quiet and elegant mother as anything but devoted to her father.

"No. But then she did. And do you know what?"

"What, Papa?" She felt her eyes widen as her father brought his face close to hers.

"It was enough." He reached up and caressed her cheek. "It will be enough for you, too."

"What if it isn't?" Nicole couldn't help asking, her voice a whisper.

"You are my daughter, too, Nicole. You will make sure it is."

"I will?"

"You will." Michel St. Sylvain pulled her to him and kissed her gently on the forehead.

Together they held each other on the stone bench in the garden as her father's words sank in. It would be enough because she loved both her father and her queen. And beyond them both, she loved her mother's secret wild heart. Her duty and her desire were to make all three of them proud. She would walk the path of duty, and only she would hear the bubbling burble of the brook of her secret love, pulsing along beside.

"Can you come?" Marie de Volonté whispered. "The queen would see you."

"Of course." Nicole jumped up and hurriedly glided toward the queen's rooms. Gliding, not bouncing, when she walked was one of the many skills she had learned at court over the past three years.

As the year progressed, so did the size of the queen's belly. With Philippe gone and her marriage far off in the summer ahead, Nicole's thoughts revolved around her queen's comfort. As usual with women, what appeared on the surface of Queen Anne's face masked something entirely different going on inside her. By Lenten season, the queen was halfway through her pregnancy. She had held up well through the holidays, but now she tired easily, her face strained and worried. Nicole hoped her sovereign's weariness in the final months of waiting could be chalked up to Madame de Laval's counsel: miserable pregnancy, healthy child.

Nicole knew that the queen wished for a large family, especially another boy or two to cement the succession to not only the throne of France, but the Duchy of Brittany which she had brought to her marriage.

As Nicole had heard the ladies of the court say, "She did what she had to do, and she made it work for her." The marriage between the Duchess of Brittany and the King of France, begun as a way for the duchess, now queen, to save her duchy, had turned into a loving one.

The more Nicole learned of her queen, the more she admired her. A woman who had ascended to power at age eleven, becoming Duchess of Brittany upon her father Duke Francis's death, her prowess as a ruler and patron of the arts was nothing less than astounding. She had brought over five hundred books to her marriage from the library in Nantes her father had left to her. Since then, she had commissioned many more, engaging countless scribes and illuminators to add to the library at Chateau d'Amboise, which had been all but empty during Charles VIII's twenty one years there before wedding his well-educated wife. In their seven years together, she and the king had overseen the complete renovation and expansion of Chateau d'Amboise, hiring builders, craftsmen, goldsmiths, and artists to transform the French royal court into one of Europe's finest. In addition, she oversaw the education of dozens of young noblewomen she had personally invited to court to serve as her maids of honor. If only her skill at bringing a child into the world and then keeping it alive could keep match with her accomplishments.

Nicole felt herself pulled back to the moment as she rounded the last corner to the queen's bedchamber. At the entrance, she stopped, taken aback by the scene before her.

The queen sat slumped in her chair, doubled over in pain. Her belly was evident now, her face pale and worn. Seven pregnancies in seven years had taken their toll. But what matter if the result was the birth of a healthy dauphin?

"Come, Nicole. The queen needs your healing touch." Madame de Laval lifted a silver-ringed hand from the queen's shoulder and gestured to Nicole.

"My lady, how can I help?" Nicole cried, rushing to her sovereign's side, her glide forgotten.

"Touch me, dear girl. Touch my belly the way you touched my horse, and heal what ails me," Anne said. Her eyes were opaque, guarded, as if she were in another world, one no one else could enter at that moment.

Nicole's heart hurt to see her queen in such a pained state. She had no experience with pregnancies, but she knew about infections. Apparently the queen had heard of Nicole's success with healing Petard. What else had she heard of that had gone on at the stables over the past fall? Brushing such thoughts aside, she put her hand on the queen's belly and slowly traversed its swollen, firm surface.

"My lady, I do not wish to hurt you," she said gingerly.

"Touch firmly, Nicole. Tell me if the babe is alive."

"But my lady, have not the doctors been called?" Why was she being given such responsibility, in place of the court doctors who attended the queen?

"A pox upon them! What good did doctors do for my son?" Queen Anne's voice broke in anguish.

"Your Majesty, the midwives are on their way now. Let us wait for them to arrive," Madame de Laval suggested, looking doubtfully at Nicole.

"Let her proceed," the queen commanded. "She healed my horse. She has knowledge in her fingers." She grabbed Nicole's wrist, forcing the girl's hand to remain on her stomach.

"My lady, give me a minute," Nicole said, pressing more firmly, her fingers walking the surface of Anne of Brittany's belly until she found what she was looking for. The throb of the babe's heartbeat was clear on the other side.

"The babe lives, Your Majesty," she finally said. "Here is his heartbeat, here."

"His. Hah!" the queen snorted bitterly, batting Nicole's hand away and putting her own there. After a minute, she slumped back again against her chair.

"Breathe, my lady, breathe deeply. Madame, can we bring some rose water for my lady the queen? And lavender sachets." Now that she knew the babe was alive, she would turn her attention to calming the queen with another one of her favorite scents: Rose de Provence. But what calm could there be for her sovereign until the babe was safely delivered? Even then, there could be no final sense of security for the queen after what had happened to her time and again with her other newborns, either born dead or dying hours or weeks after their entry into the world. Silently, Nicole pondered the heartbreak of motherhood her queen had suffered thus far. Would she herself take such a journey?

Madame de Laval clapped her hands twice. An attendant scurried out of the room in search of rose water and lavender.

"My lady, are you in pain?" Nicole questioned.

"I felt a cramp."

"Was it—was it the kind of cramp you've felt before?" She didn't dare mention the queen's three previous stillbirths. No mention of the past should sully the present moment. All signs should point to an auspicious outcome for this child, the seventh that had quickened in the queen's womb.

The queen's eyes closed as she nodded her head ever so slightly.

"No matter, my lady. It has passed, and the child's heartbeat is strong."

"Just do something, Nicole. Do something differently than what those quacks have done in the past." The queen sounded angry. Better that than resigned to failure.

"I will, my lady," Nicole promised. To begin, she would treat the child inside her queen as if it were her own. "May I put my hands on your belly again?"

"Please. Do what you did for my stallion. Do what you did for his mare. You are gifted with your touch, Nicole. We know.

Just don't go touching stable-boys," the queen laughed, the first moment of levity since Nicole had entered the chamber.

Blood rushed to Nicole's head. Saying nothing, she turned to take two sachets of lavender from the silver tray the noble-woman had brought back. She felt her face redden as she watched Madame de Laval put a graceful white hand to her mouth to suppress a snigger.

Head down, Nicole tucked a sachet under each of her sleeves then ran her hands over the queen's belly, through her gown. She had no idea whatsoever what to do to keep the child inside alive, but this much she did know. Babies like to be touched. She sensed they like to hear their mother's voices, too.

"My lady, would you speak to your child while I warm him with my hands?" she suggested.

The queen smiled wearily. "My child, stay inside awhile longer. And when you come out, stay on Earth until you have done your duty."

There it was again: the call to duty, this time coming from the queen. Nicole didn't like hearing it from her father, but from her queen it was different. Even the unborn one in the queen's womb was being called to serve a fixed role: either to one day rule France or to marry someone who would. No wonder the queen's children had resisted life on the outside. What freedom did they look forward to as royal heirs?

As Anne of Brittany, Queen of France, murmured to her unborn child, Nicole moved her hands over her belly as if she were caressing the babe itself. Within a minute, she felt a flutter under one hand. Her heart leaped for joy.

"My lady, did you feel that?"

"Dear girl, I have felt such a flutter countless times." Again, the queen shut her eyes.

Nicole couldn't imagine what her sovereign must suffer to have felt such stirrings of life through seven pregnancies, only to have not a single child to show for her labors. No wonder she had turned her mind so energetically to overseeing her castle and court. The paintings on the wall behind her had just arrived from Milan. They had been brought back by Charles VIII, from his last campaign there. Once the babe arrived safely, she had heard Madame de Laval say the queen planned to commission the painter himself to paint the child, perhaps the future dauphin. From past experience, one hardly dared hope.

"My lady, may I smooth your face?" It was best to act rather than think, especially upon the grim subject of the queen's previous pregnancies.

"By all means. Take off my headdress so you may massage my head. I am so tired of—" she waved away her thoughts with her hand, and rested it in her lap.

Nicole understood. It wouldn't do for her monarch to voice her fears to those beneath her. It would not be seemly for the queen of France to express weakness before her subjects.

Yet every woman in France knew her story, its barren outcome. How many of them at this moment were lighting a candle and saying a prayer for their queen, that this time the result would be different and France would celebrate the arrival of a dauphin in a few short months? Again, Nicole caught herself. Best not to speculate. Past experience did not bode well for future success when it came to the queen's pregnancies. Even worse, all of France knew of her trials.

Nicole took another lavender sachet and ran both of her hands over it, rubbing so that her skin absorbed its scent. Then she carefully tucked the sachet into the neck of the queen's gown. Thinking too much, especially on past events, would be best avoided by the queen until the babe's birth. Nicole would help her to feel rather than think. Distraction was where her sense of touch could accomplish the most good. And calming the queen would soothe the babe inside, just as her mother had calmed the mothers of sick children they had brought to her, knowing the children would be soothed if they sensed their mothers were.

She dipped her fingers in the bowl of rose water the attendant held out and lightly ran them over the queen's brow. At age twenty-one, Anne of Brittany's skin was still smooth and unwrinkled.

"Harder, dear. Don't be afraid to touch my face. It won't break," the queen directed her.

May your heart not break either. Nicole willed away the thought by pressing her fingers down more firmly. She smoothed the queen's face, circling each side of her brow, then worked her fingers back into her hairline.

"Ahhh," the queen sighed.

Nicole smiled to herself, gaining confidence, and began to massage the queen's head.

"Let your fingers work their magic like they did with my horse," the queen exclaimed. She leaned back in her chair, her head falling to one side.

Nicole worked silently, enjoying the half smile playing about her sovereign's mouth. She prayed the queen wouldn't mention Philippe again, nor would Madame de Laval either. Well she remembered running her hands through Philippe's thick *châtain* hair, a shade somewhere between brown and blond. Thinking of it made her fingers stronger, more imaginative in their romp through the queen's hair. She would massage the worries right out of her sovereign's head while she secretly conjured up the memory of Philippe's head in her hands. Would she ever see him again?

Mournfully, she contemplated a future without him. Then she thought of the sadness her queen must feel in contemplating her own past. First, the loss of both parents by age eleven, her sister at age twelve, then the loss of every one of her children, six in all. But the worst had been the death of Charles Orland less than two months after his third birthday.

What was the loss of her own one true love compared to the many loves her queen had lost? Still, it hurt to think she would never have Philippe de Bois to call her own. Just as Anne of Brittany, Queen of France, had never had any of her children to call her own for longer than a few hours or a few weeks, save for her ruddy little toddler.

Nicole's hands surged into the back of the queen's slender neck. Which loss could be worse? The loss of a child one has come to know and love, or the loss of a child one has never known outside the womb?

Undoubtedly the loss of Charles Orland, she mused. Who could forget the day the queen arrived home to learn the news? Nicole shook her head in memory, her fingers digging deeper into the queen's scalp, working hard to make her sovereign forget the past and think of nothing at all while she carried her still-living child.

CHAPTER SIX

A Queen Like No Other

No one had been able to deliver the news when the royal coach clattered into the courtyard that gray early December day in 1495. The king and queen had been escorted out hastily, faces pale and white, their eyes questioningly upon their staff. What they saw in their courtiers' eyes only whitened their faces further, and tightened the mask of composure that a monarch worthy of his or her title must wear in public.

It had been Jeanne de Laval who had rushed to the queen's side. Her voice was low, but Nicole could still hear the fateful words she delivered.

"He took with fever suddenly, Madame. No one could do anything."

"What do you mean? How is he?"

A horrible silence ensued. Not a single courtier spoke. Neither did anyone dare to look at the queen's face. Finally, Jeanne de Laval spoke again.

"Madame, you must be strong." She reached out, wrapping an arm around the queen's waist.

A heartrending cry broke from Anne of Brittany's lips. Nicole's insides twisted at the sound of it. She turned and hugged Marie de Volonté, who had come to court just weeks earlier. Mostly, they had been rivals, but they needed to support each other now, in order to help comfort the queen later when the full realization of what had happened overcame her.

Jeanne de Laval hustled the queen away from the staring eyes of the court, up the stairs and into the castle, to the bed-chamber of her son.

"*Mon bébé*, no-o-o-o-o," Anne of Brittany's anguished words carried down the stairs and into the courtyard, wrenching and terrible.

Nicole stood rooted to the spot along with the rest of the household. A chill fell over her heart, like an ice-cold stabbing pain. Hugging Marie de Volonté again, she willed it away. Then she opened her eyes onto the staircase and realized she would never see the bouncy, joyous Charles Orland run down them again, his nurse chasing him from behind, and the pain returned. If her own heart felt stabbed through by the thought, what must her queen's grief be like?

The dauphin was dead. There was nothing anyone could do to bring him back. It hadn't yet been officially announced, but everyone on the castle grounds already knew. Three nights before, the boy had come down with a fever after playing as usual during the day, then having supper with his nurse and attendants. Charles Orland had turned three less than two months earlier. His parents had been away, his father campaigning in Milan, and his mother staying in Lyon near the French-Italian border, where she could more quickly receive news and visits from her husband as he waged war on the other side of the Alps.

When Nicole had woken at dawn two days earlier to the sound of horses' hooves in the courtyard, she had rushed to the top of the gallery stairs just in time to see a messenger gallop away in the direction of Lyon. She had known instantly that the dauphin was gravely ill. By the time the king and queen arrived, he was already gone, carried to heaven on angels' wings deep in the night.

The king was as beside himself as the queen, although less vocal about it. Losing a child was terrible for parents, but losing the heir to the kingdom was another thing altogether. The death of the dauphin, the only direct inheritor to the throne of France, was a catastrophe for the country, as well as for every member of Charles VIII and Anne of Brittany's court. Charles Orland, the king and queen's robust and merry son, had been the flower of their hopes, with no other living children.

After two miscarriages and the loss of her only child, Queen Anne was beside herself. She shut herself away in her rooms for the entire Christmas and New Year's season, and was seen only twice over the following six weeks.

The beginning of 1496 dawned dismal and gloomy. The king's older cousin, Louis, Duke d'Orléans, was now heir to France. Anne had admired him as a child, but she wanted her own children to inherit the kingdom she ruled with her husband the king, not his cousin and his issue, although Louis had none yet. She had brought her own Duchy of Brittany to the throne, and she wanted her own child with Breton blood to rule her inherited lands one day, along with France. To that end, it soon became apparent as winter turned to spring that the queen was with child again. At least she had not let her grief overwhelm her instinct to try again.

The death of Charles Orland chilled Nicole's heart. Everyone said it was the first year of life that was the most dangerous for an infant. Yet the young prince had been strong and lusty from the moment he was born, and look what had happened to him. A fever or an accident could carry away anyone at any time. If even the king and queen's firstborn son couldn't be saved, how much hope did anyone else have for a child to grow into adulthood? All these worries Nicole hid in her heart and tried to keep out of her mind. It was enough just to live for the day, she told herself. It was all anyone had, really.

That September, before the harvest was picked, the new dauphin arrived. The court hummed with happiness, the king and queen beside themselves with joy. The child was named Charles, after his father. His arrival was heralded as a gift from heaven to replace the loss of Charles Orland of the year before. But on the first of October, the mild fall weather turned blustery; with the winds came a chill that caught the new prince and weakened him. Unbearably, on the third day of October, 1496, Charles VIII and Anne of Brittany lost their second dauphin.

That October 11th marked what would have been Charles Orland's fourth birthday. Instead it marked the loss of two living sons for the king and queen, and two dauphins for France. Queen Anne disappeared for the entire day, the king with her.

Nicole couldn't imagine what grief they shared between them. But perhaps because they were young and still in love, they turned to each other in their time of despair. This the court knew, because, by Christmas of that year, it was whispered that the queen was again with child.

In July of 1497, Anne of Brittany, Queen of France, delivered another son, Francis, Dauphin of France. Within hours he was dead.

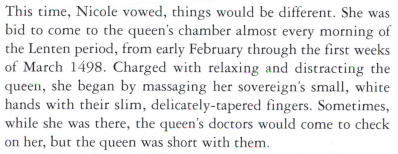

This time, Nicole vowed, things would be different. She was bid to come to the queen's chamber almost every morning of the Lenten period, from early February through the first weeks of March 1498. Charged with relaxing and distracting the queen, she began by massaging her sovereign's small, white hands with their slim, delicately-tapered fingers. Sometimes, while she was there, the queen's doctors would come to check on her, but the queen was short with them.

Nicole understood. They had succeeded neither in keeping her sovereign's toddler alive nor her two sons who had followed. What did they know?

"She is cramping again," Madame de Laval murmured to one of the senior ladies of honor, one rainy March day just before spring's arrival. Nicole caught their hushed conversation as she hurried past in the hallway outside the queen's chamber. She had just finished massaging the queen's fingers as well as her feet. They had been swollen, as had her face.

"Her time will come soon," the other remarked.

"She is not due until late spring," Madame de Laval observed, her face a tight mask.

"Let us keep her feet elevated and—"

A cry came from the chamber within. It was a cry every adult woman recognized, whether they had uttered it themselves or assisted one who had.

"Madame!" Jeanne de Laval rushed into the room as Nicole turned and followed behind.

The queen lay back in her chair, moaning. The ladies helped her up then began to walk her up and down the room. Nicole saw the cushion where the queen had sat. It was soaked. She peered closer. Water, not blood. Thank God.

"Get the midwife," Madame de Laval barked.

"Yes, Madame," Nicole ran from the room to the kitchens, where she knew the midwife and her assistants would be, warming themselves at the fire and on alert for the queen's needs.

At the entrance to the kitchen, the midwife and the head cook sat to either side of the giant hearth, mugs in hand.

"The queen has need of you," Nicole breathed out, holding her side where she felt a stitch. If the stitch hurt, what did a contraction feel like?

"Is she—"

"She is laboring." Nicole caught her chest with her hand. Out of breath from running, she couldn't imagine the true meaning of the words she had just spoken.

The midwife and cook jumped up, but not before Nicole caught the glance that passed between the two women.

"Boil the water and have the sheets brought up," the midwife instructed.

"God bless her this time," Cook said, shaking her head slightly as she turned to her task.

"God bless her and the babe," the midwife echoed, adjusting her headdress and following Nicole from the kitchen.

Next, Nicole was sent to the king's quarters.

"The queen's time has begun," she breathlessly exclaimed to Hubert de St. Bonnet. Soon enough, he would be her brother-in-law. Strange to think of, but the new relationship would bind her family closer to the king's men. Duty calls, she reminded herself. If the queen had to do her part, she could, too.

Hubert's brow knit together. Motioning her out of the room, he hurried after her.

"Is it not too soon?" he asked quietly.

Nicole looked up at him, willing her mouth not to quaver. She had heard the child was due at the end of spring, yet the vernal equinox had not yet come to pass. Spring began the next day. She nodded, saying nothing.

"What signs have you?" he asked.

"The queen's water has broken," she told him.

"Ahh. Then it will come."

Again, Nicole nodded. It was good to know that Hubert knew something about women's concerns. Perhaps one day he would be asking after her own birth pangs, and counseling his brother on how to help her. Shuddering, she shook off the thought.

"I will tell the king," he said. "Send someone for us at the stables when he is needed. He is down there now, inspecting a horse."

Nicole nodded and hurried back to the queen's quarters. From far down the corridor, she heard the queen cry out again. She prayed the babe that was coming would make as lusty a sound, although not so heartrending.

This time, the queen's chambers were crowded. Attendants murmured, and rustled by, carrying linens, smoothing the queen's bed sheets, preparing the place where the babe would rest, once born.

"The king?" Madame de Laval asked.

"He is down at the stables, Madame. Monsieur de St. Bonnet said to send someone there when he is needed."

"It will be a while yet," Madame de Laval remarked.

"What can I do?" Nicole asked.

"Pray for your queen."

"The babe comes early, no?" Nicole whispered.

Wordlessly, Madame de Laval shooed her away. What more could anyone say?

$$\clubsuit$$

Nicole returned to the kitchen, where it was warm and where most of the staff not attending the queen had congregated.

"My young lady, what news have you?" Cook asked, handing her a steaming mug of mulled wine.

"She labors now." Nicole gulped, and rejoiced at the taste of the cloves and cinnamon in the wine that warmed her stomach. "But is this her time?" she asked, in a lower voice.

Cook said nothing, but shook her head then went to the cupboard.

"Bring this to Mistress Midwife." She handed Nicole a vial containing a yellowish brown liquid.

"What's this?" Nicole asked.

"Myrrh for the queen's contractions. If she stops, this will stimulate them again. Mistress Midwife will know."

Nicole gulped down another mouthful of wine then set down the mug. How lucky she was to enjoy life's simple pleasures at that moment. Meanwhile, her queen suffered agony. Even with a successful outcome, Anne of Brittany faced the uncertainty of not knowing if her child would live. Based on past experience, the chances were not good.

Rushing back to the queen's chambers, she thought about the future with Gilles de St. Bonnet. Would there be a bouncing infant on the lap of the queen to mark his arrival for their wedding in July? And what about the following summer? Would there be one on hers as well?

"For Mistress Midwife, for the queen," Nicole breathlessly exclaimed, handing the vial to the assistant midwife. Across the room, she caught sight of her laboring monarch sprawled across her birthing stool, while an attendant smoothed her hair back from her head. Then someone blocked Nicole's sight line.

"Aarghh" the queen screamed.

"Shall I get some lavender?" Nicole asked, shaken to the core. Was this how life arrived? It sounded more like imminent death to her tender young ears.

"Too late for lavender. Or for myrrh." The assistant midwife shook her head. "The babe will come any minute. Tell the kitchen to send more hot water."

Nicole hurried back to the kitchen, relayed the order, and returned. She had never seen anyone give birth before. She doubted the senior ladies would allow her to witness the queen's moment, but perhaps she could slip in next to one of them, unnoticed. Didn't she need to know what would happen to her soon enough, once she was a married woman?

Quietly she entered the room and made her way over to the queen. Never had she seen her sovereign look so out of control. Anne of Brittany's hair and face were slick with sweat as she panted, her eyes shut. No wonder men were not allowed to attend births. No woman Nicole knew would want any man to see her in such a state.

"Your Majesty, we will try for the next round," the midwife was saying.

The queen's only response was an animal-like pant. One of her ladies put a cup of water to her mouth, and she drank, liquid dribbling down the side of her mouth.

Nicole was shocked. Anne of Brittany was a fastidious woman, careful in dress and behavior. Was this what giving birth did to a woman?

"Rest now and save yourself for the next—"

"Shut your trap!" the queen roared. Nicole had never heard her sovereign utter anything so coarse. Half terrified, half impressed, Nicole tried to move toward the laboring woman to put her hand on her, but the assistant midwife blocked her way.

"Go. This is not for you to see," she hissed.

"But I—"

"Go!"

"May I—"

"Get out!"

"Get it out!" the queen screamed, simultaneously with the assistant midwife's command. Immediately, the older women closed in around the birthing stool as the queen's next contraction began.

Nicole tried to make her way back to her, but Madame de Laval took her by the shoulders and propelled her toward the door.

"Go."

"But, Madame, I want to see what is happening," Nicole protested.

"No you don't," Madame de Laval said.

"But I do," Nicole replied.

"You will never let your husband near you, if you do. Now go!" With a shove, the older woman pushed her from the room.

Behind her, Nicole heard a long drawn-out scream, unlike any human voice she had ever heard. Shuddering, she felt the vibration from the doors slamming shut behind. Perhaps Madame de Laval was right—best not to witness such a sight if she were to go to her marriage bed willingly, which she would not. Already she was terrified to think of what lay ahead on the road of duty.

Back in the kitchen, she had just taken another long draught from her mug when one of the queen's attendants came in.

"She is delivered," the noblewoman announced curtly.

"Praise God," the head cook exclaimed as others in the kitchen crowded around, murmuring cautious thanks.

"And the babe?" Cook asked.

"Alive," the noblewoman's tone was flat, muted.

"Thanks be to God!" the cry went out.

"Is the babe well-formed?" someone inquired carefully.

"That is for the king to ask first, not for you," the noblewoman barked. "I'm here to tell someone to get him."

"I'll go!" Nicole volunteered. "I know where he is," she added, not saying where, so that she alone would be sent.

"Tell him his wife and new child await him."

The noblewoman's careful language told Nicole all she needed to know. But before she could ask, someone else did.

"And is it a dauphin who awaits him?"

The queen's lady-in-waiting glared at the owner of the voice. "It is not," she replied sharply then turned and disappeared back down the corridor, but not before taking the mug of mulled wine held out to her.

⚜

"Monsieur, the queen is delivered," Nicole exclaimed to Hubert de St. Bonnet, who stood on the other side of the fence inside the paddock where she and Philippe had trained Petard. The king stood well inside the paddock, his hands resting on a new horse that had been sent up from the South.

"Is it, is it a—?" Hubert stumbled.

"The babe is alive, Monsieur."

"And is it—?"

"It is a girl, sir." Nicole shook her head but smiled. Who cared if it wasn't a boy? What mattered was that the child lived. Certainly the queen was adept at becoming pregnant. She was young; she could try again for a boy.

Hubert nodded his head, looking thoughtful. He was no doubt formulating how he would break the news to the king.

"At least she lives," Hubert remarked.

"She lives, sir. And I am to tell you the queen and babe await the king."

"Go now. I will tell him." Hubert waved Nicole away. Quietly, she made her way up the path a few steps, then turned to see if Hubert was watching.

His back was toward her as he approached the king. Quickly, Nicole slipped behind a tree to see how Charles VIII would take the news.

The king faced toward her, his eyes on Hubert. Whatever Hubert was saying to him, Charles VIII nodded, then beckoned to his other men. In a minute, a group of four was on its way up the path, the king leading. As they passed, she caught sight of his face. Her heart leapt as she saw it was lit with joy. Charles VIII was not the handsomest of men, with his long nose, but he looked attractive now. Perhaps it was the thought of a daughter that lit up his face.

"This one I will name Anne, after the queen," she heard him say to Hubert de St. Bonnet.

"Nobly done, my lord," Hubert replied.

The king looked pleased. As he passed, he picked up his step, and the men following had to run to keep pace.

Later that afternoon, as she sat in the kitchen watching Cook prepare a cake in honor of the new princess, Nicole overheard a conversation behind her.

"When will they ring the bells?"

"This evening, perhaps. They rang them too soon after the last one."

Nicole turned to see who was talking. Two kitchen maids conferred, their expressions guarded. The older one was shaking her head, fingering her rosary beads.

"'Twas sad, the little Francis so quickly gone."

"'Twas worse the one before."

"You mean the second Charles? The one named for the king?"

"Yes. That one lasted a few weeks. The queen was beginning to get about again. She looked happy, like her old self, before her sweet boy died. Then just before what would have been the dead prince's fourth birthday, the new one caught cold and died." The older woman sighed. "Imagine."

"God save the queen." The younger kitchen worker crossed herself.

"God keep the new babe alive." The older woman followed suit.

Nicole couldn't bear to hear anymore. Hurrying from the kitchen, she made her way to the queen's chambers to see if she could catch a glimpse of the new princess.

This time she was in luck. The doors to the queen's quarters were open, and attendants passed back and forth, the younger ones with joyful faces, the older ones more neutral. The corner where the queen lay was blocked by attendants, but when Madame de Laval turned and crossed the room, Nicole moved toward her.

"How is the princess?" she asked.

Madame de Laval gave her a guarded look.

"She is small," she said shortly.

"But is she well-formed?"

The noblewoman said nothing. Her silence spoke volumes.

"May I see her?" Nicole asked, her throat closing.

"Not now."

"Is there a risk of—of—?"

"My child, the babe is here before her time. We will do all we can to keep her alive."

"How can I help then?"

"Pray." The older woman's eyes flickered then looked away. "Now leave me; I must go to the queen."

As Nicole made to leave, she heard rustling behind her, then the scent of male bodies. Turning, she saw the king and Hubert de St. Bonnet coming from the small room off the queen's chamber, where she knew the infant princess must be. The king's face beamed, making Nicole's heart jump for joy. Charles VIII did not look disappointed in the least that his queen had delivered a daughter.

Nicole smiled and curtsied as he made his way past. When she rose, still smiling, she caught sight of Hubert de St. Bonnet, his face like stone. It was strange because Hubert was a good courtier, one of the best. As Nicole was learning fast, the best courtiers were the quickest and most adept at reading their sovereign's expression, and then adopting a similar one. Perhaps he knew something the king didn't. Nicole looked at him carefully. He wasn't young, as Charles VIII was. Had age and experience taught him to guard his heart?

She shrugged off her thoughts and tiptoed toward the room where the new princess lay. Could she not just pretend she had something from the kitchen for one of the attendants inside? She picked up a pitcher of water from the table she passed on her way to the small inner room, its door firmly shut.

"You may not enter," one of the senior ladies snapped.

"The king has sent me. He would like a word with you," Nicole ad-libbed.

"The king was just here. What do you mean?" The woman eyed her suspiciously.

"He thought of something more he wishes to know. He waits in the hall now."

"What does he wish to know? I cannot leave here. I am charged with not allowing anyone to enter this room."

"He didn't tell me what he wanted; he just asked for you."

"For me? Personally? The senior noblewoman looked puzzled. But behind her frown, Nicole thought she detected a hint of pride at the thought that the king had asked for her personally.

"Yes, Madame! You! I will guard the door while you go to him," Nicole encouraged her.

The woman hesitated, looking around for help. The other attendants were at the side of the queen's bed, their backs turned to her and Nicole. "Promise you won't let anyone inside?" she finally said.

"Yes, on my heart." *Except for myself, of course.*

"Well, then, keep the door shut, will you?"

"Of course; I will ensure it stays shut." *Because I'll be on the other side, with my back against it.*

The noblewoman gave her one last look then hurried off.

Quickly, Nicole opened the door and slipped into the room. Inside, it was warm and dark, with the same cloying scent she had smelled outside in the queen's chambers. It was the aroma of blood, birth, and new life. She breathed in deeply to embrace it. One day soon, she would be scenting it in her own birthing chamber, if God was gracious.

"No one is allowed in here. Get out!" the nurse barked.

"The king sent me to check on the princess." Nicole stood tall, her face a courtier's mask.

"The king was just here. Get out, you impertinent girl!"

"He wishes to know if—if the princess—" What should she say? She just wanted to get a peek at the new princess, swaddled in linens and lying deep in the crib behind the nurse.

"If the princess, what?"

Inspiration struck. "If the princess cried when she was delivered. . ."

"Why would he send *you* to ask such a thing?" The nurse came toward her, as if she would push Nicole from the room herself.

"Begging your pardon, Madame, but the king told Monsieur de St. Bonnet to ask a maiden to come to you."

"For what reason?"

"I have no idea." Truly, she didn't. But banking on the bad luck that had befallen the queen before, she hoped the nurse would believe that the king might be feeling superstitious at that moment. Nicole had noted already at court that when her elders felt helpless in the hands of fate, they turned to symbols of purity and innocence to help them commune with the higher powers. Maidens, unicorns, and saints took center stage at such moments.

"Then you can tell him the babe did not cry." The nurse's mouth pursed.

"How wonderful," Nicole breathed out. The babe had held herself like the royal child she was from the moment she arrived.

"Wonderful it was not," the nurse rebuffed her.

"No?" Nicole tried not to show her ignorance. What did she know about newborns? Nothing.

The nurse snorted. "When a babe just delivered doesn't cry, it is never a good sign." She glared at Nicole. "But say nothing to the king. Just tell him the babe didn't cry."

"May I see the princess?"

"You may not." The nurse crossed her arms over her ample waist and moved to block Nicole from approaching the crib.

Nicole summoned all of her powers of imagination. This would be her last chance.

"The king has asked that I gaze on the princess's face."

"What is it you need to know?" the nurse hissed.

"I cannot say. He charged me with looking upon the princess's face then reporting back to him."

The nurse looked doubtful.

"For good luck," Nicole murmured. "He wishes me to give her a maiden's blessing." She cast down her eyes, trying to look as maidenly as possible, opening her hands palms outward to the nurse in supplication.

The nurse studied her for a moment, while Nicole held herself like a statue.

"You may not touch her," the woman finally said. "Just a peek. Then be on your way."

"Of course not. I will just do the king's bidding." God forbid that it got back to the king that she had spun this tale. She sucked in her breath, thinking of the trouble she would be in.

A knock came at the door. The nurse looked uncertainly at Nicole then went to answer it.

Quickly, Nicole moved to the side of the crib. Bending over she peered into the babe's crib.

"What is that girl doing in here?" a voice angrily exclaimed from the doorway.

"She said the king sent her," the nurse replied.

"I have just seen the king. Get her out of here!" The lady-in-waiting who had been guarding the door had returned.

Nicole felt the nurse's meaty hand on her arm.

"Go now. The princess sleeps and mustn't be disturbed."
Firmly, the nurse dragged Nicole away from the crib and toward
the door. As they passed the lady-in-waiting, she reached out
and slapped Nicole's face.

"I told you to guard the door, not enter the room."

"My lady, I thought you meant to guard the door from the
inside." The sting distracted her from what she had just seen.
It almost felt good to hurt on the outside the way she did on
the inside.

"You thought no such thing, cheeky girl. Go!" The noblewoman slammed shut the door behind her.

On the other side, Nicole quickly exited the queen's chambers before Madame de Laval could catch sight of her and discover what she had been up to.

It wasn't before she had escaped to the herb garden outside
the kitchen that she was able to sit down on a bench and consider the tiny creature she had just viewed in her crib.

The princess had been very small. Her face had been almost
as white as the linens against which she lay. Her eyes had been
shut, her eyelids translucent. She had almost looked like a doll,
but for one point: her face had been wizened. Nicole's heart
caught to think of it.

She knew almost nothing about newborn infants. But from
what she understood from bits and pieces of conversation she'd
overheard from the married ladies, babies were supposed to
be noisy, sucking, red-faced creatures. Perhaps the little princess had just looked so fragile and pale because she was asleep.
She shuddered, thinking of the other possibility. Perhaps the
queen's daughter had arrived in this world much too soon.

By vespers, the chapel bells still had not rung in honor of
the princess's birth; nor by complines, the hour when the royal
household usually retired for the day.

Nicole couldn't sleep. She needed to help her queen and if possible, the infant princess, although she had no idea how. To begin, she returned to the chapel after complines, and prayed.

Then she made her way to the queen's doors, but was shooed away. Down in the kitchen, there was more activity at that hour than usual with women gliding by, their expressions worried, their mouths grim-set.

Nicole sat at the kitchen table, fingering her rosary beads. As she did, she felt her eyes close.

"Go to bed, my lady, "Cook's voice jolted her awake. "There is nothing more to be done here. You will be of more use tomorrow if you have slept," she told her. She motioned for Nicole to drink from the mug she'd put in front of her. "To help you sleep," she explained.

Obediently, Nicole drained the mug then got up and slowly climbed the stairs to her chambers. On her way, she passed several female members of the queen's household, all silent, some of them holding their rosary beads as they passed. None made eye contact with her.

As she drifted off to sleep, she prayed to God to protect the little princess. And to protect her queen who had borne so many losses at such a young age. Then she fell into a sound sleep and didn't dream at all.

The next day, Nicole awoke with joy in her heart at the princess's arrival and with it the start of spring. What time of year could be more propitious for a new life to enter the world? She pulled on her clothes and hurried down to the kitchen to hear how the queen and babe were faring. As she entered, she smiled at the noblewoman leaving, but her senior peer did not smile back.

Nicole's heart froze. With it, her mouth formed itself into the tight neutral line she had seen on the faces of the women attending the queen after her delivery the day before.

Cook came over and hugged her. Her embrace was unexpected. When she released her and stepped back, her face told her everything. The gruff but kind Breton woman was not one to remain silent. If even *she* was at a loss for words, then surely what words were to come were not ones anyone wished to speak or hear.

Nicole gasped. "The babe?"

Cook shook her head, her mouth a tight line.

"But she was well-formed, wasn't she?" She thought back to the babe's wizened face and Madame de Laval's silence, when she had asked her the same question. Other courtiers had said the babe was well-formed, but it was something courtiers said because it was what their sovereigns wanted to hear.

Cook continued to shake her head. "She came too soon."

"Oh, God, what happened?"

"What usually happens to babes who arrive before they are due." Cook crossed herself.

"Dear God, dear queen, dear princess. . ." Nicole felt as if her heart was breaking. How could it go so badly for the queen time after time? "What happened?" she asked again.

"The babe wouldn't suck. She drifted off to sleep before midnight, and when the nurse checked her awhile later, she was gone for good, flown home to Heaven."

"Oh, God." Nicole couldn't bear it. One minute here, the next gone forever. "How is the queen?"

Cook closed her eyes. "As you might imagine."

"What can I do for her?" Nicole's voice came out in a wail.

"You can take this hot drink to her."

Nicole reached for it and turned to go, but Cook laid her hand on her arm and stopped her.

"You are young, my lady."

"I've seen plenty," Nicole replied. Now she had.

"You love her, don't you?" Cook's face was tender.

"I love her like no other," Nicole said fiercely. "No one is as noble as she."

"I know. So here's my advice when you see her." Cook stopped a moment and thought, her eyes faraway. They were remote; the eyes of a woman, not of a girl. "Don't say anything. Don't show a sad face. Whatever look is on her face, wear it, too. In such a way you will comfort her."

"Cook, you would make a good courtier."

Cook made a snorting noise and crossed her arms in front of her. "God saved me from such a false profession. I'd rather make real food to fill real stomachs."

"Do you say my job is not important?" Nicole pulled herself up, staring down Cook.

"I say, my lady, that some were born to serve and others were born to serve those who serve."

"And the king and queen?"

"The king and queen serve us all." Cook crossed herself. "But you must be strong for her now. She can't show sorrow and you mustn't remind her of it. Do you understand?"

"I understand." Nicole gave Cook a small smile. "Your words are as wise as your soups are delicious." She needed to patch things up fast. Although her station was above Cook's, it wasn't entirely secure. If she didn't marry into the nobility, her own half-noble roots would fall back into her father's merchant status with her mother gone. Cook was the closest thing she had to a mother; she couldn't afford to lose her love.

"Soon the queen will enjoy my soups again," Cook said. "But today, let her grieve, and do not look her in the face. Just give her this."

Nicole wondered at the strange line of her mouth she felt on her own face. It was a different configuration than the one she had worn waking up that morning: tighter, more tempered by worldly woe. The events of the past twenty-four hours had changed her. She would serve her queen by bearing her sorrows with her, while putting a good face on it. As much as she felt useless to help the queen, she knew it was important to support her. Perhaps if there was a next time, Nicole could do more to ensure that the queen's newborn lived.

On that inauspicious first day of spring, Anne of Brittany, Queen of France, did not appear. No one expected her to. Before anyone could ask where the king was, it was announced that he had gone out hunting. Not a good time for him to put on a good face either. The Princess Anne had been his first daughter born alive. She would be his last.

In the days that followed, the weather slowly warmed until finally the doors to the queen's chambers opened again, the windows were unshuttered, and the sounds of early spring made their way into the royal rooms, along with Nicole.

Back to massaging her sovereign's face and helping smooth her petite figure back into place, Nicole wore a new, more careful expression around the woman she admired most. Reflecting her sovereign's composure, she worked quietly and told herself there would be another chance for the still-young queen: another live birth, and, hopefully with it, a child that lived beyond a day. With spring's unfolding, Nicole reasoned, the queen's misfortune could not possibly get worse.

Except that it did.

⚜

After twenty days of mourning, the queen emerged on the Saturday afternoon before Palm Sunday to accompany the king to a tennis tournament. In a hurry, and not wanting to bump into too many sets of sorrowful eyes and whispered asides, they took a discreet route to the courts, using the corridors through the underground cellars to make their way to the tennis grounds.

Nicole watched as they slipped through the cellar door from the kitchen, her heart full to see them on their way to spend an afternoon together. Both were still young, the king twenty-eight, the queen twenty-one. Hope would return, Nicole thought, watching the king put his hand on the small of the queen's back. If the afternoon's entertainment proved enjoyable enough, perhaps a seed would be planted that very night.

Soon after they left, a messenger arrived, requesting the king's physician to come immediately. Someone had hurt himself on the tennis grounds. Nicole turned to Madame de Laval to ask why it was the king's physician and not a lesser one being asked to attend.

"I don't know, Nicole. I don't know, but we shall soon find out." Madame crossed herself as her handsome face settled into the same worried lines Nicole had seen on it the day the princess had died.

The afternoon passed uneventfully until the sky streaked with pale rose and blue, then deepened into indigo and purple.

Nicole shuddered as she sat with Marie de Volonté on the bench in the herb garden after supping in the kitchen. Something about those crepuscular shades seemed somber that evening. Perhaps it was residual grief from the passing of the newborn princess.

"Why is the queen not back yet?" Marie de Volonté asked. "The games must surely be over." She looked pleadingly at Nicole, almost as if asking her to give an answer that involved no bad news. Marie was only just fifteen. She had seen too much already for one so young, with the recent loss of the queen's daughter as well as the queen's newborn son the summer before.

"I don't know, Marie. Maybe they're at a reception for the winners," Nicole guessed. She was happy to think the king and queen were tarrying on their afternoon outing. Perhaps they were enjoying themselves for the first time since the death of their daughter.

"Then why was the court not invited?" Marie pressed.

"Who knows? Unless it's because the king and queen don't want the court all around them now while they heal from—from what has passed."

Marie followed Nicole upstairs, where they readied themselves for bed. But as she tried to fall asleep, Nicole felt the same restless feeling she had felt the night the princess had died. Finally she drifted off.

From a deep, dreamless sleep she was awoken by voices in the courtyard. Men were shouting, barking orders as they carried someone into the outer courtyard. Peering out an upstairs inner window, she saw a form on a pallet being carried by four courtiers. She knew it must be someone important. Then she heard words that chilled her heart.

"Make way! Make way for the king!"

Frozen, she watched as the men struggled to mount the staircase with the pallet in hand. The figure upon it was indeed the king, but he lay motionless, his eyes shut. Feeling a small movement next to her, she turned and saw Marie de Volonté in her nightdress, staring down at the sight, her clear brown eyes wide with horror.

Quickly she hugged the younger girl to her.

"Don't worry, little one. The king must have taken a fall. The doctors will take care of him," she reassured her.

Marie de Volonté looked up at her with mournful eyes. "Do you think he lives?"

"Yes, little one. Of course," Nicole told her, less certain than her words.

"As you thought the princess would live," Marie said tearfully.

"Little one, what will be will be. It is not for you to worry." She squeezed her sometimes-rival to her tightly. There were times to fight. There were times to comfort. This was a moment to comfort. Neither could bear the thought that the king might be in mortal danger.

Just before midnight, the bells of the chapel tolled. They rang slowly, letting members of the court and in the surrounding countryside know the news. Nicole and Marie de Volonté were already in the kitchen where they had heard already. Unable to sleep, they had dressed and slipped downstairs, where they had sat mute in one corner, ears perked, taking in the story of what had happened as various of the king's men came into the kitchen for food and drink then left.

Charles VIII, King of France, was dead. On his way to the tennis courts, he had struck his head on a low-hanging lintel over one of the doorways in the underground passageway he and the queen had taken to avoid being seen. The force of the blow had knocked him out for a minute but he had recovered. They had continued on to the courts, where he had greeted his courtiers, made small talk, then fell to the ground unconscious. Never regaining consciousness, he succumbed an hour before midnight that same day.

For the next two days, the queen didn't leave her rooms. Nicole heard in the kitchen that Anne of Brittany had refused all food, and was saying she wished to follow her lord and children to the grave. No one knew what to do or how to console her. In the space of three weeks, she had lost both her only living child and her husband. It was beyond unthinkable. Not yet fully recovered from the delivery and death of her daughter, the queen, in her bottomless grief, had no one to turn to as a peer. In the past, she had recovered from the deaths of each of her children with the help of her husband. But now it was the king himself, at the age of twenty-eight, who had followed his four sons and three daughters, three of them stillborn, to the grave. The date was April 7, 1498.

Within days, Charles VIII's cousin, Louis, Duke d'Orléans, arrived at the Chateau d'Amboise to comfort the queen, make the necessary funeral arrangements, and secure his succession to the throne of France as closest male relative to the late king. Knowing Anne since her childhood, he was her only peer support as well.

Nicole had overheard Madame de Laval whisper to one of the other ladies that the Duke d'Orléans had offered to pay all expenses for the funeral of Charles VIII. Not only was the new king paying his respects to his predecessor, but he was providing practical support for Anne of Brittany, no longer queen upon the death of her husband. It was a generous gesture, one that immediately told the court that Louis d'Orléans wished to impress the late king's widow, for reasons unclear.

Orders were given, and by Easter Sunday it was evident that the funeral of Charles VIII of France would be sumptuous indeed.

Soon a letter arrived by courier for Nicole. Her father and uncle would attend the king's funeral and, at that time, would speak with her about plans for the summer ahead. The vague wording of the message informed her that a change might be in the works. Her intended, Gilles de St. Bonnet, had been the target of her father and uncle because of his brother's close connection with the late king. But with the Duke d'Orléans soon to be crowned Louis XII, King of France, would her male relatives wish to rethink their marriage plans for her?

Nicole's insides tingled. There was nothing wrong with Gilles de St. Bonnet. But a change in prospective husbands would mean a reprieve from her wedding day. Perhaps fate would grant her another chance to see Philippe before that day closed in on her. After what she had seen with her own eyes regarding birth, she was in no rush to begin breeding. God alone knew what lay ahead for her on that score.

In the weeks that followed, Nicole tried not to show her high spirits at the thought that her father and uncle might have new plans in mind for her future. Her father was a good businessman, her uncle even better. She knew both were now evaluating the winds of change that blew across the court with the new king's installation. She could only hope that whatever plans were being laid would take some time to come to fruition. Meanwhile, she would keep an ear to the ground and find out if Philippe de Bois was due back anytime soon.

CHAPTER SEVEN

Summer of Uncertainty

Strolling down to the stables, Nicole peered ahead to see if Petard was in his paddock. The day was mild, with a pale blue sky overhead. A light breeze played with her headdress, and the birds chattering in the trees along her path seemed to be trying to tell her something. Looking at them more closely, she saw a mother bird feed food from her own mouth into her chick's mouth. How sweetly the mother tended her child. Would that the man she might have her own child by one day be the man she loved to tend so closely.

Turning the final corner before the stables came in sight, Nicole spotted two men up ahead. One was middle-aged, the stable-yards manager. The other was older, and limped as he walked toward the paddock railing. Coming up behind them, she moved as silently as possible to catch their conversation before they became aware of her presence. It was a tactic she had learned at court. With every official word as studied as the expression one wore in front of others, the only way to learn any real news was to listen in on private conversations without making one's presence known. That had been one of the side benefits of learning how to glide noiselessly when walking. It had been the queen herself who had taught Nicole that skill.

". . . to train him for tilting." she heard the tail end of the stable-manager's words.

"I would if I could, but my foot is troubling me these days."

"Is it age, then?"

"Aye, and that bitch of a mare that stomped on me in Agen. I've never been right since."

Nicole sucked in her breath. Was this the king's trainer Philippe had spoken of in jest? The one Philippe had replaced when he had come to break in Petard?

"Jeannot, you've got the training. No one else has your way to train a horse for tourneys."

It was Jeannot, Philippe's master back in Agen. Nicole did her best to catch every word.

"I like the honey in your words, but it's not true," Jeannot replied. "There is one. . ."

"And who might that be?"

"The lad who helps me in Agen."

"A lad?" The stable-manager's voice dripped disdain.

"He's twenty now. Grown to manhood. He helped break in the stallion last year. Knows the horse and how to train animals for the jousting ring."

"Aye, I know the one. Where is he now?"

"Back in Agen."

"When does he come next?"

"He's to be married there this summer, so he'll be busy."

Nicole stood rooted to the spot. Had she heard correctly?

"Aye, that's busy work for a lad of twenty," the stable-manager laughed.

An icy chill moved up her insides at the sound of the stable-manager's crude laugh.

"Yes, and a good match for him. 'Tis a widow with a small dowry; she's young, and some say fair."

"What happened to her man?"

"He had an accident while out with the duke's men, falconing."

"A shame."

"Yes, but a stroke of good luck for the lad. His parents are dead, and he had no prospects. The widow will saddle him."

"Aye, and ride him well, I'll wager."

The men's coarse laughter rang in her ears. She turned and ran back up the path, toward the chateau and the future she had been avoiding. What was the point? Fate would have its way with Philippe de Bois, too, and there was nothing either of them could do about it.

Just before the kitchen doorway, she turned into the storeroom where the barrels for ale and wine were kept. She sank to the floor and sobbed until her insides heaved.

In the weeks that followed, Anne of Brittany surprised not just Nicole, but the entire court. There were many who had feared for her life in the days immediately following the king's death. But there was work to be done surrounding the passing of Charles VIII. No longer queen, her uncertain situation sharpened her focus. Anne of Brittany had been raised to rule, as well as to swim the uncertain tides of political change.

The death of yet another of her children had devastated her, but had not stripped her of political power. The death of her husband the king was another thing altogether. Her present status was uncertain. As astute as Louis d'Orléans, soon to be crowned the new king, Anne recognized the need to grasp the reins of whatever political power she had, in order to show her people she was still a force.

The former queen was still Duchess of Brittany. It was a role Charles VIII had not wished her to actively play. He had let her know at the outset of their marriage that he would be the one to manage the lands she had brought him as her marriage dowry.

But with Charles VIII's death, Anne quickly stepped up to take the reins of leadership over her own inherited lands. Within a fortnight of her husband's death, she had sent large bolts of black cloth to all of Brittany's noble families, with instructions on how to mourn the death of the king of France. White had traditionally been the color of mourning, but Anne decided that deep purple or black would be the new colors to wear and to display to mourn the king properly. She had gotten the idea from reports her husband had given her on Milan, from whence came all the newest fashions and designs.

Charles VIII had overseen Brittany himself, but with him gone, and no infant nor children to occupy her time, Anne immediately took over administration of her own lands. In addition, she invited the top Breton noblemen to attend the service she organized to memorialize the dead king on May 15, in Amboise.

The morning of the ceremony dawned glorious and fair. Nicole's father and uncle had arrived, and the court was abuzz with what looked to be amicable relations between the former queen and Louis, Duke d'Orléans, in line to become next king of France. It was rumored that Anne of Brittany would leave for Paris the following day, there to stay for the remainder of the spring and part of the summer, mourning her dead husband and planning her next steps. Charles VIII had left her a large house there, known as the Hotel d'Etampes, a residence traditionally set aside for widowed queens of France. Now it would prove a strategic spot from where she could chart her future.

Nicole had heard from her father that wedding plans were to be delayed. But with Philippe to be married, what difference did it make? Whoever and whenever she married, she would not marry the one she loved, but the one her family thought the best match to further their political and social interests.

Scanning the crowd, Nicole prayed that Gilles de St. Bonnet was not in attendance. Instead, she looked for a blondish-brown-haired head attached to a young slim body. If only she could see those mutable gray-green eyes again, eyes that had sparked blue then sometime gold in the sunlight when they gazed at her a certain way.

Fortunately Madame de Laval was busy: first with the memorial service, then with preparations for the former queen's trip to Paris the following day. She would accompany her, along with other senior members of the court. Nicole and Marie de

Volonté would stay behind, lightly chaperoned. Already she looked forward to it. The only dark spot on the horizon was the thought of Philippe being married off. She wished desperately she could see him again before he disappeared forever from her life.

As Anne of Brittany passed, Nicole craned her neck to see her noble employer. She had barely seen her since the day of the king's accident. Petite and erect, Anne slowly walked the length of the courtyard from her chambers to the chapel, where the memorial service would be held. Behind her, the tall form of Louis d'Orléans matched her pace, his eyes riveted on the former queen ahead. From what she could see, the future king of France, with his longish aristocratic nose and soulful blue-gray eyes, wasn't bad-looking.

"Where is the wife of the Duke d'Orléans?" Nicole asked her father beside her.

"That hunchback? They live apart. I'm sure Louis wants her out of the way," Michel St. Sylvain said, looking over Nicole's head at his brother on her other side.

"Especially now," her uncle agreed.

"Why especially now?" Nicole asked, curious.

"Worry about your own future, not the queen's, *ma petite*," her uncle dismissed her.

"Not the queen anymore, is right. But not for long, if she plays her cards right," Michel St. Sylvain joked.

"Papa, she is mourning, not thinking of playing cards! How can you say that?" Nicole cried, indignant.

"Daughter, do you think Anne of Brittany is so beside herself that she hasn't considered her own future?" He shook his head, looking at her affectionately. "Think again, dear one. The woman who brought you to court is no ninny. She will not relinquish the Crown of France easily."

"Not if there is any other way to keep it on her head," Benoit St. Sylvain added, eyeing Louis d'Orléans behind the former queen, his eyes glued to the tiny female figure he followed. "Who is that man behind d'Orléans?" He pointed toward the procession.

Michel St. Sylvain strained his neck to see who his brother spoke of. "You mean behind the new king," he corrected him.

"Yes, the one wearing the crest of Orléans."

"That's Gerard d'Orléans," Nicole's father replied. "the duke's cousin, I believe."

"You mean the cousin of the new king, as you pointed out." Benoit St. Sylvain specified, looking meaningfully at his brother.

"Yes. That would be him." Michel St. Sylvain returned his brother's look with one of his own.

"Is he not the one whose wife died in childbirth last year?" Benoit continued.

Nicole's father shrugged. "He may be. I heard talk of it. Why?"

Benoit's voice became lower, "He has not yet remarried, I believe."

"No?" Nicole's father lowered his voice to match his brother's. "Is he betrothed then?"

"Let's find out," Benoit breathed back. Both men glanced at Nicole in the same instant.

"What are you thinking, Uncle Benoit?" Nicole asked, alarmed.

"Shhh, *ma chére.* We think of your future, of what is best for you."

"You think of what is best for our family, not what is best for me," Nicole railed.

Her father's eyes sparked with anger then became icy. "My daughter, what argument do you make? What is best for your family is what is best for you."

"Papa, I am not a horse to be paired off with the most highly-bred stallion," she objected.

"No. You are my daughter, to be paired off with a husband who is most closely allied with your sovereign," Michel St. Sylvain's tone was clipped, as if laying down the law.

But which law was it: the one of the old regime or the one of the new? Nicole wondered. Everything seemed to be changing around her. The only thing that didn't change was that Michel St. Sylvain would always be her father, and her duty would always be to obey him.

"But the man you chose for me is closely allied to the king," Nicole began then paused. "I mean the old king."

"Precisely," her father agreed.

"Precisely," her uncle echoed. He shot his brother another look and as Nicole took it in, a sudden breeze gusted past, lifting the ends of the black silk cape she wore over her shoulders. Change was in the air.

⚜

Within the next two months, it became apparent that Anne of Brittany couldn't imagine herself as anything less than what she had been already. She was no longer technically queen of France, but she remained the queen of people's hearts. More importantly, she remained queen in her own heart. The household at Amboise received regular reports from Paris that the bereaved widow was being comforted with almost-daily visits from the new king, Louis XII of France.

At the beginning of August, a messenger clattered into the courtyard with news that the king had asked for an annulment from Rome for his marriage to Jeanne of France, his hunch-backed wife for over twenty years.

Everyone knew what that request meant. Louis XII was clearing the way to marry the former queen.

"A message, too, for the young lady Nicole from Michel St. Sylvain," the messenger announced.

"A message from my father?" Nicole asked, half excited, half alarmed. "What is it?" She rushed down the stairs to the courtyard, forgetting to glide for the moment.

"I am to tell you that your father wishes you to know of the successful outcome of recent negotiations. . ."

"What negotiations?" Nicole interrupted him.

The messenger looked blank. "I do not know, my lady. I am just to give you the message."

"Yes. Continue, please." What plans were her father and uncle hatching for her now?

"He bids you to await the arrival of your betrothed in the final week of September, and to prepare for your wedding shortly thereafter."

"Of my betrothed?" Nicole asked. "Do you mean Monsieur de St. Bonnet?"

"Monsieur de St. Bonnet?" the messenger repeated, looking confused.

"Yes. Is that who you mean?"

"I do not know what I mean, my lady. I mean, I am charged with delivering you this message but I know not what the meaning of it is." The messenger looked at her blankly, at a loss for further words.

"Do you know of whom my father spoke?" she asked impatiently.

"Do you mean the man in question for your hand?"

"Yes! Of course I mean the man in question. Do you speak of Gilles de St. Bonnet?"

"My lady, I am sorry, but I do not mean this Monsieur de St. Bonnet," the messenger stammered.

"Don't be sorry. I don't care!" Nicole caught herself as laughter trilled on the stairway behind her, most probably from Marie de Volonté, who knew well that Nicole was reluctant to be married off to a stranger. "I mean, I do care. I would like to know who the man in question is." She straightened her gown, thinking how ridiculous it was to receive such an important message and not know who her intended was.

"My lady, your father mentioned his name, but it escapes me." The messenger looked helpless as well as fatigued.

"What do you mean, his name escapes you? I would like very much if you could recall it, so that I may know who I prepare for," she scolded him.

"I cannot remember if your father mentioned a name. No, I don't think he did."

He paused, looking blank, but then caught himself. "Oh, yes. He gave me something for you." Reaching into his saddlebag, he pulled out a small package.

"Thank you." Hastily, Nicole ripped open the package and found a small locket within. Holding it up to the light, she saw the crest of a porcupine on it. It was the device of the House of Orléans, the family of Louis XII, of the lesser Valois line. The greater Valois line was now extinct, with the death of the son-less Charles VIII. Even more reason for the new king to quickly secure his claim to the throne before someone else challenged it.

Oohs and ahhs from those close to her in the courtyard resounded. Was nothing ever private amongst the courtiers and staff of the household of Amboise?

"'Tis the device of the king," Marie de Volonté breathed out, peering over Nicole's shoulder. The younger girl's envy was as palpable as a cold rain shower.

"'Tis indeed," Nicole sighed. The meaning was clear. She was to wed the one from the House of Orléans, the man her father and uncle had noticed at Charles VIII's funeral. The locket must be from the king directly, as only the king had permission to use the image of the porcupine. But it signified that it was Louis XII himself who approved the marriage. Her father and uncle must have made a very good negotiation this time. Out with Gilles de St. Bonnet, and in with Gerard d'Orléans. Either way, it was all the same to her.

She fled up the stairs and ran toward the kitchen, her haven and refuge. Her upcoming marriage was more than just a possibility. With the new king's seal of approval upon it, it would come to pass. How strange to feel that it made no difference who her husband was to be, since her heart had no part in either man.

Angrily, she kicked at a heap of sacks piled outside the kitchen doorway. She would not disappear into married life without any exercise whatsoever of her own will. She would find a way to her heart's desire.

"Will the pope grant an annulment because the king's wife is too ugly to bed?" Nicole asked Cook in the kitchen, her source of news untrammeled and unvarnished by courtiers' flattery.

"Bah—'tis not her looks, 'tis the fact that they live apart, with no children to show for twenty-two years of marriage. She will give him up because she knows she does not have the love of the people," the Cook opined, a wellspring of information as usual.

"And does he?" Nicole asked. She knew next to nothing about the new king or his family. She wondered if she would be finding out more soon.

"He will if he marries your queen," Cook said, her eyes shining. "She is such a one who knows how to gain the people's hearts. Is she not?"

"She is indeed!" Nicole agreed. "She taught me how to glide when I walk." Nicole jumped up to demonstrate, sailing across the kitchen like a swan.

"Aye, she knows all manners of tricks to appear as one born to rule," Cook observed, rolling her eyes. She slid a tankard to Nicole as she sat at the large kitchen table.

"Do you call them tricks? I call them social graces," Nicole lifted her chin to remind Cook of her rank. Nicole had a position to uphold. Every once in a while it seemed that Cook needed reminding.

"Yes, whatever you might call them, they do the job they are meant to do."

Nicole nodded. She couldn't wait for her queen to become wife of the new king so she could resume her school for her maids of honor. Then she remembered. She would not be a maid of honor for much longer, but a married lady of honor. She wished there was someone like her mother or Madame de Laval to help her navigate the changes going on around her. At least there was Cook.

"The queen is clever. She is not going to give up being queen if she can help it," Cook continued.

"But she also cares for Louis d'Orléans — I mean, the new king — does she not?"

"Oh, indeed. When she was a little girl, I worked in her household in Nantes. Louis d'Orléans came there as a young man, when she was about seven years old. My, she had a crush on him! And he admired the little duchess most strongly."

"Then why weren't they betrothed then?" Nicole had forgotten Cook was a Breton. She had come to Amboise from Nantes, far to the west in Brittany, soon after Anne had married Charles in 1492.

"'Twas sad. The young man had been married off by his father to the hunchback when he was barely more than a child.

She was daughter to Louis XI, King of France. 'Tis said the boy's father threatened to lock him up in a monastery if he didn't go along with the plan."

"How old was he?" So she wasn't the only one who hadn't wanted to wed the one chosen for her by others. Even the king of France had found himself in such a helpless position.

"I think about fourteen."

"That's younger than I am!"

"'Tis a good age for a woman to find a match. But for a man, 'tis young." Cook scowled and shook her head. "He had no say in the matter at all."

Nicole silently agreed. Not that she was ready to be wed, but to imagine a fourteen-year-old boy being married off was ludicrous. Even thinking of Philippe marrying at age twenty seemed absurd. "So when he met our queen, how old was he?"

"He was . . ." Cook counted on her fingers. "He was about twenty-two."

"Oh . . ." Nicole drifted off, imagining her queen as a seven-year-old duchess meeting the tall, handsome Louis d'Orléans at age twenty-two.

"Oh, indeed. Think on it."

"I am." She sipped the cool elderflower drink Cook had put in front of her, feeling as light as the summer breeze wafting in through the open double doors next to her. With almost no supervision and Cook's chatty remarks to absorb, Nicole was having a carefree summer. If only she could share it with the one she loved. Under the table, her leg tingled as she thought of Philippe's own leg next to hers as they had lain on the hillside overlooking the stables the fall before.

"The duchess was besotted with him. And he was taken with her. Already she was a fine lady; well-educated and giving orders all around like the born ruler she was," Cook continued.

"Did her parents encourage her?" Nicole asked.

"The Duke and the Lady Margaret worshipped the ground she walked on; none of that nonsense about boys only inheriting the family fortune where I come from." Cook smacked the tabletop for emphasis.

"As it should be," Nicole agreed.

"As it should be, indeed. And because the Duchess Anne was raised that way, she isn't going to let anyone or anything stand in her way to get the Crown of France back on her head."

"But what if the Pope won't grant the annulment?" Nicole asked worriedly.

"Mark my words, the Pope will grant it." Cook smiled knowingly.

"How do you know?"

"I know the queen. I've known her all my life. And I had a good enough look at the new king when he was a young man to know what he's all about. They're peas in a pod," she observed.

"How so?" Nicole pressed.

"They both go after what they want. Did you see how fast Louis got here when the king died?"

"'Twas about three days, wasn't it?"

"It would have been sooner if he hadn't had to come all the way from the North."

"And our queen?"

"Both you and I know what the queen's been through these past years." Cook's face darkened as she dipped one meaty hand into the bowl of dough she had set out to make bread and scooped out a large handful.

"A happy marriage, no?"

"And seven pregnancies with seven dead children to show for it." She slapped the dough ball smartly then flattened it on the table into a squashed pancake.

"God comfort her." Nicole crossed herself, silently praying that nothing similar would happen to her on the path laid out ahead. Yet who was she to ask fate to serve her better than the queen herself had been served?

"And always carrying herself well and caring about others around her," Cook continued.

"Like bringing me to court."

"Exactly so. Bringing me here, too. Our queen knows what she's about. Once the king had his accident, what did she have left?"

"Brittany, no? She is still the duchess of her own lands, is she not?"

"That's not good enough for a woman who's been queen," Cook snorted and crossed her arms. "She remains the duchess, but she wishes also to remain queen. She will make sure the annulment goes through."

"But how can a woman influence a pope?" Nicole asked.

"Silly girl!" Cook snorted again, this time louder. "The same way a woman influences any man." Her smile was full of secrets: women's secrets, deep and not to be denied. "By being clever, of course."

"What does that mean?" Nicole had a clue but from conversations with her father about his business. She wanted to learn from a woman's point of view.

"Back-channels, my lady, back channels." She rolled the flattened dough into a perfect rectangular shape. "She knows how to work them, as does the new king."

"Back-channels?"

"Learn how to work them, too, my lady. Then the world will serve you closer to the way you wish it to, if you're smart." Cook nodded her head, as if approving her own plan.

"Do you think I can?" Could she apply such advice to herself and Philippe? If so, how?

"You admire your queen, no?" Cook eyed her.

"I adore her!" Nicole cried. As indeed she did. Everything about Anne of Brittany spoke to her, even her cunning. But the loss of her children spoke to her heart, and for that reason she loved her even more deeply.

"Then you will try to be like her. Watch carefully and learn from her," Cook advised. She placed the bread onto the cooking tray and slid it onto the rack over the giant stone hearth.

"That's what I do already." Cook had put her finger on Nicole's exact method for finding her way at court. From the moment she had caught sight of her queen limping in the privacy of her bedchamber, and realized that her trick of gliding when she walked had been a method to conceal that one leg was shorter than the other, Nicole's heart had swelled with admiration for her sovereign. Anne of Brittany was not one to give in to whatever bad cards fate had dealt her.

"So you will work with what fate gives you, but make the most of it; just as our queen does," Cook read her mind. She patted her on the arm.

"But her children . . ."

"That may change with the new king," the older woman said thoughtfully.

"How so?"

"Perhaps the combination of her with the old king didn't work for making strong children."

"How can you say that?" Nicole was shocked. Cook's words sounded like blasphemy. Then she remembered King Charles was dead and the queen was no longer queen. What would have been blasphemy a few months earlier no longer was. How quickly the world around her had changed.

"Pretend I said nothing," Cook slipped her forefinger across her mouth, as if to take back her words. "But everyone thinks it. As do you. What else could anyone think? Even the humblest peasant woman has at least one or two children to show for seven seeds planted."

"And you think things might go differently with the new king?" Nicole asked.

"It's possible." Cook shrugged as she scrubbed at a spot on the large wooden table where they sat.

"I wish there was something I could do to help, if she is to get her chance to become a mother again," Nicole remarked.

"Perhaps there is, my lady. You might put your mind to learning things now, so that when her time comes next you can help her carry a child to life."

"What things? How can I learn them?"

"I heard you were good with healing the queen's horse last summer."

"I tried." What else had Cook heard? Nothing of how closely she and Philippe had worked together, she hoped.

Cook cocked her head, evaluating Nicole for a moment.

"What? What are you thinking?" Nicole asked, willing herself not to color. Cook wasn't about to bring up Philippe, was she? Had that little Marie de Volonté spread stories in the kitchen about them? Carefully, Nicole looked down at her lap and crossed her hands, as if to put them over Marie's mouth.

"Do you want to learn more?" Cook asked hesitantly.

"Yes!"

"Nothing to do with courtly ways, you understand . . ."

"I understand. What things? How?"

"Come to the herb garden after breakfast tomorrow morning. I will show you some things."

"Oh, Cook, thank you!"

"Little one, you are a lady of the court. I'm a cook. But we both want the same happiness for our queen."

"So we do!"

"So let's work on it together."

"Oh yes, Cook; what a good idea." The last time Nicole had learned about herbs had been with her mother. Her heart swelled at the memory.

"Go now. I'll see you in the morning."

Forgetting her higher rank for the moment, Nicole threw her arms around Cook and felt her heart fill with joy as the kind Breton woman hugged her back.

⚜

For the next week, Nicole came to the herb garden behind the kitchen every morning. The summer was hot and dry but the garden faced west, so in the morning hours they were able to work in the shade from the fruit trees that lined the walkway outside the kitchen walls.

Working alongside Cook, Nicole was reminded of happy times spent alongside her mother in the gardens of her childhood home. As head of her household, Blanche St. Sylvain had been responsible for tending to the sick or injured who worked within her house or on her lands. She had known much about herbs, and had gained a reputation as a healer. But what Nicole most remembered was the way her mother had gained her patients' trust, with her gentle, sensitive manner. Nicole thought back to when Petard's ankle had been hurt. Slowly she had worked to earn the stallion's trust until he let her put her hands on his leg. Then she had used her sense of touch to find where the infection was. As she probed, she had thought of how her mother would have handled a similar situation and tried to do the same.

"Now, that's celery root there," Cook pointed to a pile of bushy greens with bulbous white balls attached. "Take heed. That one's good for keeping the babe in when mixed with mint."

"There's plenty of mint over there. But what was the one Marie was holding in the garden that day," Nicole asked. "Did you say it was called pennyroyal?"

"You want to be careful with that one, my lady. 'Tis only to be used in small amounts and certainly not to keep a babe in."

"And in larger amounts?"

Cook shuddered. "'Twill most certainly kill the babe, if not the mother too."

"What does it look like?" Nicole pressed.

"Small, white or purple and not very pretty, like the nasty weed that it is." Cook wrinkled her nose and turned down the corners of her mouth.

"And where does it grow?"

"Mostly in damp places. Down along the river below the chateau."

"Will you show it to me one day?"

"Aye, we can go weed-hunting down there one of these days. That one's to be carefully handled. I know women who drank a potion made from it to rid themselves of a babe and lost their own lives, too."

Nicole shuddered. She was getting a solid education with Cook's unguarded conversation and Madame de Laval away in Paris. Already she had learned of as many potions to stop a babe from growing in the womb as to encourage one to stay inside. Cook was an invaluable source of information.

One quiet Friday morning, Nicole and Cook slipped out to gather flowers down by the river. Not only did they pick pennyroyal, but they also found nettles and other flowers that Cook said they might use for potions to cure a wide variety of ailments.

On their way back to the chateau, they spotted dust on the road below. Men on horseback approached, perhaps with news of the queen's latest doings in Paris. It didn't look like a large party, two or three at most. Nicole shuddered to think it might be her father and uncle with the new marriage candidate they had arranged for her. If negotiations went well, her wedding would take place by the end of September. Her father and uncle were overjoyed to cement an alliance with the house of Orléans, the family from which Louis XII came, although some said the king's father had not sired him. Who knew? Another mystery Cook was filling her in on in the garden as they worked was that not all babies who arrived were necessarily sired by their mother's husbands. But Cook pointed out that it served no good purpose for either the child or the head of household to know such details, and if the mothers were clever, neither ever did.

Nicole sighed and thought of what lay before her. Nothing she could do or say would change the inevitable. If not Gilles de St. Bonnet as her husband, then it would be another who wasn't Philippe. At least she would be sixteen by the time she embarked on married life.

Within fifteen minutes, Cook and Nicole were at the outside gate to the chateau. The men on horseback were nowhere in sight.

"News from Paris then?" Cook asked of the man nearest to them as they walked in the gate.

"No, Mistress, just a few men up from Agen to work with the horses," the man replied.

"Did you send them to the kitchen?"

"No, Mistress. We knew you were not about, so we told them to go directly to the stables."

"I'll have something sent down. How many were there?"

"Three, mistress. Two men and a youth."

Nicole picked up her ears. A youth? What youth from Agen might it be? She knew of only one who worked with the horses at Amboise. Careful to conceal her excitement, she followed Cook into the kitchen, where she laid down the flowers they had collected and began sorting them into separate piles.

"Let me see what I've got here to feed our visitors," Cook mumbled, bustling about.

"Shall I store these on the cellar shelves?" Nicole asked. She would not suggest taking food and drink down to the men at the stables herself. She would wait for Cook to suggest it. Hadn't Cook herself advised using back-channels when women needed to get something done? Was there one she could use now to get Cook to ask her to deliver the food to the stables?

"Leave them on the counter," Cook ordered. "I know better which ones go where. And I don't want you touching the pennyroyal. Not till I've shown you the way to handle it."

"Then what can I do to help, Cook?" Nicole asked casually.

"Do you want to run this down to the stables for our guests?"

"Yes, of course." Nicole thanked the kind fates who had befriended her for the moment. "Shall I bring ale as well?"

"It's too much to carry all at once. You bring down the food and I'll bring the ale behind you."

"No, Cook, I can bring it all at once. You need to attend to the pennyroyal so no one else comes in here poking about and poisons himself by accident."

"Hmm, perhaps you're right." Cook disappeared into the storeroom where the ale barrels were kept.

Nicole moved to the cupboard where she knew the silver pieces were kept for fine occasions. She pulled a silver tray out and wiped it off, glancing at her face in its reflection. Quickly she smoothed her hair down on either side, removing bits of flower and nettles that had caught in it on their excursion to the river.

"Don't waste that tray on stable-hands. Take the basket. The big one there." Cook had returned from the storeroom and was pointing to the corner away from Nicole, her back turned to her.

"Alright." Nicole put back the silver tray, not before peeking again at her face; it was flushed, excited. She pursed her lips, practicing a disinterested expression. Finding the basket, she loaded it with provisions and three tankards while Cook filled a leather skin with ale. The travel-worn men from Agen would be grateful to see her, one in particular if it was the one she hoped it was.

⚜

One glance told her Philippe had grown, by two finger-lengths at least. She looked away quickly, as befitted a maiden in the company of strange men. Carefully, she busied herself with unloading the contents of the basket and pouring the ale.

She handed the tankards to the two older men, who took them gratefully, then stepped away and quaffed greedily. Immediately they resumed their discussion of the horses.

Pouring the third tankard, she kept her head down as Philippe moved toward her. The scent of him filled her senses as he neared. Fresh, virile, sweaty, too, but above all, young. Different from the hard-living scent of the older men.

"Thank you, my lady," Philippe murmured as he took the tankard from her hand. His own brushed against hers as he grasped its handle. From under her eyelashes, she glanced up to see the same gray-green eyes from the year before staring straight into hers. Quickly she looked away.

The men drained their mugs and held them out for refills. She complied, not raising her eyes. She didn't want them to take note of her, to sully the picture in any way of her first moments of seeing Philippe again after eight months of absence.

Her eyes on the ground, she looked at his shoes. Dusty and travel-worn from the journey, still they looked a higher quality, the toes pointier than the shoes he had worn the year before. Had he come up in the world since the December before? Did marriage to a wealthy widow have anything to do with it? If so, how dare he stare so boldly at her? She tightened her body, as if to squelch the unruly thoughts jumbling inside her head at the sight of him.

Nicole held out the basket to the older of the two men, and motioned to them to sit in the shade while they ate. Then she squinted at Philippe out of the corner of her eye and turned to go to the well to draw water. She would bring some for Petard and the other horses, so the men would think she had duties there and would not be surprised to see her in the stable-yards again.

Behind her, Philippe followed, saying nothing. She understood. Best not to speak in the men's presence. What they had to say to each other needed to be said privately. As she drew the water up from the well, she felt his voice brush her ear.

"It is good to see you again," he breathed out as he leaned toward her to take the bucket.

She looked up, saying nothing. The lines of his face had become more defined, less boyish. The hint of a beard smudged his chin, but his eyes were the same gray-green with flecks of gold shot through them in the midday sunlight. Their gaze was direct, as if memories of the fall before danced in them.

"They will fall asleep after they eat," he murmured. "Meet me on the hill in an hour if you can." His eyes flicked to the hill behind the pasture where they had spent so much time the autumn before.

Nicole narrowed her eyes at him and said nothing. Then she returned to the men, who had sat down under a tree and were busily cutting bread and eating the sausage and cheese Cook had provided. Nicole refilled their tankards once again.

"My lady, we will not get much done in this heat if you keep pouring for us," the one with reddish-brown hair joked.

"Monsieur, take your rest. The horses rest, too." She looked toward the paddock where the new mare grazed under a large, shady tree. "Time enough to begin work later."

"Aye, well said," grunted the other man, holding out his tankard for a second refill.

Holding in a smile, Nicole filled both their vessels then put the skin of ale down next to the tree.

"I will leave this here for you to finish," she instructed. There would be no uncertainty if the men took a nap or not. She would see to it that they did.

Turning to go back to the house, she didn't make eye contact with Philippe. But as she passed him, his scent filled her nostrils once again, and she knew she would find her way to the copse of trees on the hill behind the pasture in an hour's time. She wanted to know all that had happened to him in the eight months they had been apart. If congratulations on his recent marriage were in order, she would try to offer them. Her own nuptials were coming soon enough, to a stranger she knew even less about than the one her father and uncle had chosen for her before. She would look into Philippe's eyes again and guess what memories swam there. It was all they had left to their story, she told herself.

It would not be enough. She straightened the corded belt on her gown as if to yank out the unruly thought passing through her head: She knew as surely as she knew the queen would get her way and be queen once more. Did Anne of Brittany not pursue what she wanted? Then so would she. Her father had arranged one match for her, but then flung it away when a better one presented itself. She felt no bond with the man who would be her husband, nor did she have any certainty that she ever would. All she had was total certainty of her feelings for the youth who had just asked her to meet him in an hour. She prayed he was yet unmarried.

⚜

An hour later, she crept out of the house. In the early August afternoon, everyone had found a place to rest after the noonday meal. Cook had gone to her room behind the kitchen to lie down, and no one at all was about the courtyard, save for a gray and white cat licking its paws in the shade of the staircase. It hadn't been hard to steal away.

As she spotted Philippe on the hill above her, she put her hand to her throat. Sweat trickled down between her breasts from the exertion of climbing under the hot sun. He would scent her once she was near. It would stir him, she knew. The autumn before, they had both tried to quench the flames they had fanned together. This time, she would see. To begin with, was he married? And if not, would she feel the same way about him as she had eight months earlier?

Her head bursting with thoughts, her senses on fire, in a minute she reached the small copse of trees on the hill. She walked to the other side of the widest tree, out of sight from the paddock.

Suddenly, there he was: taller, more manly, yet the same; only more grown up, as was she. The sight of him made her heart throb.

"How have you been, my lady?" Philippe asked as he took in Nicole's face, his green eyes scrutinizing hers.

"I have been well. And you?" She kept her face composed, her tone neutral.

"Well, indeed." He lowered his voice, "But missing you."

"I heard news of you in April after the king's accident." She would cut to the chase. No point keeping him in the dark as to what she knew.

"What news was that?" Was she mistaken, or had Philippe's face colored slightly?

"News of a widow you were to wed." She looked straight at him, curious to see what color his eyes would turn with mention of the other woman.

The roses in Philippe's cheeks deepened. But his eyes stayed the same, clear and gray-green as he held her gaze.

"My lady, 'tis not what you think."

"What do you know of what I think?"

"I think you missed me. As I missed you," he breathed out to her as he leaned near and reached for her waist.

She stepped back.

"What difference does it make if you missed me, if you are a married man?"

"I am not . . . "

"You are not?" Nicole was confused. What did he mean?

"Not now."

"Not now?"

"Not yet." He breathed out heavily, then looked away.

"So you will be, then." Best to state the facts. They would have less power over her if she gave voice to them.

"It looks to be that way," he mumbled, looking at the ground.

"And are you not pleased? Your Jeannot said it was a good match for you, one that will raise your position."

"Aye. All of that. 'Tis a way to gain a higher place in Agen, and Jeannot has arranged it for me."

"He was ill last year?"

"Aye, he was ill, but he recovered. I tended him with the same kind of poultice you healed Petard with."

"The moldy bread?"

"Aye, lady. Your remedy did its job. When he got better, he told me I had saved his life and he wanted to better mine. He made me promise to let him arrange for my future."

"And so it is my poultice that leads you to another woman now?" Her heart panged to think of it. How strange life was.

"Not now, lady. Soon."

"And when is this to take place?"

"I will tell you, but first news of you." He searched her eyes as his hands sprang to either side of her waist. "How have you fared these months?"

"Many changes have taken place." This time she didn't shy away from his touch. How could she? So little time was left before they would never be able to touch each other again.

"And you? Have you changed?" He searched her face.

"In what sense?"

"Has your father married you off then?"

Nicole turned her head away. "Not yet."

"But you are promised?"

"Yes."

"And when is this to take place?" Philippe's words were teasing, echoing hers. Both shared the same fate, one assigned them by duty.

"Toward the end of September, my father has told me." Nicole tried to brush away the thought. But the day was approaching soon.

"And are you happy?" He peered at her closely, his eyes boring into hers.

"About what?" To have him near her again, within reach, made her deliriously happy. Everything else, she wished she could push away forever.

"About upcoming plans . . ." His words sounded brittle, as unnatural as the plans themselves seemed to Nicole's unwilling heart. Both his plans and hers.

She stared at him, anger rising inside like a sudden gale wind. What did he think? Then anger turned to frustration as she thought of how unfair it was to be with the one she loved, to know they both would soon be bound to others. Hot tears welled up behind her eyes at the thought.

"My fair one. Do you cry?" Philippe's hand shot out, touching her face and wiping the tear from her cheek.

Nicole shook her head silently, helpless to prevent the tears from welling afresh. They came as insistently as the end of September would come, as the day Philippe would be bound to the widow in Agen. Fate was a voracious wolf, too big to fight against, too powerful to resist.

Philippe pulled her into his arms, "Nicole," he breathed out, "don't cry." He reached under her headdress, stroking her hair down the back of her head and digging his fingers into her neck as he did.

She melted against him. All the long months of his absence, the queen's babe's long-awaited arrival then sudden death, the king's freakish accident, and her queen's departure welled up inside her and came pouring out in tears of frustration and lost hopes. There was nothing she could do to stop fate's drumbeat. It was coming for her next, as soon as the end of the following month. All she had now was this moment with her true love's arms around her.

CHAPTER EIGHT

Summer of Love

Philippe was to stay for a month, more or less, until Petard was fully trained as a jousting steed. There was also a new horse that needed to be broken and saddled, a condolence gift sent to the queen in July from her Breton nobles. The mare's name was Châtillonne. Fiery and spirited, she had a reddish-brown coat that blazed red in the sunlight.

Nicole longed to help Philippe with both horses, but she knew from the queen's and Madame de Laval's comments that they had been indiscreet the autumn before. She would not make the same mistake again. Fortunately, Madame de Laval was attending the queen in Paris for the summer. Rumor had it she would not be back for a while, at least until the new king got his answer from the Pope. All Nicole needed to do was keep Marie de Volonté away from the stables and distracted from asking questions at the end of the day when they retired.

That night, she spoke to the younger girl as they prepared for bed.

"Cook needs me up early to tend the herb garden, so I'm to sleep in the room next to hers starting tomorrow night." She chose her words carefully, leaving it vague as to whose orders these were.

"Until when?" Marie stared at her with big eyes filled with interest at this news.

Nicole's heart sank. Had Marie heard that Philippe was back? If the younger girl caught wind he was at Amboise, she would watch Nicole like a hawk.

"Until the weather turns. Till next month sometime." *Until my love leaves and my heart goes with him.* Nicole busied herself with plumping up her pillow.

"Why do you do that dirty work?" Marie sniffed. "'Tis not a lady's job to scrabble in the dirt and labor under a hot sun on hands and knees."

"What do you know?" Nicole shot back. "My mother used herbs to heal ailments, 'tis a skill she would have wanted me to bring to my own household and Cook knows such arts." Nicole crossed herself for good measure.

"We are meant to learn how to manage our future servants, not work beside them," Marie scoffed.

"Cook is a good woman, and she is from the queen's own lands."

"From Brittany?"

"Yes, from the queen's childhood home in Nantes."

Marie de Volonté looked disdainful, saying nothing.

"I hope you won't be lonely," Nicole added. "Shall I ask Clotilde if she'd like to share your chamber with you?"

"No! I'll be fine," Marie said quickly. She looked down, her eyes fluttering.

Nicole studied her. Something in Marie's face told her she had plans of her own that might be affected by the new sleeping arrangements. Had her friendship with the youth from Naples progressed? Or was there someone else? Her eyes swept over her bedmate's form, noting Marie's new curves. Her breasts were evident now. Her hips and waist had curved in opposite directions since the year before.

"Oh, good. Well, you'll have plenty of space. I'll stay near the gardens until the weather changes next month," Nicole tossed out, her tone casual.

Marie's eyes flitted ever so restlessly to the side, as if to say that Nicole's change of sleeping arrangements worked perfectly for her.

Back-channels, Cook's words echoed in Nicole's head. *Work the back-channels.* "So, your beau will be happy to hear of these new arrangements?" she asked, narrowing her eyes at Marie.

"My beau? Which beau?" Marie's face colored red, confirming Nicole's hunch.

"You know." What luck. Not only had she guessed right, but it sounded as if there was indeed more than one. In that case, one would be taller. "The taller one," Nicole ad-libbed. Marie was a dark-haired beauty of fifteen, so the possibility did not surprise her.

Marie narrowed her eyes back at Nicole. "What do you know of him?"

"I know this is a good time to spend with him, before the queen's ladies return." She raised her eyebrows to drive home her point.

"Do you know when that will be?" Marie looked hungry for information.

"No." Nicole leaned toward her and smiled. "But now is your moment," she said in a low voice. "Take it, and don't delay."

"Why do you say such a thing?" Marie asked, flushing red again.

"Because with your looks and the queen's planning skills, you'll soon be married off."

"To the one I love?" Marie looked hopeful.

"What do you think, little one?" Nicole put out her hand and stroked Marie's lush, dark hair. At the unexpected turn their conversation had taken, she felt a poignant kinship with the younger girl. Fate had befriended them both for the moment; but the moment was short.

Marie shook her head, looking downcast. It seemed that she, too, knew that her path ahead was not aligned with her heart's desire.

"Heed my words, and seize your moment," Nicole whispered to her.

"Promise not to say anything?" Marie de Volonté held up her pinkie finger.

"Promise." Nicole hooked her own pinkie finger with Marie's. "Not a word."

⚜

The next day, Nicole met Philippe in the early afternoon on the hill above the stables. Neither had made the appointment. Both just found themselves there.

"My lady, how fare you today?"

"I am well. And you?"

"I am happy to see your bright eyes." His expression was keen, like a hunting dog at the start of a fine day of hunt.

"As am I to see yours." She couldn't help but smile at his compliment. She hadn't felt such joy since the autumn before.

Philippe's hand came up to push a strand of hair back from her face that had escaped her headdress.

"A request," he murmured, his other hand coming to rest upon her waist. Instantly, they were back to where they had left off the December before.

She quivered under the warmth and firmness of his touch. It felt sure of itself, sure of its rightfulness in seeking her waist. She was sure, too. No longer was she the tentative young girl she had been the year earlier.

"A favor for a favor," she said.

It was his turn to smile. "Very well," he replied, the flash of his eyes lending seasoning to their exchange. "You first, my lady."

She paused then summoned her courage. Time had run out. If they were to deepen their story, the moment to act was now. He had handed her the key to their next steps, a courtly gesture. She had it to do with what she wished.

"No, you. You spoke first." She would hand it back to him. In any case, she wanted to know his request before coloring it with her own. "What do you ask of me?"

"Would you take off your headdress?" he asked. His face was expectant, hopeful. But his eyes glittered in the brilliant August sun, as keen as his tone was soft.

Nicole smiled with relief. Not difficult at all. With pleasure, she complied.

"Now what favor do you ask of me?" Philippe continued as his fingers stroked through the silken locks of her long hair.

She thought fast before thought left her altogether under the touch of his hands on the back of her neck. It was the secret spot he had discovered on her the autumn before. How quickly he had found it again.

"Could you take off your jerkin?" she asked, wondering if the outlines of his chest under his shirt would have broadened since last she had seen him.

"I can do better than that," Philippe replied. He loosened the leather strings of his jerkin, then pulled it over his head along with the shirt underneath.

Nicole sucked in her breath. Philippe's chest was a thing of beauty, well-defined, sprinkled with a golden down that reminded her of the wheat fields ready for harvest. She stared as the muscles that defined his slim shape flexed beneath her gaze. She had never seen him without his shirt on before. He seemed more manly without clothes.

She put up her hand to cover her mouth.

With gentle authority, Philippe pulled it from her lips and put it on his chest.

In the days that followed Nicole and Philippe met most early afternoons on the hill above the stables. Then, again at dusk at times they would meet, sitting in the shadows and watching the sun disappear over the horizon in the direction of Nantes and the great sea beyond. Nicole had never seen it, but Philippe had been there.

"What is it like? Is it a kind of large lake?" she asked, trying to imagine the sea she had heard about, the one that had carried the Genoese Christophe Colomb to the land that he had returned to report on to the king and queen of Spain.

"It is as unlike a lake as you are to your friend with the dark hair."

"Do you mean Marie?" Nicole asked, a twinge of jealousy shooting through her.

"If that is the one who saw us at the stables together last year, then yes."

"What do you mean about her?"

"I mean nothing about her. Well, there is a little something, but no matter. What I mean about you and her is that you are both women, yet as unalike as night and day. That is the difference between the sea and a lake."

"How so?" Nicole's curiosity was piqued.

"I mean one is quiet, calm, placid."

"You mean me?" Nicole gathered her hair and draped it over one shoulder. She hoped she looked demure.

Philippe chuckled, then threw back his head and laughed loudly.

"No, I do not. You are the sea, my lady."

"I am the sea? And what is that to mean?" Indignantly, she crossed her arms over her chest.

"I mean you are always changing: planning, moving, thinking." He leaned toward her and pulled a lock of her hair.

"Or not," she reached out a hand and traced the line of muscle firmly outlined from the center of his chest to one shoulder. Over the past few days she had indeed been planning and thinking; all to do with how they could steal some moments together without the eyes of others upon them.

"You are the sea, *ma chère*. Believe me. Always changing before my eyes."

"You're a fine one to talk. It's your eyes themselves that are always changing. From green to gray to blue, then sometimes with gold in them . . ."

"We're brother and sister then," Philippe jested.

"No, we are not," Nicole corrected him.

"Aye, most certainly we are not," he echoed, this time his voice low as he moved her hand down his chest, to areas below as changeable as the sea he had spoken of.

⚜

Mornings were spent learning from Cook in the herb garden. There was weeding and watering to be done; also pulling herbs for meals as well as flowers to grind and store in the storeroom, ready to be made into tinctures and potions.

Afternoons, once the household had risen from their naps and Nicole had returned from meeting Philippe, Cook spent time explaining formulas for potions to Nicole. Some were for reducing fevers and healing infections, but the vast majority seemed to be for women's ailments.

"This one here is meant to flush out poisons and whatever else from a woman's womb," Cook explained one afternoon as she pulled out a handful of small purple wildflowers from the back of the shelf in the storeroom.

Nicole recognized them as the ones Cook had snatched away from Marie in the herb garden the year before. "Whatever else?" she asked. Usually Cook was straight to the point. This time, not.

"Whatever else shouldn't be in there for whatever reasons," she said, narrowing her eyes at Nicole.

"Do you mean the result of a flux that hasn't fully washed out?" Nicole guessed.

"That, perhaps, and also its opposite." Cook looked carefully at Nicole. "Do you understand?"

"I—I think so."

"I think so, too, my lady, but, just to be sure, I mean washing out whatever shouldn't be inside."

"What are they called again?" Nicole stared at the scraggly little purple flowers thoughtfully. She wanted to be a healer. As a woman, she knew there were situations that women found themselves in frequently that weren't practical. What was a healer's responsibility to a woman in need who came to her?

"They're called pennyroyal. You grind them into a tea and give whoever needs it two cups daily, then watch for results." Cook gave her a long look, then took her arm and led her out into the garden. They walked to the far end of the enclosed area, where Cook sat down on a bench under a fruit tree and patted the spot next to her for Nicole to sit.

"How old are you, my lady?" she asked.

"I've just turned sixteen," Nicole told her.

"A good time to learn the facts of a woman's life."

"I know the facts, Cook! I've had my courses for almost two years now," Nicole exclaimed.

"And what happens when those courses stop coming?" Cook asked.

"Then something else comes instead," Nicole replied.

"And what if that something else should not be on the way? Say, if there is no father to provide for it?"

Nicole stared at her, open-mouthed. Finally, she spoke.

"But the law, Cook; the law forbids stopping a babe from coming."

"And the law has never stopped a woman from doing what she has to do, should she find herself in a situation that cannot be." Cook crossed her arms and gave Nicole a level look.

Nicole continued to stare. She knew, of course, that there were herbs and potions to flush out the womb, usually not written down, but shared between women privately.

"But what if it is discovered that a woman has taken something to end an—an unwanted situation? Will she not be charged with a crime?"

"Let me ask you something. How often do you hear of such a thing happening?" Cook asked.

Nicole searched her mind. "I—I've never heard of such a thing happening." She couldn't think of any story she'd heard where a woman was charged with ending a pregnancy. Yet she knew women sometimes took a part in not bringing to the light of day what had no welcoming home there.

"Steps are taken in such cases," Cook observed vaguely.

"I know, Cook. You've shown me a few." She remembered potions her mother had had on hand for women's ailments. There had been many different concoctions, always to remedy problems referred to in the vaguest of terms.

"It's not just about potions. There are other things that might take place, too, to ensure no woman ever gets pulled before a magistrate to explain herself in such a situation." Cook nodded, her face full of mystery.

"Such as?" Nicole was unused to Cook beating about the bush. Usually she was the most direct of souls. Clearly the mysteries she spoke of were mysteries indeed, if even Cook was unable to speak of them directly.

"Many events can cause a seed planted not to take root and grow," Cook explained. "Most of them befall women without them even knowing what it was or why. 'Tis a great mystery."

"Yes." Well Nicole knew. Everyone at Chateau d'Amboise was aware of the great mystery of the queen's repeated pregnancies, all ending so tragically.

"But if the woman knows very well why the pregnancy has stopped, she can take measures to ensure that no one will ever question the reasons why."

"And what would those measures be?" Nicole asked.

"A fall, say, down the stairs or from a horse; maybe just tripping on a loose paving stone."

"Anything else?" Judging by the ripe look on Cook's face, there was more.

"Too much travel. A coach a woman's riding in going over a heavy bump in the road."

"Is that all?"

"No." Cook looked thoughtful. Nicole had never seen her act so indirect.

"Then what?"

"A husband hitting his wife."

"But what if he is not of a mind to hit her?"

"Then she can put him in a mind to do the job."

"How so?"

"Talk too much. Damage his most prized possession. It doesn't take much for a woman to irritate a man."

"Truth indeed," Nicole agreed. She thought of her father. It hadn't taken much to irritate Michel St. Sylvain. The last time they had conversed, he had wanted his way, and she had wanted hers. It seemed that was largely the case in relations between men and women.

"There are ways to make sure that whatever ways and means have already been taken are never discovered or discussed."

"But 'tis a crime, no?"

"Is it a crime for a woman to manage her own body?" Cook's look was sharp.

Nicole said nothing. Searching inside herself, she remembered her mother helping women from her household or the fields of their estate who came to her for help with women's problems. At times, Blanche St. Sylvain had spoken to them in front of Nicole. Other times, she had ushered them into a private room and shut the door. Nicole knew her mother helped any and all in her household who came to her in need. She would never know if any of those women had needed to end a pregnancy, but she knew beyond a doubt that her mother would never have turned away any woman with such a story. Any one of her sex could be in a similar situation.

Carefully, Nicole got up from the bench and followed Cook back to the kitchen. She had much to think about, and not just as it might apply to other women. She was fast on her way to having her own secrets. Already she could see that a woman's life was full of them.

⚜

That evening, she met Philippe on the hillside after supping. Together they watched the sun disappear behind the horizon in a great ball of fiery red.

"'Tis said when the sun's red at night, it will be a fine day on the morrow," Philippe remarked.

"And a warm night, too, I suppose."

"Warm enough to sleep outdoors, I'd say," Philippe remarked, his hand finding hers as they sat shoulder to shoulder, their backs against the widest tree in the copse.

"Yes, and probably more comfortable," Nicole agreed. The small room she slept in off the kitchen was hot those August days; partially from the summer heat and partially from the kitchen's hearth being so nearby.

"A full moon tonight too," Philippe continued.

Nicole glanced at him from the corner of her eye. "So the calendar says." She watched as Philippe's features grew taut. His eyes gleamed green-gold in the setting sun.

He leaned toward her. "What say you we meet back here an hour before midnight?" he asked, lacing his fingers in hers. He squeezed them, then released.

Nicole breathed deeply. *Have courage and be bold.* "But what if someone finds out we're not in our rooms?"

"Easy for me," Philippe shrugged. "My room is wherever I make my bed in the stables. No one cares where I sleep."

"I care where you sleep," Nicole remarked, pulling her hand from his and leaning back to gaze at him.

"I would sleep in your arms, if I could," Philippe murmured, taking her hand again.

"But we fall asleep here at times. Is it not pleasant?"

"Very, my lady. But 'tis stolen moments. I long to spend a night with you in my arms."

"But what if someone finds I'm not in my bed?"

"Do what your little friend does. Shape a blanket into a long lump and stuff it under your bed sheet."

"My little friend?" Nicole asked, confused.

"Little Marie."

"What do you mean?"

"I mean she has a friend she visits at night."

So even Philippe knew. "Who is he?" she asked, wondering if he would name the garden designer's son from Naples.

"My lady, it is not for me to tell tales."

"It sounds like this is more than a tale."

"Let me keep the secret I have promised to keep. You would not want me to do less, would you?"

"Of course not." It was good to know. Useful.

"I will bring a blanket from the stables for later," Philippe said. He reached under her hair and stroked the back of her neck. "You will come?" he asked. The gleam of his eyes held a yearning urgency. They were more blue than green now.

She gazed at him as she held her breath. Exhaling slowly, she felt her mouth form itself into a teasing smile.

"You will have to wait to find out."

"I shall wait all night if I must," Philippe said, his mouth forming into a similar smile.

Nicole turned and made her way down the hill toward the chateau. She would be circumspect, as careful as she could be until she reached her heart's desire that night. Then she would abandon all caution to the wind, along with her reason.

⚜

The moon was halfway to its zenith when Nicole made her move. It shone as bright as a lantern; she would need to stay in the shadows as she made her way from the chateau. If Marie de Volonté's night-time movements hadn't gone unnoticed, then she herself would have to be extra careful not to be discovered herself.

Instead of wearing her nightdress, she put on the dark purple gown Madame de Laval had given her to wear while the court observed the mourning period for the late king. Choosing a dark shawl to put over it, she covered her hair with the black veil the queen had had made for her maids of honor to wear. Nicole silently blessed her for choosing such new mourning colors, instead of the traditional white. Perhaps it was a sign the queen was on her side.

She bunched up her night dress along with an extra straw pillow she had found in the chest where the items for her trousseau were stored. It was not yet full, since Nicole's wedding plans had taken a backseat to the queen's more urgent agenda of securing her place on the throne of France again as soon as possible.

Satisfied that she had fashioned the lump under her blanket to look like a human form, Nicole slipped out the door.

The night was balmy, the moon brilliant. Flattening herself against the stone of the chateau walls, she hugged them till she reached the wall enclosing the herb garden. Only one small patch right before the garden gate was bathed in moonlight. The rest stood hidden in the dark.

She crept along the wall until reaching the moonlit patch. Then she got down on her hands and knees and pressing the blanket to the front of her gown to keep it clean, slid along the ground to the darkness on the other side, where the gate was located. Quickly she lifted the latch and let herself out, closing it carefully behind her.

The click was louder than she had expected. Immediately, a dog barked from the direction of the kitchen.

Nicole darted to the nearest copse of trees and hid behind the broadest one.

The dog continued to bark then suddenly yelped. Someone had stopped it. Who? And was that person now coming to see what the dog had been barking at?

Her heart sank to her feet. Hugging the tree for comfort, she prayed that whoever had silenced the dog had gone back to resume his or her sleep. Still as stone, she waited another few minutes then crept out from behind the tree.

No further barking broke the night's silence. Nothing at all moved in the moonlit night except the flutter of the breeze and Nicole's silent form.

As she climbed the hill, she scanned the trees ahead for Philippe. Listening for the dog or worse, her senses sharpened until she realized the night air was filled with the croaking sounds of the cicadas. Their ceaseless whirring would provide good cover for them. Her heart beat faster as she thought about what might unfold ahead.

At last she arrived at the tree where they usually sat. No one was about. Sitting down, with her back against it, she breathed deeply.

Before she had time to wonder where Philippe was or when he would arrive, two hands covered her eyes. The heart-stopping scent of him filled her nostrils.

"You!" she whispered, stifling a laugh.

"No, you, my lady!"

"No, you, my lord!"

"If only it could be so, my lady!"

"'Tis so, but if only the world could know."

"Aye, but 'tis our secret to guard forever," Philippe said, suddenly serious.

Nicole drew back. "And not just this night?"

"Lady, what do you think? Could I forget you ever?"

"Did you not forget me when your widow showed up?" she challenged him.

"I have not yet laid eyes upon her," he told her, his eyes grave.

"No!" Nicole exclaimed.

"Yes. First I heard of her was after the falconer's death."

"But you met her, surely!" Nicole cried.

"I saw her from a distance a few times in early spring. But she was in mourning, all covered in veils. Like this one." He lifted the material of Nicole's veil, now lying in a crumpled heap next to the tree.

"But haven't you seen her more recently? Over the summer?"

"She works in the Lady of Agen's household, and they have gone to the sea for the summer. I haven't seen her since the summer solstice."

"How could you marry someone whose face you've never seen?" Nicole asked, incredulous. Yet the news made her happy. Better to be with Philippe knowing he had not been near the woman who would soon take him from her. As Gerard d'Orléans would do the same with her. Their positions were reasonably the same, yet she felt anything but reasonable about it. How dare he take a wife if it couldn't be her?

"They say she's fair, and that's all I know. Jeannot told me he wished to be a father to me and that he had a good plan for my life. What does it matter, since she's not the one I want?"

"And who is, then?" How dare he mention she was fair? Nicole curled her fingers into her palm.

"You know, my lady." His hand sought hers, uncurling it. "You know who you are."

"It's me you would marry if you could?"

"Of course it is, my lady. It is and always will be."

"Philippe, why can't we have what we want in this life?" she cried. She felt like a bleating lamb, vulnerable and incapable of reason.

"Shhh, my love. Let's not ask questions with answers that don't please us, when so much that does please us is right here, now."

"You are here and you are the only one who matters."

"Now you speak to my heart."

"Philippe?"

"What, love?"

"Don't push me away this time." She looked at him carefully, to discern if he caught her meaning.

His eyes locked onto hers, letting her know he did. "Are you sure?" he asked, his voice low.

She nodded. "I am."

"My love, I want what's best for you."

"Then let me decide what that is."

"And have you?" His voice was hoarse, his eyes lit with gold.

"I have." She reached up and pulled his mouth to hers. The memory of what they were to share would have to last a lifetime.

Their wonder-filled nights continued over the next few weeks. Nicole had not expected many of the aspects of what went on between a man and a woman. She had guessed at the messiness, heard about the initial painfulness from other women, but had had no idea of the exquisite pleasure that took her over once her body had gotten its bearings. She was beginning to understand why women didn't always use their heads when it came to men. She had known that long before about men, but had thought her own sex was more sensible.

Philippe was considerate. He had not been content to take his pleasure without introducing Nicole to hers.

"I wish you to be mistress of your own bliss," he whispered to her on the third night they spent together.

"What do you mean? Am I not?" Mistress of what? Whatever he meant, the idea of it rang agreeably in her ears.

"I mean you must know what it is and how to find it," he told her.

"But have I not? You are here with me now; that's all I need."

"My lady, we will not be with each other forever. You do not need my presence to find your own pathway to heaven."

"Philippe, what are you saying?" Was he getting at the same thing Madame de Laval had alluded to when she had spoken of extreme pleasures?

"I am telling you these things, because I want to give you something that is yours forever, if it cannot be me."

"Do I not have your love?" she asked.

"You have my love." He spoke gravely, "Now I want you to have your bliss." His mouth twitched slightly.

"My bliss is to be with you, Philippe."

"No, *ma chère*, your bliss is yours alone, and I wish to lead you to it so that when I'm gone you will have the key to unlocking your own body."

"I don't know what you mean." Truly, she didn't. Was he telling her there was something she needed to know that she didn't yet?

"It is my pleasure to show you, my lady, if you will let me."

"Show me what?"

"Don't talk, just feel," he urged.

"Feel what?"

"Your bliss," he whispered, his hand moving down her torso.

She lay back and surrendered to his hands and tongue moving over her secret parts. As she did, an exquisitely full feeling began to overtake her, specific and localized. It was different from the feelings she had experienced up to that moment with him. The new sensations were more acute, with a driving rhythm of stop and start to them.

"Don't try to understand," he murmured. "Just let your feelings overtake you. Don't think. Respond. Then rest."

She lay back. Was this the path that led to extreme pleasure? If so, she had no idea how to proceed. Soon, she was writhing and trying as hard as she could to escape his insistent touch.

"No, my love," he counseled, his eyes gleaming, a hint of merriment dancing at his mouth. "No escape. Surrender. Give in to sensation."

"But my love, I do not know what is happening. It is as if my body is on fire."

"Exactly as it should be. You are safe with me," he calmed her. "You are safe, but fearful, no?"

"Yes. Exactly!" She stared at him, wondering why he wouldn't release her. After a few more seconds, the full feeling inside began to prickle, then burn. "My love, let me go!" she cried out.

"You will not get to where you need to go, if I do."

"But I do not know where that is! I'm afraid!"

"*Ma chère,* sometimes it is good to be afraid. In the horse being broken in. And in love."

Telling herself it was her true love who was leading her to unknown places, she gave herself over to his hands. Underneath them, she felt herself drawn taut then released, not once but twice. The third time, after the most pregnant pause, he touched her once again and wouldn't relent.

"Ahhh," she screamed out as she hurtled over the edge of control and into a world beyond any she had known before. There, she shattered into a million shards of glass.

"Ahhh," Philippe responded in a different tone, one that bespoke of witnessing his beloved's pleasure. His eyes gleamed with what appeared to be a mix of admiration and pride.

She rested; then his hand was upon her and she shattered again. Then again. The fourth and final time it was as if she had traveled beyond oblivion.

She fell back, spent, as a languor unlike anything she had ever felt before infused her entire body. So this was *le petit mort*, the little death the married ladies at court whispered about. She had never understood what they meant when they had used the phrase in hushed tones and discreet giggles.

Now she knew what Madame de Laval had referred to as extreme pleasure. Philippe had called it the pleasure of being oblivious to all else. The driving urgency she had felt only seconds earlier fell away from her, replaced by a divine serenity, a sense of being fully alive and floating in the moment.

"Good," Philippe murmured then fell into a deep sleep. Nicole was too excited to join him. She marveled as she watched the moon above illuminate their bodies like white marble. What she had just experienced was beyond anything that had ever happened to her before. Never again would she be the same.

When thought finally returned, with it came the image of Châtillonne. She was a fine, noble animal. Now she knew that she was more like her than she had thought. Perhaps the new mare was as terrified of being forced into a bridle as she had been moments earlier of being forced toward an unknown destination.

The queen's new chestnut mare had never been ridden before. Nicole had never been shattered by ecstasy before. Now that she had experienced it, she knew she would long for the feeling again. Would Châtillonne long for the right rider one day? She would help the men with training her, she vowed. If they couldn't do the job, she would use a few of the techniques Philippe had just shown her. She would offer safe, tight, unrelenting control. She smiled, thinking of how she had fought Philippe's hand on her, the same way Châtillonne had resisted bridling. Who could blame the mare? Everyone longed for the right sense of touch upon them; humans and horses alike.

Nicole's gaze lingered on Philippe's inert form, one strong hand relaxed and resting on a marble-muscled thigh. How had he known so much about how to awaken her? Did all men know such secrets about a woman's body? Whatever the answer, one thing she knew: no one could ever take away from her the knowledge of herself that Philippe de Bois had just given her.

In a state of bliss beyond any she had ever known, she fell asleep and dreamt that she slept next to the stallion Petard and the mare Châtillonne, deep in the forest while Philippe stood nearby, gazing at her with gold-shot hazel eyes. A voice that was hers said, "I wish this gift was for us only to share," to which Philippe put his finger to his lips and shook his head.

"No, Nicole. The gift is for you to know your own pleasure wherever you go. Remember that I showed you the way."

"You are my love, Philippe. My first and forever love," she told him.

"As you are mine. Always." He put his hand on his heart and turned, vanishing into the woods.

⚜

Nights, neither of them could stay away from each other. During the day, they would catch sight of each other near the stables, or when Nicole was asked to deliver provisions to the stable-hands. For the most part, they stayed far from each other when others were about.

But the sensations of the past few weeks she had experienced with Philippe had washed away some of her discretion, along with most of her reason. Fortunately, she was able to keep a level head when stealing away then back again under cover of night. Her motivation ran deeper than just to remain undiscovered for the sake of her upcoming marriage. More importantly, she wanted what Philippe and she had together as hidden from others' knowledge as they themselves remained hidden from sight as they explored each other through the hours of deepest, darkest night. She couldn't bear to think of their story discussed by others in coarse talk.

"My lady, are you satisfied?" Philippe asked one moonless night about a month after they had first come together. In that time, he had learned about her body, patiently, with skill and zeal.

She had not sought her own bliss that time, but had reveled in his.

"I am more than satisfied, my love. Why do you ask?" she asked, reaching up to touch his face, invisible above her in the ink-black night.

"I want you to feel what I do," Philippe said, his hand smoothing her hair back from her temple.

"I am different from you, dear one. As a woman is different from a man," she said, choosing her words carefully. She wanted to give an answer that was true, not just one to please him. No longer a courtier in his arms, unobligated by any bonds of marriage or duty, she could tell him the truth.

"Tell me what you mean by such words," he breathed out, heavy against her chest.

"I mean there are times I seek my own pleasure, and other times my deepest pleasure is to enjoy yours."

"Well spoken, my lady. 'Tis the same with me."

Already, she knew that. There was something selfless about Philippe. He made her feel as if she was his entire world.

"At times I don't care whether my tide crests or not. I just wish to see yours roll over and drown you in pleasure," he told her, stroking her cheek.

"Your words are strange to me, Philippe. I know not of what you speak."

"The sea, my lady. I speak of the sea. It is like you and you, like it: changing and mutable; different every time in your requirements, your satisfaction."

"Then I must visit this sea one day, for I know not of what it looks like, but I know well of what you speak. Never try to understand my pleasure the way you understand your own."

"Aye, my lady love. Well spoken. But one thing I insist to you."

"And what is that?"

"That you seek your own pleasure and refuse to rest until you have found it."

"Shall I tell my future husband that?"

"You shall teach your future husband the way to satisfy you. And if he doesn't, promise you will come and find me."

Nicole pulled him closer to her, her hand circling the broad ribbons of muscle on his back.

"I will teach him the way to find me," she replied. "But I won't come find you if he doesn't," she added.

"Why not?"

"Because you will belong to another woman, and if I were that woman I wouldn't want that." Already, she felt jealous of this widow whose face Philippe had not yet fully seen. Yet the widow was a woman like herself. Life was hard enough for her own sex. Did they not pay for their pleasure with the labor of birth, and sometimes death thereafter? She shuddered to think what the consequences of childbearing had been for the two women dearest to her: her mother and the queen.

"I understand." Philippe nodded gravely.

"I will just think of you in my mind."

"How often?" he asked teasingly.

"When the moon is full and the weather fair," she told him.

"That is when I, too, will think of you."

Nicole closed her eyes and pulled him down to her. She would think of Philippe far more times than just when the moon was full and the weather fair. But no need to mention it. He would be thinking of her, too, she knew. It would have to be enough. The memories they were building now would make it enough. Because, likely, memories would be all they had of each other to hold onto forever. Her heart panged to think of it, so she clung to him until his ardent response chased all thoughts from her head.

Just before dawn they slipped down the hillside together, emboldened by the moonless night. No dog barked as they rounded the corner of the stables into the yard where they had first met. Even the cicadas had ceased their whirring. It was as if every living being at the Chateau d'Amboise was sunk in the deepest of sleep. Indeed, every living creature or being was, save for one whose form slipped silently behind the horse shed as Nicole and Philippe embraced one final time.

PART II

1499-1500

CHAPTER NINE

Married Life

It wasn't as bad as she had thought it would be. As much as she hadn't wanted to bind herself to Gerard d'Orléans, the wedding had taken place as planned in late September. Her father and uncle had come for the ceremony then left two days later. Gerard had stayed on at Amboise through the Christmas season. Just before Christmas, news came that the Pope had granted Louis XII his annulment. In return, the king was to provide the Pope's illegitimate son, the infamous Caesar Borgia, with a pension, a Duchy of France, and promise of a French princess's hand in marriage. It was outrageous, but Louis XII understood the cost of doing business. He complied eagerly with all of the Pope's requirements in order to marry

Anne of Brittany, the duchess who had captured his heart as a young girl.

They were wed in Nantes, in early January 1499. Gerard had asked Nicole if she wished to attend the ceremony, but she had said no. She would see the queen when she passed through Amboise on her way to Blois, the king's royal residence, and soon to be her new home.

There were reasons that she didn't wish to make the trip.

There were reasons that she didn't wish to see the queen.

There were reasons that she was content to remain behind when Gerard left for Nantes to attend the wedding and offer his services to the combined new court of Louis XII and Anne of Brittany, again Queen of France.

The conversation with Gerard had been brief.

"Would you like to go to the wedding?" Gerard asked one night, in the week between Christmas and the New Year as they prepared for bed.

"No, my lord. I don't care to travel at this time." Nicole busied herself turning down the bedclothes and arranging the fur coverlet on their canopied bed. It was a wedding gift sent from the queen, trimmed with the tails of ermines, the device of Brittany that Anne had taken as her own on her coat of arms.

"But you will wish to see your queen on her wedding day, no? You speak of her highly, and she is your patron."

"Yes, Gerard, but I don't think it's wise to travel right now," Nicole said carefully. Squeezing her eyes shut, she willed him to realize her meaning.

"Do you mean the roads?"

"No." She sucked in her breath, then looked straight at him. "I don't." It was time to share her news. She had hoped he would guess. If Jeanne de Laval and the queen had been back they would have figured it out months earlier.

"You mean . . .?" Gerard d'Orléans looked down his long nose at Nicole, his gaze uncertain, as if out of his element. He was an athlete, a horseman, and one of the best jousters in the tourneys it was said, although Nicole hadn't seen him in any yet. Women's affairs were not his strong suit.

"I mean . . ." She looked down and crossed her hands below her stomach, holding them close against her body. She was no longer the slim sylph she had been the summer before.

"Are you . . .?" Gerard asked, coming closer and putting his hand on Nicole's shoulder.

"I am, my lord." Squeezing her eyes shut, she couldn't help but smile. Private thoughts flooded her, along with a feeling of inexplicable contentment that was her constant companion these days. She bottled them up and returned to the present moment.

Opening her eyes, she shared her smile with her husband. She knew whatever appeared on her face he would mirror on his own. In just three months of marriage, she had learned that Gerard was privately as malleable as he was rigidly unyielding on the sports field. It wasn't a bad combination of qualities for a husband to possess.

Gerard stared at her a second then broke into a smile. "Fast work, my lady," he grunted, then reached out and squeezed her shoulder.

"Fast work, my lord," she agreed. Whose fast work it had been, she would not specify, nor could she with any certainty. She was a married noblewoman with a babe on the way. It was as it should be, and she was happy to share such good news with her husband so soon into their marriage.

For the next ten days, Gerard d'Orléans was extremely considerate, offering her the choicest morsels of meat at meals they shared and showing restraint at night. By the third of January, he had ridden off in the direction of Nantes to attend the royal wedding. Nicole didn't doubt he would mention her news to those he met there. She only hoped that when she next saw her queen, Anne of Brittany, again queen of France, would be in a similar condition.

"You seem distracted, my lady. Is everything well?"

"Don't be silly, Philippe. I am fine. It is women's secrets, that's all." She was overjoyed to see him again. Since five months earlier, so much had happened, so much had changed.

"An extra secret these days? Or the usual ones?"

How could a half-grown man be so perceptive? He was twenty-one going on thirty-two. She couldn't keep him from guessing what most men were blind to until confronted by obvious evidence. But Philippe wasn't like most men. He was more sensitive. Or was it just that he was more sensitive to her?

"You have the third eye, Philippe. A woman's gift, usually, but you are lucky to have it as a man," she told him.

"So there is something." He eyed her carefully, his eyes roving over her face and hair, then down.

"There is nothing I have to tell you, cheeky boy. And what about you? Any news you have to tell me?" She felt her face flame as she thought of the widow in Agen. Was she now Philippe's wife?

"There is something, and it's thanks to you."

"What is it?"

"Remember the poultices you made for Petard when he hurt his hoof?"

"So what?'

"Word of it got back to Jeannot in Agen."

"And?"

"They asked me to help with the horses there when they got injured."

"And you healed them, didn't you?"

"Mostly, yes, thanks to your moldy bread and spider web ideas."

"Bravo, then!"

"That's not all."

"Yes?" She hoped none of his news led to the widow. She knew she was being unfair, but she couldn't help herself.

"I'm going to Milan to join the king's army there, as assistant horse master."

"And not back to Agen to your wife?" she asked, surprised.

He shook his head. "I am not yet wed. I go as soon as I'm done here."

"'Tis a good step up for you, Philippe. I'm happy to hear of it," she said, happy to hear he would be nowhere near his future intended bride.

"Thank you, my lady," he replied, his eyes wandering down to her swelling stomach.

"Let's get back to Petard," she told him. There was nothing she could do if Philippe guessed her secret, other than to not confirm it. But how could she keep such momentous news from the one who shared her heart?

She tried to ignore Philippe's scrutinizing gaze, but her hands instinctively crossed in front of her belly. Turning from him, she pretended not to see the knowing smile that lit up his face at her gesture.

"Petard! Come here, boy," Nicole called to the queen's stallion. It was a warm day for February, but still chilly. The handsome black horse had filled out from the summer before, his muscularity more evident under the sleek shine of his coat. Happily, he trotted toward Nicole then tried to nuzzle her under the shoulder. Ever so gently, she pushed him away, then reached up and scratched his ears. The horse snorted gently in response, his warm breath tickling Nicole's belly. She felt a slight flutter, most likely the vibration of the horse's breath on her mid-section.

"Will you ride him today?" Philippe asked.

"You ride him," she told him. "He must get used to you again since you've been gone so long." Philippe had returned to Agen the first week of the September before.

"Have you been riding him regularly?" he asked.

"I've had other things to do," Nicole hedged. She had stopped riding Petard in November, at the first sign.

Then, in December, after a messenger had arrived with news that the king's annulment had been granted by Rome, on her way to tell Cook in the kitchen, she had realized she could no longer run, even with the special glide her queen had taught her.

"The king has gotten his wish from the Pope. He will marry our queen next month, they say," she had panted out as she leaned on the doorway to catch her breath.

"Good news indeed." Cook eyeballed Nicole thoughtfully. "And more on the way, I'd wager."

"What do you mean?" Nicole asked, feeling her face flush even more than it already had from the exertion of running down the hallway.

"Are you staying off that horse?" Cook's eyes swept her figure then returned to her face.

"Yes, Cook." Cook knew how fond Nicole was of the horses, especially Petard.

"Still no courses?"

"No." Then she clapped her hand to her mouth. She had told nothing to Cook of her courses not coming over the past few months. Cook had trapped her in the same way she herself had trapped Marie de Volonté the summer before.

"Then something is on the way," Cook's face rounded into a smile as she put an experienced hand on Nicole's belly. "You must guard your secrets, little one," the older woman added in a lower voice.

"I know, Cook. You are the one who taught me that."

"'Tis a blessing the queen's away; she will not wish to see your joy until she can share in it herself," the older woman continued.

"There's nothing to see, is there? I can't eat, and my bodice fits the same."

"Little one, the news is written on your face, but not yet on your body. You are glowing. How happy your lord must be."

"I haven't—I haven't said anything yet."

Cook looked closely at Nicole, a sly smile playing at her lips.

"Are you waiting for Christmas to gift him with such news?"

"I'm waiting until—I can be certain." *I'm waiting because I cannot be sure of certain things.*

"Focus on what you can be certain of: that your lord will be pleased." Cook's eyes narrowed slightly. "You must let him know, so he will share in your joy."

Whatever Cook knew or guessed, Nicole was sure that the woman who had taught her so much about herbs and healing knew how to keep secrets. Women healers always did.

"I'll bring some apples to Petard," she said, moving toward the storeroom. She wanted to get away before the older woman asked any more questions. Reaching clumsily into a basket in the cool room off the kitchen, she pulled out two dried apples left over from the fall harvest. She couldn't bear to bite into one herself; she would offer both to Petard.

"Don't go inside his paddock," Cook told her. "You are guarding a life now. Protect it with your own."

"I will, Cook. I surely will."

Heeding Cook's words, she had taken care over the Advent season not to run or jump, anchoring herself to the ground beneath her, just as the babe was anchored inside. Gerard had left for the wedding the first week of January and was still gone when February arrived, and with it the first intimations of spring.

She watched Philippe as he awkwardly tried to climb onto Petard's back. He had grown in the five months since she had last seen him. The fine muscles in his thighs had thickened. They flexed and danced under the rough material of his leggings as he clumsily tried to mount the horse. Finally, he succeeded in getting one leg over, fully seating himself.

Petard tossed his head back as Philippe squeezed the stallion's flanks. The horse seemed happy to be ridden and soon broke into a canter. After a moment, Philippe pulled the reins to circle back to Nicole, and Petard whinnied; whether in protest or for joy, she couldn't tell.

She threw back her head and laughed loudly. Everything felt so good at that moment. She prayed that the next time she saw her queen, Anne of Brittany would feel a similar joy.

"My lady is happy, although full of secrets today," Philippe observed.

"Yes. Both." The secret she guarded was one that she herself didn't know the answer to. Fortunately she had enough to focus on with the secret she had that she did know of. Soon enough, it would no longer be a secret to anyone with eyes to see.

"I am happy to see your roses." Philippe slowed Petard to a walk and sidled up to the fence on the other side of Nicole.

"What roses?" She could feel even more heat than usual spring to her face. Over the past few months, she had felt like a small oven warmed her from within. And so it did, with something precious growing inside.

Philippe leaned down and put his head near Nicole's. His scent was intoxicating, a heady, bracing aroma that made her senses dance. She felt dizzy.

"The roses in your cheeks," he whispered, looking intently into her eyes.

At that moment, the babe leapt in Nicole's stomach. Startled, she stumbled sideways. In a flash, Philippe was off the horse and at her side, steadying her with his arm. "Come. Sit down. I will get you some water," he said gently.

In a daze, Nicole waited for the slight internal movement to happen again. Now, she understood what the flutter had been the moment before when Petard had snorted and exhaled his warm breath onto her stomach. The babe had kicked. The moment of quickening had come: in Philippe's presence, not Gerard's. Thinking back to Cook's words, she realized the older woman had counseled her to guard her secrets, not just one. Had she known Nicole had more than one secret, or did she simply know that every woman did?

Philippe returned with a leather skin of water, and crouched beside her.

She took it and drank thirstily.

"Did you feel faint?"

"I felt something, but not faint." she told him.

"What did you feel?"

"What I felt, I cannot share with you. But it was a good thing. Do you understand?"

"A happy secret?'

"Yes."

"Then I am happy, too."

"Even though your happiness belongs to your future wife?" she couldn't help asking. She hoped she didn't sound bitter.

"About that—"

"Tell me nothing about that," she said sharply, cutting him off. She reached up and touched a finger to his mouth. "I don't want to know." She wished to hear nothing that might pain her. Not for her sake, but for the one on the way.

"Then let me tell you your laugh is my happiness. The roses in your cheeks are my happiness. You are—"

"Enough, Philippe. Now is the time for you to keep such thoughts as your own secrets. You must put them out of your mind."

"I cannot, my lady." His green eyes blazed; he seemed almost angry. "They are my thoughts, and mine to do with what I please."

"Then you mustn't share them with me." He felt exactly the way she did, she now knew. Her thoughts were a verdant field, alive with memories of the summer before and the autumn before that.

"You are the cause of them," he told her.

"You are the cause of some of my secret thoughts, too," Nicole confessed. The scent of him so near jumbled her senses.

"Really?" His face lit up, eager and open.

The babe kicked again. In protest at Nicole's words or in celebration? She couldn't tell, but the slight flutter elated her. She couldn't share either the news or the sensation with the man who stood before her, but she could treasure it in her heart. Instantly, she knew that Cook had spoken of all women when she had told Nicole to guard her secrets. Women had many, if they were lucky. Nicole was beginning to feel fortunate indeed.

"Listen to me," she whispered to Philippe.

"I do. Even when you are not near, I hear you in my thoughts," he breathed back, his breath warm on her face.

"You must guard all these thoughts and whatever other ones you have, and put them in a secret place," she told him sternly. She would faint in a minute, dissolved by his scent and breath.

"Only if you promise to do the same."

"I do, Philippe. I truly do." She spoke sincerely. She had kept her thoughts of Philippe secret ever since they had first met.

"And the other thoughts, too. You have them?"

"Many."

"Many more than the ones I know?"

"Many more." She smiled as the tiny flutter inside began again. Was the babe warning her or cheering her on?

"Then, when I ask you where you put them many years from now, you will have them carefully hidden away but not forgotten?"

"Many years from now, Philippe?"

"Yes. God willing." He looked earnestly into her eyes.

"I will be an old woman many years from now." Was he implying the time they both knew would come sooner rather than later, when her present husband no longer walked the Earth? Who knew if she would be alive by then? Especially after childbirth. She shuddered to think of how many women she knew whose lives had ended with that experience, her mother among them.

"And I an old man."

"I will not be alone, God willing," she spelled out. Hopefully, the babe in her womb would live, if God could forgive her for seizing her own happiness.

"Then I will take what comes with my heart's love," Philippe promised.

"You speak of that which we have no power to control. But if ever such a time comes . . ."

"You will not forget me?" His eyes searched hers, the green of them flecked with gold.

"I will not forget you." The weight of Cook's counsel cloaked her like a mantle. What transpired now between Philippe and her had no place in the present moment. Yet their feelings were as real as the fluttering she had just felt inside. For that reason, their conversation must remain secret, known and remembered only by them. It was good counsel to guard her secrets. Now she realized not only women had them.

"Good," he breathed.

"Good, my foolish one," she told him to lighten the moment. "Now, get back on that horse, and ride him like I would if I could." She needed to recover herself before she fainted from emotion. Either that, or from the flutter of the babe inside, reminding her that the deepest of all of her secrets would forever remain a secret, even to herself.

CHAPTER TEN

A Ma Vie (To My Life)

Her face was serene, a marble mask. She seemed taller than before leaving for Paris the previous spring.

As the queen strolled through the castle garden, Nicole and the other ladies of honor in tow, Nicole saw that she also looked more rosy than the last time she had seen her. Marriage to the new king apparently agreed with her.

In her loose pale yellow gown, Anne of Brittany flowed as she walked. As she turned the corner of the rectangular formal garden,

Nicole saw that she was less slim in profile than she had been in May, at the late king's memorial service. Was it because she had worn black for the entire season when last Nicole last saw her, and black made every woman look slimmer? Or was it something else?

Nicole dug her elbow into Marie de Volonté's side. "What do you think? Is the queen looking fuller now, or am I imagining things since I am a round ball myself?"

"Madame de Laval says the queen has been blessed again," Marie de Volonté said, looking down at Nicole's large tummy then up again. "Soon, she will bring another dauphin into the world to make her smile and laugh again." Her mouth wavered, as if she wasn't quite convinced.

"Pray God his smiles and laughter continue to his adulthood this time." Nicole replied, crossing herself. Marie de Volonté followed suit.

"And may yours, too," Marie added. "When did you say it will come?" The look she gave Nicole was as blank as her face was sweet.

Nicole stared at her a moment. "Toward the end of spring. Why?"

The younger girl giggled. "You are so big, I thought maybe sooner." Eyes half-lidded, she glanced again at Nicole's midsection then looked quickly away.

"Nicole, come," the queen's fluid, yet authoritative, voice floated toward her, cutting through the spring air like a crisp tuft of wind.

Nicole hurried to her side. "Your Majesty," she curtsied clumsily, as she did everything else these days. Fearing to look into the queen's eyes, she kept hers downcast.

"I see you have been busy since your marriage," the queen teased, her eyes on Nicole's enormous egg-shaped tummy.

"My lady, I have not wished to—to—"

"To flaunt your belly in front of me when mine is flat?" the queen asked levelly.

"I—yes, my lady." Her queen didn't lack for courage. She knew how to call a spade a spade.

"Do you see me in my black gown now?" Anne's tone was teasing.

"No, my lady. I am happy to see you in this pretty yellow one," Nicole replied uncertainly.

"It was time for a new one," the queen commented. "Besides, my black one no longer fits."

Nicole looked questioningly into the queen's eyes. Joy danced there.

"Your Majesty?" It wasn't for her to speculate as to what the queen was implying. She would wait for her monarch to lead. If she didn't care to share whatever news she had, Nicole would find out soon enough from the other ladies before they left for Blois, where the king and queen would make their home.

Anne of Brittany laughed aloud, the first laugh Nicole had heard from her lips since the winter before, when King Charles had been alive and his child on the way. At the queen's gay humor, the other ladies began to laugh, too, brightening the spring day. Did their sovereign have good news?

"I am happy to hear you laugh, Your Majesty," Nicole confided, recovering herself.

"And what about your babe? Does he kick at our pleasure?" the queen put a hand on Nicole's belly and felt it carefully. Sure enough, the little one inside kicked in response, evoking a giggle from the queen.

"It seems he does, my lady!" Nicole cried. She could faint from happiness at the sound of her liege lady's laugh. It had been a long winter.

"And what about mine? Are you an expert now on feel-ing the flutter of a soul within?" As she spoke, the queen took Nicole's hand and put it on her own belly.

A murmur went up from the ladies around them.

"Your Majesty?" Nicole stammered.

"Is it true?" one of the more bold amongst the court ladies asked.

"May we congratulate you on your happiness?" another chimed.

"My happiness lies inside, yes. You may pray for me that this one enters the world safely, and stays longer than my Charles Orland," the queen said bravely. Her face neither flinched nor changed color as she spoke the name of her dead son.

Nicole's heart swelled. Royal down to her fingertips, Anne of Brittany had been trained from childhood to mask weakness. How well she demonstrated the courtly virtue of self-control.

Joyous cries rippled through the soft spring air at the queen's news. Her maids of honor crowded around her, smiling and chattering. Little Marie de Volonté's face beamed as tears of joy streamed down it. She had seen much at court already at the tender age of fifteen.

"*Ma chère*, do not cry. This is the time for joy. You must amuse me and keep our little dauphin entertained until he is ready to join us. Wipe your tears," the queen commanded.

Nicole felt tears spring to her own eyes. Quickly, she turned away so the queen wouldn't see them. Never in her life had she met any other woman as brave as her sovereign. She had lost seven children, then her husband the king. God grant that the babe she now harbored, planted there by Louis XII, would live to adulthood.

"Why do you cry, Nicole? Especially you, favored among others?" the queen asked.

"Because you are so brave, my lady." Nicole could barely get the words out. "So brave and strong. No one who has ever ruled a kingdom is above you in courage and grace."

"My little one," the queen murmured, putting a dainty hand on Nicole's shoulder. Some of the ladies tittered. Nicole was as large as a giant eggplant, the birth of her child looming only a month away. She had prayed for many months that her own babe would be a girl, so that the queen would not feel downcast at the arrival of another woman's son after losing all of her own. But if the queen was expecting her own son, it wouldn't matter. If he survived. She shuddered. Of four live children Anne had borne, all four were dead. Then there were the three others that had been born dead. The odds were horrendous. Best not to think of them at all.

Instead, Nicole considered the possibility that it might be a boy inside her. Still, she clung to the idea that it was a daughter to keep her company night and day. Gerard had returned to Amboise from Nantes in February, but then had been sent off to Blois in March to prepare the castle for the king and queen's arrival. Philippe was gone, too, back to Agen. For now, however, she didn't much care; with the final months of pregnancy upon her, she had low appetite for male company. All of her thoughts and actions wrapped themselves around the life inside her, protecting the little soul and talking to it in countless inner conversations.

"I was trained to lead my country from the moment I began to walk," the queen spoke, cutting into Nicole's thoughts. Anne of Brittany's tone was suddenly serious.

The ladies grew silent around her. "At age eleven, my parents were dead and I became Duchess of Brittany. The following year, I lost my sister, Isabeau, and two years after that, almost my country."

The ladies moved closer, eager to hear her words.

"In the years that followed, as all of France knows, I lost every one of my children and then my husband," she continued.

The garden had become so still, even the birds had stopped twittering.

"But now I have moved through my season of loss, and spring is here." She paused, her face radiant, proud. "Yet none of us know what lies ahead. For any of us. For our lords in war and for us in childbirth."

Nicole's heart stood still. Her time would be upon her soon, within weeks. She prayed to God and to her mother's soul to send a quick labor and safe delivery. Guilt twinged her as she considered that she asked for an easier hand than her queen had been dealt. Silently, she crossed herself, as did every woman present.

"Whatever lies ahead, it is my duty to be strong. Not just for myself, but for my people. For all of you, for all of Brittany, for all of France." Her words swelled to a sweeping volume, precise and clear as a bell. At the mention of France, every woman present curtsied before her. Many wiped tears from their eyes as they rose.

"Follow my example and be strong yourselves, my ladies. I ask you to help me to bring this babe I carry to life; and to survive, once born."

Every woman before her murmured their assent to the queen's request. Nicole didn't doubt that all of them harbored the same thought in their hearts: seven previous pregnancies, not a single child surviving beyond the age of three. The queen's road ahead was not clear to see. What was clear was the fortitude and courage of the petite woman among them, who seemed the tallest of them all at that moment.

"And for any of you who save this coming babe from harm or death, I will grant you one request that you ask, no matter what it is." Queen Anne's voice rang with promise, the promise of spring, the promise of a monarch's authority.

As the ladies weighed the queen's words, Nicole drank in Anne of Brittany's regal self-possession. She hoped she would remember every one of her queen's qualities, and store them inside to use in the face of future storms. One thing life had already taught her was that there would be many, as surely as day turned to night.

"But, Your Majesty, what if that one request is not to the liking of your husband the king?" Only Madame de Laval could have dared to ask the question that likely many of the ladies present were thinking.

Anne of Brittany's eyes sparkled as she turned to her close friend, first among her ladies of honor.

"What do you think, Jeanne?" the queen challenged, looking down her short nose at Madame de Laval.

"I think my sovereign queen will move her lord to grant whatever request she makes in light of her bearing him a child," Madame de Laval answered in the same playful vein as the queen.

"Exactly so," the queen agreed, a smile playing at her lips.

"Long live the queen!" a voice cried.

"Long live the queen and her children!" another voice rang out.

"Long live Queen Anne!" others joined in. The tone of the afternoon had turned as gay as the fair spring sky above.

"To my life," the queen agreed, to which the ladies' cheers grew even louder. *A ma vie* was her motto, one that didn't lack for confidence, as a woman born to rule would not.

Queen Anne held up her hand. "Hush, now. Do not disturb my prince's nap," she chided the women playfully. She turned and continued her walk. "Nicole, stay by my side. You will bring me luck," she bade her.

Nicole kept pace with the queen, her heart bursting with love for the brave, regal woman next to her. Side by side, they strolled through the gardens, Nicole aware of the queen's almost imperceptible limp. She admired her sovereign even more for so carefully concealing her defect. The April sun beamed down on them, blessing them both, as well as their precious charges within. Warm, sun-drenched days would follow black nights, and Nicole vowed to endure whatever nights came with the example the queen had set. Then a new day would come and they would laugh again. It was all they could ask for, Nicole told herself, trying not to ask for more.

⚜

Nicole's prayer was answered. At the end of May, she delivered a healthy daughter whom she named Blanche, after her own mother Blanche St. Sylvain.

Gerard had been pleased. As was customary, he had stayed clear of the birthing chamber, coming to congratulate her after the child was born.

Nicole's labor had been hard, but mercifully short. After labors she had seen the queen endure, with no live issue as reward, Nicole counted herself blessed to have delivered a beautiful, rosy babe. She prayed the same would happen for the queen in the fall, although a dauphin would be preferable for the king and queen to cement the line of both Brittany and the house of Valois on the throne of France.

Gerard proved a devoted father. His delight in his new daughter warmed Nicole's heart, and his delight in his wife soon warmed her bed again.

He wasn't bad. He was energetic, enthusiastic and considerate. What he lacked was not his fault. Nicole looked to her infant daughter to fill in the gaps.

Blanche's every movement, every murmur, ravished her heart. A warm shower of love washed over her at moments when she watched her daughter kick her limbs in the morning sun or lock her eyes onto her mother's. Nicole counted herself abundantly blessed. She thanked God for all she had been given, including rich memories of what had also been taken away.

In June, the queen's court moved to Blois, to the childhood home of her new husband, Louis XII. It was a much larger castle, with far more rooms than the Chateau d'Amboise.

There, Nicole attended her sovereign almost as tenderly as she looked after Blanche. Daily, she massaged the queen's hands and feet with the violet musk-perfumed oil she loved. At least twice a week the queen bathed; a practice previously unheard of at court. Nicole made sure to scent the water with a few drops of Rose de Provence each time.

Two kitchen boys were on call at all times to prepare the fire for the queen's frequent baths. Although some at court whispered at the lavish taste of the diminutive duchess from Brittany, most at Blois Castle felt proud to be part of what was becoming known as one of Europe's most sophisticated royal courts.

The king denied his new queen nothing, doting on her in a way Nicole hadn't seen Charles VIII do, although he, too, had been a loving husband. Perhaps it was the age difference, with the queen almost fifteen years her new husband's junior. More likely it was because Louis XII had admired the young duchess as a commanding seven-year-old at her father's court in Nantes. She had been trained to rule from birth, a fact that showed in her firm decision-making skills, her opulent tastes, and her supreme self-assurance. For understandable reasons, the king appeared besotted with his new, young wife.

Nicole knew well how childhood bonds sometimes tightened with age rather than loosened. Similar cords of affection had tightened around her own heart, although she told herself she had everything she could desire.

On languid summer days when she nursed Blanche in the garden, she would wait for her daughter's mouth to move off her breast, her eyes suffuse with satiety then shut, and her small head drop back into a deep contented sleep. While Blanche napped, Nicole reveled in her own thoughts. To others, both mother and daughter looked fast asleep, but Nicole's head swam with memories of the summer before when she had behaved as her own mother's daughter, giving herself up to the one who had not been chosen for her.

She had chosen him herself, as he had chosen her. Time with him counted among her most treasured and sacred memories, although she wasn't sure what a priest would make of such thoughts. God knew plenty of men of the cloth, from the Pope on down, had given themselves over to similar pleasures while in the line of sacred duty.

Nicole treasured her naps with Blanche after nursing her. To others, she looked the paragon of motherhood, a noble lady too besotted with her child to allow a wet nurse to do the job, as most did.

It was all that and more. Those quiet moments were the one time she could count on not being disturbed, neither by Gerard nor any of the ladies of the court who thought it rather common of her to nurse her own child. Perhaps it was, but she delighted in her time alone with her babe as well as her memories.

Cook had told her she would not get with child again until she gave up giving the breast to her. That was fine by Nicole. She didn't want to be rushed along the tidal river of fate that had brought her to Gerard d'Orléans' marriage bed. It was pleasant, agreeable. But it lacked what another bed had offered. A bed of her own making, on a blanket laid on a grassy hill, where sensation and emotion had melded together in rapturous waves of bliss she had never felt since.

She had had her moment before duty swallowed her up. And she had seized it, just as her own mother had. "To my life," had become her own motto.

Looking down at Blanche's sweet face, Nicole's heart swelled. It was too soon to know the true color of her daughter's eyes. They changed every time she opened them.

CHAPTER ELEVEN

The Queen's Desire

By late summer, the rumor of plague coming to Blois had been confirmed, with several cases in the village, but none as yet at the castle. Word of it was sent to the king in Milan. His return was swift, his directives firm.

"I am taking you to Romorantin where my cousin will care for you until the child is delivered," the king told the queen. Chateau Romorantin, the home of Louis XII's cousin, Louise de Savoy, was a two-hour journey from Blois, to the southeast.

Nicole and Madame de Laval had escorted the king to the queen's chambers, where they had plastered themselves to the

other side of the door, their ears to the narrow gap between
hinge and wall as soon as he had shut it behind him.

"I do not want my child born in that woman's home," the
queen's voice was shrill.

"No signs of plague are at Romorantin, and Louise will see
to it no one visits from any towns touched by pox while you
await your time," the king counseled.

"I hate that woman," the queen wailed." She wants my sons
to die, so she can put her own son on the throne." She referred to
Louise's son by her late husband, Charles, Count of Angoulême.
Francis, Duke de Valois, was a child of four, who was next in
line to the throne of France should the king and queen produce
no male heirs.

"You know how strict she is. She will see to it that no plague
enters her home to protect her boy," the king argued. "Do you
not see that her interests are aligned with ours?"

"She is as fierce as a mother hawk about that boy. Do you
know she calls him her little César?" the queen snorted in disgust.

"That is precisely why you will be in the best hands, far from
Blois, under her protection. Her only goal in life is to safeguard
her son. She will guard him and everyone else in her household
better than anyone can here, where pox already lurks."

"What if she tries to kill our son, if I have one? She will not
be pleased."

"My lady, I am sending a doctor to you as soon as I receive
word your time has come. He trained in Milan. I've charged
him with watching over the health of the babe once it's born."

"I don't want any of that lot near me," the queen railed.

"He will attend to the babe, not you, my lady. And he is
from my personal staff, so I trust him."

"What good have any of them done for any of my children?" the queen cried.

"My lady, this one has skills I saw myself. He is young; he has new ideas."

"What good are the ideas of men for the mysteries of women?"

Nicole and Madame de Laval exchanged glances; the queen's question was apt.

"My lady, you ask a question to which I have no answer," the king replied judiciously. "But our child will be attended by this man who served under me, and is loyal to our house. You may also bring some of your ladies to attend you, so long as they are healthy."

"I want Nicole to assist," the queen told him.

On the other side of the door, Nicole felt herself blush with love and pride.

"The wife of Gerard, you mean?" The king had been away in Milan the past few months and was only now getting to know the inner circle of his wife's court.

"Yes. She has a sense of touch. I want her to be with the babe after it's born. She will know what to do, not like those charlatans with their mumbo jumbo."

"Then I will see to it that she also assists the man I am sending."

"A pox on your doctors!" the queen's voice rose.

"This one is different. He comes from an unusual background," the king replied. "I trust him and you must trust me."

"What do you mean?" the queen demanded.

"You will feel safer having your babe attended to by the man I send than by a doctor from my cousin's household," the king said.

"Truth to that, husband," the queen's voice was calmer. Louis XII had reached out to her and she had accepted his peace token.

"Now rest, my lady," the king's tone softened. "You will need your strength for the battle which only women are given to do."

"Shut up and bring me one of those Venetian treats, if you brought any back this time."

"You read my mind, my lady love. I have some here that I saved for you."

Holding back a giggle, Nicole smiled at Madame de Laval. The king and queen's relations were wonderfully informal. It was a good sign, boding a loving alliance, one that a child together would cement.

Madame de Laval smiled in return, and silently they slipped away from the door.

As expected, Nicole was chosen to be part of the attending team. Two midwives would assist at the queen's delivery; the new physician would attend to the health of the infant. The king had returned to Milan, but would come as soon as he received word that the queen's pains had begun.

Louise de Savoy's welcome was surprisingly warm. She stood in the courtyard of the Chateau de Romorantin, personally greeting each member of the queen's escort, bowing dutifully as Anne of Brittany, Queen of France, was helped out of her litter. Louise de Savoy was an efficient manager of her household as well as her son's safekeeping. Every one of the attendants who accompanied the queen to Romorantin had been checked carefully for sickness by Louise's own doctors, before being admitted across the bridge over the moat surrounding the chateau.

Cook numbered among the women the queen had brought from Blois. The wise woman had packed large bags of clove heads, cinnamon, orange and lemon peels, and sage and lavender, meant to safeguard from plague. No one was more expert than Cook on how to ward off illness. Plus she was a Breton, someone the queen trusted, from her own childhood home in Nantes.

On the evening of October twenty-fourth, after a sumptuous supper with Louise de Savoy, the queen's pains began. Quickly, her team of attendants and midwives prepared her for the birth. A messenger was dispatched to the king on the fleetest horse in the Chateau de Romorantin's stables. Louise de Savoy kissed the queen, wishing her a safe delivery, and retired to her own quarters per instructions from her cousin the king. The queen had told him, under no conditions did she want Louise anywhere near her during labor and delivery, and Louis XII had relayed the message, rephrased in more diplomatic terms, saying that his wife would be more at ease to have her own women attend her when her time came.

By early the next morning, the queen entered hard labor.

"Get the physician sent from the king," Madame de Laval snapped to one of the attendants standing behind Nicole.

"Yes, my lady." The woman rushed from the queen's chamber to the hall outside. Nicole could hear her ordering the guard to summon the doctor.

In a minute, heavy steps were heard in the hall outside, and the attendant appeared in the doorway.

"The doctor is here, my lady."

A tall man in a black cape and traveling hat stood behind her, his face in shadows. Just beyond him, the first rays of breaking day filtered through the windows.

Madame de Laval put up her hand. "Tell them to stop there. We will be done in a few minutes, and when the babe has arrived, the doctor can check him."

Him. It was doubtful, but one could hope. Nicole leaned over the queen, then clutched the laboring woman's forearm firmly to help her through the final agonies of the birth passage.

"Breathe, Your Majesty. Breathe in now," the first midwife urged the queen, who half stood, half sat on the birthing throne.

"Shut up!" Anne of Brittany, Queen of France, screamed in anguish.

"Hold her up," the second midwife instructed Nicole and the woman who clutched the queen's other arm. Firmly, Nicole grasped the queen's arm with one hand and slipped her other arm around her back, forcing her more upright.

"Get it out!" the queen shrieked.

"Yes, Madame. He is coming now. He is almost here. Don't push yet; wait until I tell you," the midwife instructed.

Nicole dipped a linen in the basin of rose water next to the birthing stool then wiped her sovereign's glistening face. She smiled at her, but the queen noticed nothing. She was in another world, one Nicole had been in herself. As with all mothers everywhere, she knew how desperately the laboring woman wanted to escape it as soon as possible.

"Now, Your Majesty. Push now!" the midwife ordered.

"Ahhh!" the queen moaned.

"He is coming, Madame. Keep pushing."

"Damn you to hell!"

"Very good, Madame, his head is showing."

"Arghhhh!"

"Push, Your Majesty. Push out your babe," Nicole cried, urging her on.

The queen exhaled again, a mighty groan escaping her, and, with it, the child. Expertly, the midwife caught the babe. The second midwife moved in to cut the cord. Nicole wiped the queen's face again, and watched as Anne of Brittany's eyes came back into focus and sought the being she had just delivered.

Silence blanketed the room. The child began to cry: a loud hardy wail.

"Bless God," Nicole said, although she knew what the silence meant.

"The babe is alive, bless God." Murmurs echoed all around the room. Every remark was positive, except for the one not stated. Nicole knew what the absence of that one remark was.

The queen's eyes closed then fluttered open.

"What have I?" she asked weakly.

"Your Majesty, your daughter is born," the midwife announced. A cheer went up around the room.

"Get the doctor," Madame de Laval ordered Nicole. Her face revealed nothing, neither joy nor sorrow. How well all of the queen's attendants knew the tenuousness of their sovereign's infants' grip on life.

With a final swipe of the queen's sweat-drenched face with a wet cloth, Nicole left the room and went into the next.

"Come now. The child is born. A girl," she said to the back of the man in the black cape.

He turned. "Good news, indeed."

A melting warmth came over Nicole, as if spring had gotten mixed up and arrived in late fall. Someone else's voice had sounded like that when her heart had first awakened from girlish slumber to womanly joys.

"I've always preferred girls," the man continued, his cape brushing her gown as he passed.

Her senses sharpening, she breathed in. "You are among the few," she replied, thinking she did too, with one exception. The man's face was partially hidden by his wide-brimmed hat. But his scent enveloped her, filling every pore of her being with aching familiarity.

"One in particular," he added, turning his head to look at her over his shoulder.

Again, she inhaled, feeling dizzy. *Could it be?*

Quickly, she re-entered the room and busied herself with tidying up the queen. When her eyes fluttered open, Nicole greeted her. "Your Majesty, well done. Your daughter lives."

"My daughter lives," the queen repeated tonelessly.

Nicole watched as her monarch adjusted her face. What fortitude it took to be queen. The woman had just missed yet another chance to give the Kingdom of France a dauphin. Louise de Savoy would be lighting a candle to whichever saint she had prayed to to deny the queen a son and heir to the throne yet again. Anne of Brittany, Queen of France, needed to face the outcome with fortitude and resolve.

Nicole knew her queen well enough to know that both the king and the queen were determined that one of their children would succeed them, either by direct succession in the case of a son, or by marriage of a daughter to the male member of the king's family in line to succeed him, in the event that no son was forthcoming. The birth of a daughter meant the only way to get their child on the throne of France was to marry her to the four-year-old son of their host, Louise de Savoy. The queen had no alternative but to resolve herself to this outcome, although it most likely meant that her beloved Brittany would become part of the Kingdom of France, something Nicole knew the queen did not wish to come to pass. It would be interesting to see if her sovereign found a way around this problem. Nicole had no doubt she would use all her powers to try.

"Madame, may I get you something? Something to eat or drink?" Nicole knew that Queen Anne would get over whatever sacrifices she must make to accomplish her overall objective: to secure the throne of France for one of her children. She was too politically astute not to do whatever needed to be done to achieve that goal.

"Find out if the babe is healthy," the queen commanded her. "And don't leave my husband's cousin or that doctor alone with her. Check her yourself."

"Yes, Madame." Nicole made her way to the other room, her heart beating fast. Not for the queen's sake, but for the sake of meeting face to face with the man in the black cape. *I'm a married woman; my husband awaits me in Blois.*

"Her Majesty asks after her daughter. How is she?" Nicole addressed him, her face composed in a serene mask. All of her senses were afire. Was this the man she thought it was?

"She is completely healthy. She has all her fingers and toes. A good strong heartbeat and lungs. Tell her that she has given birth to a beautiful, strong babe." Under the brim of his hat, his eyes searched hers as he spoke. His gaze was far too forward to belong to a stranger.

Everything inside Nicole tingled. Sensations that had lain dormant for so long she had forgotten she possessed them began to vibrate. Surrounded by others, nothing could be said for the moment.

"How is she?" Madame de Laval inquired, coming up to them.

"She is perfect in every way, Madame. Perfectly formed, perfectly shaped," the doctor announced.

The newborn princess let out a wail. Nicole smiled at how loud and lusty it was. It sounded the way she felt inside. She wanted to fling her arms around the neck of the man in front of her.

The king arrives," a courtier boomed at the door.

"Go to the queen and give her the news of her healthy babe, so the king hears it from her lips first," Madame de Laval commanded Nicole.

Her heart beating as fast as the queen's new daughter's, she rushed to the spent woman's side. Nicole was sure of it. Philippe de Bois was no longer a horse-trainer.

"The doctor says she's perfect," she exclaimed. "He said to tell you your babe is both beautiful and strong, Your Majesty!" Nicole's joy swam in her eyes, blurring her vision.

"We will call her Claude," the queen replied matter-of-factly, "after St. Claudius de Besançon. I prayed to him for a safe delivery." She looked as if she wanted to say more, but her thoughts were her own. A born ruler, she had spent a lifetime practicing the discipline of keeping her troubles to herself.

"Your Majesty, are you not happy? You have delivered a princess to France," Nicole exclaimed, full of fresh awakenings, of love thought lost now found.

"I am queen; it doesn't matter whatever else I am. All that counts is that I am queen." Anne of Brittany looked as composed as she had looked like a madwoman only minutes earlier.

"But I want you to be happy, too, Your Majesty." She caught herself. It was not her place to speak of her own wishes for her sovereign. It was her duty to simply carry out whatever charges the queen gave her. Perhaps the queen wanted power more than happiness. Or perhaps the attainment of power was her happiness.

"Yes, silly goose. I am happy." The queen's smile was small, but her eyes shone, putting Nicole's heart at ease.

Because her queen was happy, she gave herself permission to feel the full extent of her own joy. Inside, the dam broke; cool, rushing water flowed over it. Philippe de Bois was alive and in the other room. Everything else seemed immaterial. She hoped, unreasonably, that he was yet unmarried. But even if he wasn't, to have the one who had fired her youth so close by was a joy beyond measure. The feelings he awakened in her were feelings she had never held for Gerard. Of course she loved her husband; she was bound to him. But the history she shared with the man in the other room was something she would never share with any other man. It was as if her feelings ran on parallel tracks:

one for the world to see, the second for only her and one other human being to remember and savor at secret moments.

"Leave me now. I need to rest, and you are much too excited. It's me who has a new babe, not you." The queen peered at Nicole. "Why are you so beside yourself?"

"My queen, your joy is mine. Thank you for giving us all this healthy princess!" Nicole enthused, masking the real source of her happiness. She enjoyed it even more because it was so exquisitely and privately her own. The only other being who shared it stood in the adjoining room, making small talk as he awaited the king's arrival. Steeling herself, she told herself she was a married woman. Of course she was. Happily married, too. Still, could she not allow herself the joy of knowing that the one with whom she had tasted bliss beyond words was so close at hand? It was enough, she told herself. It had to be.

CHAPTER TWELVE

Secret Garden

Marie de Volonté had not accompanied them to Romorantin. Further plague cases had stopped in Blois and, after it was clear the queen's newborn was healthy, plans were made to return.

The first week of February, the royal entourage rode into the courtyard of Blois Castle. Nicole accompanied the queen to her chambers, then got her own daughter settled into her rooms. Gerard was away, summoned to join the king in Milan, where he had returned after Princess Claude's baptism in the chapel of Romorantin.

The following day, Nicole went down to the kitchen to help Cook put away the supplies they had packed for Romorantin. They had not needed most of them, since the household there had been healthy. Louise de Savoy was a controlling woman, but in times of pestilence or pox, her strict oversight proved helpful in keeping her household safe.

The queen had complained of her non-stop in their carriage ride home to Blois, but Nicole had silently blessed God that Louise de Savoy had opened her home to them for the safe arrival of the royal princess. If they hadn't gone to Romorantin, the king would not have sent Philippe de Bois to attend to Claude after her birth. Nicole didn't doubt Louis had sent him not so much for his newly-acquired medical skills, but so as to have someone he could trust watch over his newborn child in his cousin's home. In the event that Claude had been a boy, Louise de Savoy's son Francis would no longer be next in line to the throne of France, something that would have displeased the strong-minded woman. Whether she would have schemed for the infant to fall ill or fail to thrive, no one knew, but better to be safe than sorry.

Seeing Philippe again had been the sweetest of shocks; one Nicole had tried to manage delicately, as a married woman and mother. It had been easier to see him away from Blois, where Gerard had stayed while she accompanied the queen to Romorantin. At least Nicole had not had to cope with the stress of hiding her joy from her husband, as well as her sorrow when Philippe had returned to Milan shortly after the princess's birth.

They had not shared a single private moment. She had not sought one and he had followed her cues, as he had always known so well how to do. Duty held her in its grip and she was not unhappy to be bound by it. She had not been able to bear the thought of spending time with him in private conversation while her eyes swam in the deep waters of his gray-green gaze, then meeting the eyes of her husband upon her return. The secrets she already had were enough to fill a lifetime.

Still, the morning Philippe was due to leave, she had stood at the window and watched as he lifted his eyes to the rooms where the queen and her attending ladies were quartered. When, finally, he spotted her, she felt as if time stopped. Then she remembered all that awaited her back in Blois and raised her hand in farewell. Hot tears welled in her eyes as she saw Philippe put his own hand over his heart, staring up at her for a long moment. Then he had turned his horse and spurred it from the courtyard, and the tears had spilled down her cheeks.

With rich food for thought, she carefully unpacked the bundles they had brought back. As she did, she glanced over Cook's shoulder into the storeroom. Surprised, she caught sight of Marie de Volonté. Her friend and sometimes-rival was reaching up for something on the shelf, near where Cook and Nicole kept the more poisonous herbs: pennyroyal, cowbane, and other herbs for women's ailments. Her profile bulged slightly below her bodice: she was not as slender as she had been five months earlier.

"Is that you, Marie?" Nicole called out. She sidled toward the storeroom to see what her friend was doing, but Cook blocked her way before she could enter.

Peering over Cook's shoulder, she took in Marie's silhouette as she clumsily stepped down from the stool she had used to reach to the top shelves. The outline of her form under her gown told Nicole that Marie had been busy in her absence. Her friend's belly was rounded, her face puffy and red.

"Good news?" Nicole exclaimed delightedly.

Marie's face blanched from red to white. She frowned at Nicole, saying nothing.

"Don't you need to take this up to the queen's chambers?" Cook asked, stepping directly into Nicole's sight line. She thrust a bunch of dried sage into Nicole's hands.

"I can do it later," Nicole protested. She wanted to know Marie's news.

"Best do it now, before visitors come." Cook gave her a push in the direction of the door. "Let's take no chances on anyone giving the queen an illness."

"But—"

"Go now, my lady. It's best for all concerned." Cook was being cryptic, protecting Marie.

Quickly, Nicole took the sage and hurried from the kitchen. But not before one last glance into the storeroom. The young noblewoman's face was peaked, her expression alarmed. Either pregnancy wasn't agreeing with her, or she wasn't agreeing to this pregnancy. Nicole would learn more later. For the moment, she would not further ruffle her friend's composure. If a babe was indeed on the way, she didn't wish to upset Marie in any way.

As she glided to the queen's chambers, she ruminated on what she had just seen. Marie's hand had been on the highest shelf where Cook kept the more poisonous herbs, the ones that were sometimes used to quietly end unwanted situations. What need would Marie have of such powerful poison, if she were protecting life inside? Unless . . . the life inside wasn't supposed to be there.

"What was Marie doing in the storeroom, Cook?" Nicole asked later that day, back in the kitchen. She had already checked the storeroom, noting that the pot that contained the pennyroyal was no longer there.

"My lady, you have your job and I have mine. Your job is to nose about in other people's business, and mine is to help keep people's business to themselves. You do yours, and I'll do mine," Cook told her bluntly, ending the conversation.

She couldn't be angry with Cook for such an honest answer. She had heard such a one from the discreet Breton woman before.

She knew how to keep her mouth shut. Nicole could hardly fault her for possessing such a rare quality at court. She had her own secrets that needed to remain so; she could count on Cook to keep them hidden away where they belonged. It was strange to think Marie de Volonté had a few of her own secrets, too.

Nicole got a chance to speak with her friend later that evening.

"Have you some news to share?" she asked, trying to broach her subject delicately.

"Not particularly," Marie snapped. "Why do you ask?"

"I—it . . . it's just that I haven't seen you for months and you look different," Nicole tried to be diplomatic.

"How so?" Marie's eyes narrowed. She was hiding something more than the obvious, which wasn't going to stay hidden too much longer, if it progressed.

"I mean you are rounder, more womanly," Nicole began. Frankly, her friend looked bloomingly rosy and luscious, except for the sour expression on her face.

"I'm married now." Marie's voice was neutral.

"That's wonderful! Who is he?" Nicole was surprised. She hadn't heard of any betrothal in the works before she had left for Romorantin.

"Guillaume de Montforet, the old king's keeper of the dogs." Marie's tone did not overly brim with the sweet enthusiasm of a newlywed.

"I'm so happy for you. He must be thrilled with your news," Nicole exclaimed, her eyes lighting on Marie's gently-rounded midsection.

"He does not know the news." Marie's face colored. "I mean, there is no news."

"Are you sure, dear friend?"

"As sure as you were when you married your Gerard," Marie commented, wrenching the conversation in an unexpected direction.

It was Nicole this time who colored.

"What do you mean by that?" she stammered.

"I mean those of us with eyes in our heads and ears to hear followed your doings closely the summer after our late king's death."

"What is that supposed to mean?" Nicole asked, her stomach twisting at Marie's jab. Men were not the only ones at court who learned the art of jousting. Women did, too, only verbally.

"It means that those of us who cared about your welfare were happy to see your life events unfold with such perfect timing." Her friend knew how to get her point across without actually stating it. She would follow her lead and do the same.

"Marie, you are among those who care about my welfare, are you not?" she probed gently.

"I might be," Marie answered judiciously. She had become an adept courtier in her five years as one of the queen's maids then ladies of honor. She owed the queen her good fortune; she had been smart enough to recognize that the man the queen had chosen for her to marry was part of that good fortune.

"As I am one who cares about *your* welfare, dear friend." Nicole reached out and stroked one long tress of Marie's dark brown hair. It was even thicker and more lustrous than usual.

"Do you?" Marie eyed her.

"And I would not see you denied one shred of happiness," Nicole continued.

"What meaning do you take, then?" the younger girl asked, looking suspicious yet in need of counsel at the same time.

"I mean that the arrival of a babe means happiness for all in one's household."

"Does it really?" The younger noblewoman looked doubtful.

"I know it."

"And if there is something not quite the way it usually is in its coming to be?" Marie asked hesitantly.

"Then that is in the past, and the past belongs to the past," Nicole told her firmly.

"You should know," Marie commented, somewhat less judiciously than the moment before.

"My happiness is deep, and it continues." Nicole clenched her hands at her sides. Now was not the time to blurt out words in haste that she would regret later. "I want you to have the same happiness. A babe is forever. The way of its coming about is but a moment in time. Which do you think is more important?"

"I—I've never had a child of my own. All I've had is something else of my own. And now that something else is gone." The light drained from Marie's eyes, and she looked away.

Nicole's heart ached. She knew of what her friend spoke, all too poignantly. She knew of whom, too. Best not to mention him, so that her own secrets would stay where they belonged.

"Dear one, that moment is gone. But if a child comes, it gives you joy for however many years it is with you," she counseled the younger woman.

Marie looked questioningly at Nicole. Her hand went to her stomach, her gesture clear.

"My friend, if you stop what has already begun, you might never again have a chance to bring life into the world."

"Why would I not?" Marie looked defensive. "I am married, after all."

"Our queen is married, too, for many years, yet the princess is her only issue," Nicole pointed out. "Accidents happen, sickness comes instead of babes, herbs don't work, or they work too well." She shuddered, praying Marie had not yet touched the pennyroyal. If made into a tea, and taken, it could induce contractions. If she didn't know how to handle it, she could easily kill herself along with an unborn babe. "If you were never again given the chance to be a mother, wouldn't you choose to be a mother now even if the situation isn't one you would have favored?"

"I don't know. I've never been a mother," Marie observed accurately, her tone glum.

"Are you not glad that your mother brought you into this world?"

"Yes, of course!" Marie looked startled, as if she'd never thought of such a parallel.

"Then bring this babe into the world and give it its own chance at happiness," Nicole counseled.

"Even if there are questions?" the younger woman's voice brushed the air, almost inaudible.

"There will always be questions. As long as there are whispering gossips, there are questions. Who cares?"

"Do you?" Another sting. Marie had learned much at court in five years.

Nicole drew herself up. "No. I don't. But neither do I wish for my child to be hurt by slanderous tongues." She waited for whatever further barb Marie might send her way.

"Your daughter . . ." Marie began, her voice trailing off along with her eyes.

"Do you have something to say about her?" Nicole pushed back.

"No. I do not," Marie replied.

"And do you have something to say about her mother?" *Take the counteroffensive. It's your best defense.* Michel St. Sylvain's words echoed in Nicole's mind. Her father was gone, but his practical counsel remained to guide her.

A long moment ensued as Marie studied the ground then brought her eyes up to Nicole. "Only that she is my friend." Her smile was faint but sincere.

Nicole's heart thumped with both joy and relief. "So let us be friends forever and guard each other's secrets, whatever they may be," she offered. She put out her hand to Marie, palm up.

"So may we." Marie put her hand in Nicole's.

The kiss on each cheek that Nicole gave her sweet, dark-haired friend was returned in kind. Marie stared into her eyes until her face broke into a wide smile.

"Friends forever?" Nicole asked, returning the smile.

"Friends forever," Marie answered.

"Secrets forever?" Nicole asked.

"Forever secret," Marie replied.

They fell into each other's arms, and laughed until tears streamed down their faces.

CHAPTER THIRTEEN

Unexpected Events

She enjoyed watching her husband joust. A year and a half into their marriage, Gerard d'Orléans was forty-seven, as fit as the day she'd first lain eyes on him, but a tad more filled out, with broad bands of muscle running across his chest. She loved the spectacle of the jousting tournaments, with the prancing, finely-muscled horses and the gaily-dressed ladies in the stands, waving and tossing their scarves to their favorite competitors. She reveled in the queen's good mood on tourney days, her eyes sparkling to match her jewels, as she reviewed the competitors riding their destriers down the lists, and then stopping before her and the king, to pay homage. But most of all, Nicole enjoyed watching her husband in his element. If she couldn't love him in the deepest possible way, at least she could admire him.

One day he would put away his lance and leave the competitions to those younger and more rash. For the moment, Gerard d'Orléans was still in fine form, and no one could deny that, for a man on the threshold of old age, he was in exceptional shape. The ladies of honor at court frequently congratulated her on the fine catch she had made. Only she knew in her heart of hearts that the prize she had truly wanted had slipped away.

As she dressed for the tournament, she glanced out the window and spotted her eleven-month-old daughter outside in the garden. She waved to Blanche, who was on her nurse's lap, holding tight to the small stuffed pony her father had given her. Already her daughter seemed as horse-obsessed as she herself had been as a girl.

At her daughter's wave back, Nicole's heart leapt for joy. Fastening the heavy gold necklace inlaid with precious red stones that Gerard had presented her with after Blanche's birth, she readied herself to attend the queen at the afternoon's games. She put on the red and yellow gown with black trim that Anne of Brittany had instituted as colors of the royal court upon her marriage to Louis XII, and attached her yellow scarf to her arm. Gerard on his horse would stop before the royal stand where Nicole sat and request it from her at the start of his match. She would place the scarf on the end of his spear, then watch as he raised it in homage to her, letting the scarf slip down then tucking it into his hauberk. There weren't many surprises in their marriage, but fate sprang so many on hapless souls, that perhaps it was a blessing.

Hurrying from her room, she took the fast route through the cellars to the tourney grounds. As she passed under a particularly low doorway, she slowed down, careful not to catch her headdress on the frame. It had been on the support lintel of one of the doorways in the same passageway that King Charles had hit his head two years earlier that same month.

She had never asked which doorway it had been. It had seemed bad luck to know such details, but she knew the accident had taken place somewhere in the passageway she was now in. Carefully, she made her way to the end and saw the light of day, thanking God He had made her short, and not at risk for hitting her head on doorway beams. Yet the former king had been short, too; shorter than the new king was. Strange, the twists and turns of a man's or woman's fate. All that could be counted on was that one's days were usually less than one hoped for, rather than more.

Thankfully, the queen's daughter by King Louis was thriving. The Princess Claude was in good health, a lively and bright six-month-old who squealed with delight when Blanche made funny faces at her. Life itself was something to be grateful for, and Nicole thanked God for the health of both her daughter and her queen's.

"There you are. Hurry, they are starting," Marie de Volonté called out to her. On the threshold of eighteen, the younger woman had grown into a beauty with her long, curly dark brown hair and almond-shaped dark eyes. Her new husband had brought two sons to their marriage, their mother dead in childbirth, delivering a third who hadn't survived. The queen had convinced King Louis to make a place for Guillaume de Montforet as master of his hunting dogs at Blois, so that she could keep Marie amongst her attendants at her new court there.

Marie's eldest stepson, Antoine, was learning chivalric skills under the tutelage of Nicole's husband. Guillaume de Montforet was in the tournament, too, but boys never trained under their own fathers. They were apprenticed to other knights, to strengthen bonds of fealty between families. Anyone knew that fathers would be too likely to go easy on their own sons, fearing for their safety. That afternoon, Antoine would assist at the games as Gerard's second squire, helping with his horse, and looking after his armor and weaponry. For a lad of twelve, it was a big responsibility.

Nicole hurried after Marie, marveling at the interplay of colors and light on the early spring day. May and June were magnificent months. September and October weren't bad either; but April was the most delicately beautiful of them all. It was a changeable month; the color of the leaves was the most translucent shade of green she had ever seen.

Admiring the pale pink and purplish blossoms that were coming out on the trees, Nicole marveled at the subtlety of their colors, the opposite of Gerard's clear-cut manly style. There was little nuance to her husband's preferences and dislikes, but perhaps it was a good thing. He was a perfect specimen to carry the royal colors of scarlet and gold with black trim; bold and not to be missed half a league away.

Glancing down at her gown, she saw she was wearing the same colors and laughed. Once there had been someone who had understood her lilac-shaded personality; someone who had vanished from her life, but whose memory lingered. How poignant it had been to see him so briefly the October before, at the birth of the young princess. Their meeting had been like a butterfly alighting on a flower: breathtaking for a fleeting moment, then gone. She shook her head to clear thoughts that had no place in her full life.

Arriving at the playing field, she climbed the steps of the queen's raised dais and seated herself a row behind, just to her right. The queen sat directly at center field, Madame de Laval next to her. She was now a graceful and dignified lady of older years, almost forty, some said more. Still the Duke d'Agincourt visited her with great regularity, their long disappearances together clucked about amongst the court ladies, not without admiration for the great lady who apparently had not let age diminish her enjoyment of life's pleasures.

"What's that barrier doing there?" a young woman who had just come to court asked Nicole, pointing to the middle of the field.

Nicole shrugged. She didn't care for sports other than enjoying the smell and muscularity of the horses, or the way Gerard behaved after a successful athletic competition or hunting outing. He would be ruddy, rosy, and full of confidence. On those nights, he would forget to ask how he was doing, to her great relief. It was strange that one of her cardinal rules for men was consideration, especially in a knight, but, in the case of Gerard, his consideration irritated her. Perhaps it was because she wished him to be as sure of himself in the private arena as he was in the public one; especially on the jousting field where he truly shone.

"Do you know what that is, in the middle there?" she asked Marie, pointing to the field. The low fence-like structure was gaily-decorated, with red, gold, green, blue, and purple fabrics covering its sides.

"It's a new device; a tilt barrier so that the horses will know where to stop," Marie replied.

"Do you think it will spook them?" Nicole asked. She had never seen such a structure before.

"Oh no, Antoine says they have been practicing with it these past two weeks now. The horses are accustomed, and the knights will better be able to aim their lances if the horses know where to stop."

"Who decorated this device?" Nicole continued.

"I heard it was the queen's favorite craftsman, the handsome one from Milan who came back with the king the last time. He must have done it last evening, because I was here yesterday morning to get Antoine, and it was just bare wood then."

Nicole said nothing. Her experience with horses told her they were highly sensitive to new or unexpected stimuli. This was especially true of destriers trained for tilting tournaments. They were the most high-strung of all and needed to be carefully handled so as not to unseat their riders. In any case, she had no fears for Gerard. His jousting horse was as steady and dependable as he was.

She sighed.

The hum of the crowd swelled in volume as the first knight approached the queen's dais. He wore black and white, the colors of the queen's own lands, representing the black tip of ermine tails against a white background, the traditional emblem of the dukes of Brittany. The queen rose and gave the chevalier her blessing, as well as her own scarlet and gold *coudière.*

Gerard appeared next. He was magnificent on his horse, regal and erect, at one with his favorite chestnut stallion. Nicole couldn't decide which looked more glorious: the horse or her husband. Her heart swelled with pride at the sight of the man she had married. His athletic posture belied his years. She thanked God the old man her father had first chosen for her had died. Then she offered a blessing for the family of the second one. She had heard that Gilles de St. Bonnet had married a wealthy widow in Paris a short time after being thrown over by her father. She said a prayer for a third man, too, one with translucent gray-green eyes whose memory she didn't dare linger on overlong.

"Why is your husband not on his white stallion?" she asked Marie, as Guillaume de Montforet came into view.

"His horse trod on a sharp rock on his run this morning. They had to find another mount," her friend told her.

"Really? Where did that one come from?" Nicole eyed the medium-sized, white and brown-dappled horse upon which Marie's husband was seated. It danced sideways as its rider tried to steady it. Was she just imagining it, or was the horse particularly high-strung?

Marie shrugged. "I don't know; Guillaume said he is highly trained."

Nicole raised her hand to Gerard as he rode past the dais then stopped below where she sat. He returned her greeting in the same manner then carefully lowered his spear toward her. She undid her yellow *coudière* and stood. Leaning forward, she loosely tied it over the end of his spear. She sat back down and watched as he raised his spear to her, causing the scarf to slip down its length. At the handle, he undid it and carefully tucked it into his hauberk.

Watching him, she felt proud that her husband still sought her scarf at the start of such events, even after a year and a half of marriage. Gerard remained in need of her approval, something Nicole felt guilty about at times. She had come to their marriage with her heart already engaged, and as much as she responded to her husband's open and boyish nature, at times it annoyed her. She hoped this might be one of his final tournaments at age forty-seven. There was no point in tempting fate, and she wanted another child, perhaps a son, especially if the queen managed to have one.

"I will make an herb poultice for your husband to put on his horse's hoof tonight," Nicole told Marie, resuming their conversation. "He should be better by morning." If infection set in, the consequences would be rapid. She had seen it happen many times with the children of the castle household. One minute happily playing, a small accident resulting in a cut or gash, infection setting in, then two days later—dead.

"He will be happy to have it," Marie said graciously. They both loved horses, especially fine destriers trained for tilting.

As the first course commenced, they watched with excitement for a few moments. Then, satisfied that the rounds were proceeding as usual, with much speed, power, and clashing of lances on shields, they lapsed into conversation, their eyes no longer on the field. Neither Marie nor Nicole was wholly focused upon jousting tournaments or any other athletic events. Giving birth then keeping one's children alive was enough of a feat for a woman, as far as either of them was concerned.

Languorously, Nicole turned up her face to bask in the warm April sun. She enjoyed quiet pleasures, unlike her husband who preferred moving with great speed most of the time. They were as unalike as night and day. Nicole didn't mind, as Gerard gave her the space she needed in which to savor her private thoughts, of which she had many.

"Look, there goes the Breton!" Marie cried as the knight with the black and white caparisoned horse charged down the field toward Gerard.

Nicole watched as her husband's horse skidded sharply to a halt before the tilt barrier. Gerard lurched forward in the saddle and engaged the Breton. Neither side prevailed, and the round ended in a tie.

Jauntily, both riders turned and rode their horses down the lists, back to their respective ends of the playing field. Nicole sensed Gerard lived for those moments between engagements, after proving himself before the crowd. She could almost feel the lazy flexing of her husband's muscles, successfully warmed up, engaged, and now in resting state, twitching in anticipation of the next round. She watched closely as he prepared for the second run.

At the trumpet's blare, Gerard galloped down the field. His horse obediently stopped at the gaily-decorated barrier. Gerard charged his opponent. This time he unseated the Breton. A roar went up from the crowd. Nicole's heart swelled.

The round was over. Next up was Marie's husband against a knight from Champagne.

"Do you think his horse is nervous?" Nicole asked Marie. The dappled horse's head was nodding from side to side. He seemed to be objecting to his rider trying to turn him around.

"No. It's probably just not used to being ridden by Guillaume," Marie said, looking unconcerned as she smoothed the voluminous folds of her dark green gown over her lap. Married life appeared to agree with her. She was unusually serene these days, wearing flowing dresses that concealed her figure and smiling enigmatically but saying nothing when Nicole at times glanced at her belly and raised a questioning brow. The pennyroyal jar had reappeared on the storeroom shelf the day after Nicole and Marie had sworn to be friends forever. Nicole didn't seek to coax any news out of Marie that her friend wasn't ready to share. The passage of time alone would tell the tale.

"Hmmm." Nicole shielded her eyes from the sun and followed the next round, then the next, in which Guillaume scored two blows of his lance to his opponent. He failed to unseat him, but it was a point in his favor. After applauding each time, she settled back into conversation with Marie. Nicole was glad to have her friendship through the years. Both of them held secrets in their hearts and both took comfort in knowing they were not alone in having them.

With the sun warming Nicole's head and shoulders, the memory of one with eyes as mutable as the month of April stole over her. She chased it away with thoughts of her daughter. Still, its sweetness lingered in the soft spring air.

A gasp went up from the crowd.

Straining to see, Nicole half rose in her seat and peered over the heads of those in front of her.

"He's down!" someone shouted below her.

"The horse is on him!" another voice rang out.

"Can you see what happened?" cried Nicole.

"Oh, God," Marie gasped.

"Oh, God," Nicole echoed. Guillaume de Montforet was down. Racing off the dais, she ran after Marie to the entrance to the field, where two knights of the court barred them from entering.

"My husband!" Marie cried.

"My lady, they are securing his steed now." One of the squires blocked her way through the lists. " It's too dangerous for you to go on the field."

"I will go to my husband!" she screamed at them.

"My lady, wait for the horse—" Their words were interrupted by Guillaume's steed galloping up behind them, running amok. As the men turned to chase it, Marie ran onto the field toward where her husband lay.

The second she reached his side, she sank to the ground.

Guillaume's body, in its full suite of armor, laid still, one leg turned out in the wrong direction. His helmet remained on, his squire trying to remove it.

Marie pushed him out of the way, throwing herself onto the heavy steel hauberk covering her husband's torso.

"Guillaume!" she shrieked.

"My lady, he is—he is—"

"Shut up!" she screamed. She pulled herself up at her husband's side and flicked open the steel helmet. His eyes were shut, his face white.

"My love!" she cried.

Nothing.

"Get up!"

A thick silence descended upon the men surrounding them. Hands reached down to Marie's shoulders to pull her back.

She resisted. "I need you!"

Nicole's heart hurt, thinking of her friend, of all their rivalries and moments good and bad, their shared secrets, their shared sacrifices. Both of them had married men different from the ones they had loved. Yet it seemed Marie had grown to love Guillaume de Montforet. A husband was a good thing; better than none at all.

"My lady, let me help you," one of the men said, as another removed the stricken man's helmet.

"Get away," Marie shook him off. "Guillaume!" she screamed. "I am with child. Get up!"

Nicole gasped. A low murmur rose from the men surrounding them. She pushed away the one in front of her to reach her friend. She would not allow them to touch her. Not at that moment. None of them could know her pain. Not one.

As she reached out to comfort her, Marie screamed again.

"Guillaume!" This time her voice sounded different, almost commanding.

Nicole winced in pain for her friend. Placing her hand on Marie's shoulder, she peered over it at the still figure on the ground.

Come back for our child!" Marie cried out, as if summoning her husband's soul to return to his body.

It was heartbreaking to hear. A rustle went up behind them, the men moving and attending to the rider-less horse and scattered equipment on the field.

Nicole stared at Marie's husband's face, thinking how sad it would be for him never to see his child by his beautiful, young wife.

"Get up, husband!" Marie roared. "I'm pregnant!"

Nicole gave her friend a gaze with all her heart in it, then looked at Guillaume again. Startled, she noted the color of the fallen man's face. It was different than when she had glanced at it seconds earlier.

As she stared, Marie put her head down next to her husband's and covered his face with kisses.

Nicole turned away to give her friend some privacy. When she turned back, she gasped.

Guillaume de Montforet's eyes had opened. Instead of staring at Heaven, they flickered open and shut, then opened again.

"It's high time you told me," he murmured weakly.

"Guillaume!" Marie shouted joyfully, throwing herself on him again.

"He lives!" a cry went up. Immediately the men moved in to attend to him.

Nicole backed away, spent with relief. It was a miracle. She thanked God for her friend's good fortune. Then she heard a roar go up behind her and turned.

Guillaume's horse had kicked someone to the ground. The body lay motionless next to the lists. Nicole craned her neck to see.

A yellow *coudière* fluttered in the breeze from the breastplate of the man on the ground.

CHAPTER FOURTEEN

Princess Claude

In the weeks that followed, it was the queen herself who comforted her, just as Nicole had comforted her sovereign so many times.

"My dear, he went quickly to a better place. He gave you good memories. Gather up what you have and live life. Live again, Nicole. Live for your daughter. You are young enough that God may grant you a son, too."

"Your Majesty, I need no son. I need nothing more than you as my example." Her sovereign had lost four sons: three born alive, one stillborn. Anne of Brittany knew loss, yet she wished for Nicole what she herself had had snatched from her countless times. Nicole couldn't pull herself together for herself, but for her queen she would do almost anything.

"Thank you, dear. But you also need to get up and give your daughter love and attention." The queen leaned in closer to her and whispered in her ear. "And I need your help."

"What do you mean, Your Majesty?" Nicole stared at her, forgetting her loss for the first time since the accident.

The queen smiled slyly and slipped her hand onto her belly; the gesture was unmistakable.

"My lady, good news on the way?" Nicole whispered.

"In the fall. I will need you to keep me amused. You are not amusing when you are sad."

That did it. After the queen left the room, Nicole got up and called for a bath to be drawn. Gerard was gone, but her daughter Blanche was alive; a ruddy, healthy child on the verge of taking her first steps. She needed her mother. Besides, the queen was pregnant. Nicole wished to offer her the love and support that the queen had shown her in so many ways during her time at court. Anne of Brittany could be brutally practical, expedient, some said, in her decision-making, but Nicole respected her ability to make decisions efficiently and without regret. On her face, the queen never revealed any sign of the hand she had been dealt. To Nicole's eyes, her monarch's marriage seemed a loving one, and with the possible arrival of a second child in the fall, she prayed that this one would cling to life, as only Princess Claude had managed to do thus far. She would do whatever she could to aid the queen in bringing her child to full term, and keeping the babe alive once born.

The next few months passed in a haze. Nicole was grateful for the queen's charge to amuse her. It distracted her from the loss of Gerard. Again and again, reliving the afternoon of the accident, she thanked God for taking her husband quickly, without suffering a lingering death. Blanche occupied her hours, along with her duties to the queen. The days passed quickly, and Nicole tried not to ask for anything more.

Yet as had happened each summer of her life for the past few years, her thoughts turned to Philippe. Memories of the two summers they had spent together played over her the way the breeze played over her hair on certain evenings. Nicole had been a child; then she had become a wife and mother. In that brief period in between, her heart had awakened to love.

On the morning of Nicole's eighteenth birthday, in early August, the queen summoned her to her rooms.

"I am not well today," the queen told her, her face pale, in stunning contrast to the afternoon before. They had taken a long walk in the gardens; the queen had been joyful and glowing.

"Your Majesty, what can I do for you?" Nicole cried, rushing to her side.

"Help me keep my babe," the queen said, her voice faint.

"Do you—are you?—"

The queen lifted her eyes to Nicole. Suddenly she squeezed them shut, clutching her stomach with one hand.

"I will bring a potion for you." Nicole took a cloth and wiped the sheen of sweat from her sovereign's brow.

The queen nodded. "Hurry."

"Shall I call the doctor?" Nicole asked.

"A pox on doctors! Did they save a single one of my sons?" Queen Anne looked away, mindful of bearing her losses alone as befit her royal position." Now go!"

"I will be right back, Your Majesty. Breathe deeply—"

"Go!" the queen cut her off and threw her head back, her face white with pain. Or was it loss of blood?

Trembling, Nicole rushed to the kitchen. As she ran, her thoughts turned to her own mother. What would she have done in a case like this? Trying to order her thoughts in time to her steps, she prayed the queen would hold on to her babe inside.

"Cook, where are you?" Nicole cried as she ran into the kitchen.

"Here. In the storeroom," Cook called to her.

"The queen is in trouble!" Nicole blurted out.

Cook's ample form emerged from the cool interior room off the kitchen, where she kept the dried herbs and bottled vials she and Nicole prepared together.

"Don't tell me it's the babe," Cook said, her face darkening.

Nicole nodded. "Can we give her something to keep it in place?"

"When a babe stops clinging to life, there's a reason for it," Cook muttered.

"Maybe it's something she ate," Nicole protested.

Cook grunted in response. Moving to a cupboard, she took out a few bottles. Pointing, she directed Nicole to the olive-wood mortar and pestle she used to grind herbs into powder. "What signs?" she asked.

"She was holding her stomach." She handed the mortar and pestle to Cook.

"And?"

"Her face was white." Nicole's heart hurt to think of the helpless expression she had seen on the queen's face before she had turned away.

"Bleeding?"

"She didn't say."

"Her face told you already," Cook guessed, looking grim.

"No, Cook. It's not possible. Didn't you say she might make healthier babes with the new king than she did with the old one?"

"I hoped." Cook turned from her, intent on her task.

"Then keep hoping. And make something strong to keep the babe inside!" Nicole cried.

Cook said nothing, but worked away. In a minute she handed Nicole a vial with a brown, cloudy liquid in it.

"Have her drink this. Then she should lie down and sleep. If she stays still, the babe may stay inside." Cook looked at her skeptically.

"I hope so, Cook. Let us pray that it does." She wouldn't say "he." It might bring bad luck to make such assumptions. The queen had had so little luck with sons thus far. None at all.

"Let us pray that the babe is healthy. And if it is not, let us pray that Nature takes its course," Cook muttered.

"Don't say that," Nicole hissed. As she exited the kitchen, over her shoulder she heard Cook's parting words.

"What will be will be, my lady. You're a mother yourself now; you know that." The resigned tone of her voice told her what she already sensed.

Back in the queen's chamber, Madame de Laval blocked Nicole's way.

"I have something for her, Madame. You must let me give it to her before it's too late," she blurted out.

"It already is," the older woman said curtly. "The midwife is with her now."

"Where is she?" She looked around Madame de Laval at the empty chair where the queen had been seated before. A dark color staining the cushion told her what Cook had already guessed. Nicole's throat closed. She mustn't cry. She needed to be strong.

"Shhh. She is in the other room. Get some linens from the housekeeper, and cold water from the kitchen. Don't say anything when you see her."

"Is she—did she—?"

"You see for yourself. We will find out more in a minute," Madame de Laval kept her tone low, her mouth a grim line. "Now go and come back quickly before they return."

Nicole hurried from the room. Quickly finding the head housekeeper, she instructed her to bring linens, then dashed to the kitchen again.

"A pitcher of cold water, Cook. Hurry!"

"If it's cold water they need, what's the rush?" Cook asked.

"Madame said cold water, not warm."

"To wash out the blood stains, I'll wager," Cook commented.

"How did you know?" She felt numb to her fingertips at the thought of what had just happened. All of the queen's wealth and position couldn't solve the mystery of what went on inside her when a babe was being formed. No amount of power and riches could assist the queen in the workings of her body, inescapably subject to the same mysteries every woman underwent.

The Cook filled a large pitcher with water kept cool in the storeroom. "Because after awhile you know these things."

"I have known the queen to give birth to stillborns."

"And now you know the queen to have miscarried," Cook said softly.

"Oh, God, no."

"Praise God, yes. Better to lose it now than to bring it to full-term, then deliver another dead child."

Nicole opened her mouth to say something then shut it again. Cook was right. Already the queen had delivered three stillborn children, all to her previous husband. Best not to deliver another born dead to the new king. At least they had the comfort of their daughter, the princess Claude. She shuddered, thinking of what had happened to Charles Orland: healthy, rollicking, ruddy one moment, and dead the next.

"Now get back to our queen and be with her when she needs you." The woman reached out with one capable large hand, and gave Nicole a firm shove toward the door. "Don't give her any sad looks either," she barked after her.

Putting on her courtier's face, Nicole hurried back to the queen's chamber, hoping she could offer the queen whatever she needed, although she knew it wouldn't be enough.

❧

Summer turned to fall, and the queen's grief began to heal. The princess Claude provided a great distraction, taking her first steps just short of her first birthday, encouraged by Nicole's slightly older daughter, Blanche. The girls were inseparable, much as Nicole and the queen had become, sisters in motherhood and also in mourning.

In the first week of October, the court hummed with excitement at the impending first birthday of the princess. The king was due to return from yet another military campaign in Milan. This time the queen had not accompanied him, but remained at Blois, intent on watching over her daughter, unlike her brief time with Charles Orland.

Nicole had heard the whispers at court after the dauphin had died. The queen had been away for fifteen of the thirty-eight months of the young prince's life. She had moved her court to Lyon then Grenoble, in order to be closer to the king, who had been on campaigns in Milan and Naples on the other side of the Alps.

It was not an unusual arrangement, but had been unfortunate in light of what had happened. Royal parents were not encouraged to bond closely with their small children, given the high rate of infant mortality. Instead, they were encouraged to produce as many children as possible, as quickly as possible, to secure a direct line of succession. The queen had been no exception. She and the king had missed almost half of the dauphin's life, arriving too late even to comfort their little boy in his final hours.

With Claude, arrangements were different. The queen watched over her like a hawk, charging the wet nurse to continue nursing her throughout her first year. With plague having come to Blois the summer before, Queen Anne would take no chances on losing her only living child. She had lost too many already.

The king had been informed by messenger of the queen's miscarriage. He had replied to say he would arrive in time for the princess's birthday, and would bring a pony with him for her.

The following week, Nicole sat on the bench in the herb garden, daydreaming after the midday meal. Her eyes flitted to the hill behind the stables from time to time then shut as she lost herself in reveries. She had tried not to indulge herself too frequently in such moments when Gerard had been alive. Now he no longer was, and she gave herself full rein to savor every memory of those days and far too few nights she had spent with her one true love.

At the sound of a trumpet blaring out from the direction of the ramparts behind the chapel, Nicole jumped to her feet. It's meaning was clear: the king's party approached.

She hurried to the staircase leading up to the rampart and lightly ran up it. Chances were slim that Philippe was amongst the king's party, but, with a new pony in tow, it was possible that the king had brought him along, knowing his healing skills with both horses and humans.

Scanning the distance on the bright late harvest day, she couldn't make out more than a cloud of dust and the king's pennant, the royal blue background fluttering in the breeze, with the gold of its fleur-de-lis design flashing as the sunlight caught it. Her throat closed as the group came into focus. Five men rode with the king. Nicole prayed that one in particular would be amongst them.

⚜

"I thought you had married."

"It didn't come to pass. The widow found someone wealthier."

"Ahhh." Nicole's heart leapt. There was no point in saying she was sorry. She wasn't and Philippe knew it. Three days had passed since the king's return for the princess's birthday celebration. Philippe had been asked to attend to the little girl's health, as the elderly court physician at Blois had come down with what looked like sweating sickness, and the queen didn't want him near her daughter until it was clear he had recovered.

They had tried to speak, but each time had found themselves soon joined by others. Finally Philippe had whispered to her to meet him in the furthermost of the queen's chambers, within earshot of her attendants should she need either of them, but out of earshot of others.

"I heard your husband died. I'm sorry," Philippe continued.

"Thank you." She thought of Gerard. He had been a good man but her heart had been locked in a secret chamber deep inside, bound up with the man who now addressed her.

"You have a daughter," Philippe spoke it as a statement. Who had told him? And what had they said?

She colored. "Yes. And what about you?"

"What about me?"

You have a daughter, too. "You were in Milan, no?"

"I was there almost two years."

"Why did you stay so long?" *Away from me.* So unreasonable, she knew, yet couldn't help feeling.

He coughed and looked at the floor. "Can you not guess?"

Without thinking, she reached out and touched his hair.

He grabbed her hand, bringing it to his lips.

"And did you find a wife there as well?" She steeled herself for his reply.

He shook his head. "No." His eyes remained steady on hers.

"Why not?" Relief coursed through her, chased by a dawning hope.

"My sweet—my lady, can you not guess?" he asked again, his expression softening.

"Because of me?" she asked in wonderment. She had never thought of re-routing her life for the sake of a sentimental attachment. It wasn't in her to do so. Her example was her queen, and always would be. Queen Anne was practical and sensible; she had taught Nicole to make the right decision for the right moment. It was what women did. Had they any choice about who they would marry, when to have children, or how many they would have? All were life events beyond their control. Better not to question, but to accept with grace, and squeeze what happiness one could out of what fate served.

But Philippe was different. Not just because he was a man, but because his character was as immutable as his eyes were not. It had been his eyes that she had first noticed about him. But it had been his character that had made her unable to forget him.

"Yes, because of you," he breathed softly. His hand reached up and stroked her cheek.

She grabbed his wrist. It had broadened from the last time she had touched it. The image came to her of washing his hair in the horse trough. Philippe had raised his arm in protest and she had smacked it down, bidding him to be still. Thinking of it, a giggle escaped her.

"My story makes you laugh?"

"Remember when I washed your hair?"

"How could I forget?" He laughed too, a low, murmuring sound that resonated below her stomach in a place deeper and wilder than where her heart was located.

She reached up and touched a lock of his hair again. This time, she pulled slightly.

The back of his warm neck shuddered against her hand. Gold flecks shot through his eyes as they bore into hers.

At that moment, Madame de Laval entered the room.

"Monsieur?" she addressed Philippe, her glance flickering between him and Nicole.

"Yes, Madame?"

"You are needed in the nursery."

"The princess?" Nicole asked, alarmed.

"Come now," was all she said, her lips in a straight, unreadable line. Nicole had seen that expression before. It was never good.

Philippe hurried after her without looking again at Nicole.

She followed them to the nursery, praying silently that the child wasn't ill or fevered. Twice it had happened that the queen had lost a child in the fall. It was all too thinkable that the same could happen again: all too thinkable, yet all too unbearable to think.

At the door to the nursery, Madame de Laval stopped, pointing to the wet nurse walking to and fro, with the queen's year-old daughter in her arms. The child whimpered weakly.

Philippe went to the nurse, quickly assessed the babe, then asked the nurse a few questions.

Returning to the doorway where Nicole stood, he frowned. "She is fevered," he said in a low voice.

"What will you do?" Nicole whispered.

"Cool her down with wet cloths. Beyond that, I am not sure."

"Then let me help you," she said with authority. Instantly she felt herself transported to their days at the stables three years earlier, nursing Petard back to health.

"What do you suggest?" he asked.

"We will make a potion for her."

"What kind?"

"Do you not remember?" she asked.

"What do you mean?"

"When Petard had the gash in his hoof," she reminded him.

"Ahhh, yes." His eyes lit up.

"You bound it, and it healed," she said, her heart full of memories. Those days seemed so long ago, before marriage and motherhood; yet it had only been three years.

"You made a poultice for the bandage," he recalled. "With spider's web and the parts that grow blue and green on old bread."

Nicole nodded. "Weeks-old bread," she specified.

"We don't have weeks to spare," he murmured, so no one else would hear. "Not even days."

She stared at him. Not another child lost to the queen. She couldn't bear it. "I'll find some in the pantry and make it into a drink."

"And what if the babe refuses to take it?" he asked, practically.

"We will give it to her nurse to drink, and the ingredients will go into her milk."

"The child still takes the breast?" Philippe asked, his voice low.

"The queen has been very careful with this one," Nicole whispered back. "After what happened with the dauphin. . ."

Philippe's brow knit together. "That may not be enough and may take too much time."

"Then I will put it in the babe's mouth from my own," Nicole said firmly. She would do whatever she had to do. She always had and she always would, following her queen's example.

"That would heal anyone," Philippe said with a smile.

"I will check the kitchen," she told him. "Maybe there's some bread lying around from God knows when."

"Hurry. We don't have much time," Philippe whispered gravely.

"Monsieur, what do you recommend?" Madame de Laval came up to them, her gaze lingering on Philippe.

Nicole struggled to remember if Jeanne de Laval had met him. She had known of him, certainly.

"We will prepare a drink," he told the older woman, his tone businesslike, as if to chase away any thoughts she might have of having seen him before in another capacity. "Meanwhile, we will bathe the child to bring down her fever."

"But what if she catches cold?" Madame de Laval asked doubtfully.

"We will keep her away from drafts and wrap her in clean linens once we have cooled her down," Philippe answered firmly. He clapped his hands twice. "A basin of cool water," he commanded the servants. "And clean cloths. Quickly."

The attendants ran to do his bidding.

Nicole shivered despite Philippe's confident tone, a deeper, more authoritative one than the one that had belonged to a nineteen-year-old youth commanding the stallion Petard. She feared for the little princess as well as for her mother. Another child lost to her sovereign would break Anne of Brittany's heart. And if the heart broke of the woman she loved most, then so would her own.

She would do whatever she could to ensure that Claude lived.

"Cook, can you find some old bread for me?" Nicole cried as she rushed into the kitchen.

"God save us, is the princess ill?" Cook knew why Nicole needed the bread. She had taught her young assistant all she knew of herbs and potions, but Nicole, in turn, had taught her what she had learned from her mother.

Nicole nodded, saying nothing. The grim look she gave Cook said it all.

Cook barked orders, and after a search by the entire kitchen staff, some moldy days-old bread was found. Quickly, Nicole scraped the blue and green bits from it and ground it with a pestle into fine dust. Rushing back to the nursery, she gestured to the wet nurse to come to her.

"I am just about to feed the princess, my lady. Could you give me a minute?"

"Even better," Nicole replied. "Don't feed her yet and come here."

Philippe stepped to her side, motioning to the attendant to bring the bowl of water.

"Before you begin, wash," he told Nicole. "You, too," he said to the wet nurse.

Nicole dipped her hands in the basin and Philippe rinsed them thoroughly, causing shivers to run up and down her spine. Then he repeated the process with the wet nurse, who looked disgruntled at getting her hands wet. The mid-October weather was cool, and the castle interior chilly. Motioning for the clean cloths, he gave one to each woman to dry her hands.

"There. Now go about your task," he exclaimed.

"Turn your back, then. This is women's business here," Nicole shooed him away. It felt good to be ordering him around again; almost as good as it had felt to surrender to his hands and let him give the orders. She pushed away the thought.

Philippe bowed, and complied, turning and stepping a few paces away.

"My lady?" The wet nurse looked baffled.

Below the woman's throat, a telltale wet stain spread in two spots on her tunic. She was engorged. Perfect, Nicole thought.

"Good woman, express your milk into this bowl here, and we will mix it with the medicine," Nicole instructed her.

"But the princess will not drink, save from my breasts."

"Will she not take a cup?" Nicole asked.

"She stopped taking her cup yesterday. I can barely get her to suck now."

"We will mix it in and coat your nipples with the solution. We'll coat your finger, too."

The wet nurse nodded. Leaning over the bowl, she unlaced her bodice and exposed one heavy-laden breast. Squeezing, she pressed out a thin stream of almost-clear milk. Quickly, Nicole mixed it with the ground-up bread mold. It was messy business, as was everything to do with producing and maintaining life as well as creating it. Would she ever again engage in messy business with Philippe, God willing? She vowed she would save the queen's child then lose herself with alacrity to Philippe de Bois.

They worked in silence for the next few minutes until the milk from both breasts was fully expelled.

"Bring the child," Nicole instructed the attendant now holding Claude. When the woman came over, Nicole took a quick look at the princess. She was listless and whimpering, not at all the ruddy girl she had seen two days earlier at her birthday celebration, laughing and playing peek-a-boo with Blanche. She shivered, thinking of how fast the course of Charles Orland's only illness had been.

"Nurse her," she told the wet nurse.

The woman put the princess to her breast, but the child wouldn't take it. She turned her head away, whimpering

"She's too weak to suck, my lady," the nurse said.

"Try your finger," Nicole commanded.

The nurse dipped her finger in the solution and put it inside Claude's mouth. Although the infant didn't suck, she didn't resist. Painstakingly they worked, but the amount of milk they got into her was meager.

Despair began to gnaw at Nicole. The magic of the bread mold couldn't tae effect unless they could get it into the child's stomach to spread through her body.

Wordlessly, Philippe handed her a cup.

Picking up the bowl, she poured the rest of the bread mold and milk solution into it, careful to capture every drop. Then she held it out to the wet nurse. "Drink it and hold it in your mouth then spit it into her mouth."

"My lady?" the wet nurse balked. She looked at the mug with distaste then back at Nicole.

"Do it, or I will," Nicole told her curtly.

The nurse remained motionless, her mouth firmly shut.

Taking a deep breath, Nicole lifted the mug to her lips and drank its contents, without swallowing. She motioned for Claude to be turned toward her.

Like a mother bird, she kissed the princess's tiny rosebud lips and slowly expelled the mixture into her mouth. The child was too weak to resist; for the first time, Nicole was glad. With her thumb and index finger, she stroked down the sides of the little one's throat as her mother had done with children in her household who had been reluctant to take their medicine. After a few seconds of soft stroking, she saw the gulp of the child's throat and she knew she had swallowed. The medicine would reach its mark. Careful not to swallow the liquid herself, she dribbled more of it into Claude's mouth. Again she stroked. Again, a swallow.

Finally, the milk was gone. The princess, after being rocked and burped, fell fast asleep.

Nicole righted herself and sighed.

"Where did you get the idea to do that?" Madame de Laval asked.

"From the birds," Nicole answered. They feed their babes that way, no?"

"You have the gift of inspiration, my lady," Philippe said, bowing deeply as Madame de Laval went to Claude's crib to ready it for the child to lay in. "I have always known that," he added softly so that only Nicole could hear.

"We shall see. I need more bread mold fast. Let us get back to the kitchen and tell Cook to put the oldest bread she can find in a warm, damp place right away," she answered curtly. Inside, her heart was opening to Philippe like spring leaves unfurling on a vine. She prayed no frost would kill them before they fully opened. If the princess died, so would her hopes for a future with the man she loved. Only if Claude lived could she feel comfortable reuniting with the man who had re-entered her life because he was summoned to oversee the princess's health at her birth.

Philippe exited the room, motioning Nicole to follow. Wordlessly, they made their way to the scullery.

There Cook helped Nicole find some old loaves of moldy bread, and set out fresh bread near the fireplace under damp cloths so that it would go bad as quickly as possible.

Nicole wasn't sure how it worked or why, but she had gotten the idea as a young girl from watching her own mother, whose healing skills had been legend in the countryside surrounding their own lands. Although Cook had been skeptical, Nicole had proven herself to her over the years; first by healing Petard's hoof with her poultice, then by using it countless other times on members of the royal court's household.

When they returned from the kitchen, Queen Anne was there, her face drawn, masking the despair that lurked nearby in the form of the ghosts of eight souls: one miscarriage, three stillborn children, two carried away within a day of birth, one within a month, and, the most heartrending of all, the dauphin Charles Orland, two months past his third birthday.

"Can you save her?" the queen asked, glancing from Nicole to Philippe, her face ashen.

Nicole knew well Anne of Brittany had a dim view of physicians, who hadn't managed to save her other children.

"Your Majesty, we will do our utmost." Claude was the queen's only living child. Nicole would not let the princess's soul fly away if there was anything she could do to prevent it from escaping its mortal shell.

"And what exactly is it you will do that will make this outcome any different than—" the queen's face tightened, "than the others?"

"We are using a potion that will bring down the fever if we can get the princess to take it," Philippe told her.

"Why should not she take it?" the queen snapped.

"She should, and she will," Nicole broke in.

"My lady has found a special way to feed it to your daughter," Philippe answered.

"Pray, what is that?"

"She feeds her as a mother bird feeds her chicks," Philippe explained.

"Then, this mother prays you save her as one of your own," Queen Anne said, giving Nicole an anguished look.

"Your Majesty, I will do my best," Nicole said, dipping her head to her queen then moving to the child's bed. Laying her hand on the princess's forehead, it seemed cooler than before. Thank God.

Over the afternoon and into the evening, Nicole gave Claude her medicine every time she awoke, roughly every two and a

half hours. She instructed the kitchen staff to prepare another
solution of the bread mold mixed with ale, for the little girl's
nurse to drink.

This combination the wet nurse accepted. Now even more
of the healing properties of the bread mold would find their
way to the princess's tummy through the milk the wet nurse
produced when the child took the breast again.

In the third hour after midnight, the princess's fever burned
hotter than it had before. Philippe slapped a wet cloth on the
little one's forehead, and Nicole hugged the girl to her chest,
putting another cool wet linen on the child's back. Meanwhile,
she overheard Madame de Laval quietly order the priest to be
called, as well as the king and queen.

"Give me the cup," Nicole hissed. It was now or never. The
fever needed to break now, or the child would succumb.

Philippe handed it to her and she took a full mouthful of
the concoction then closed her eyes and clamped her mouth
upon Claude's, laboring to get the maximum amount of liquid
into the babe's mouth and then stomach. Each time she followed with a gentle stroke of her finger from under the little
one's chin to the base of her throat.

Little by little, the princess accepted the mouthfuls,
unconscious and swallowing reflexively. After the last of the
cup was gone, Nicole gave Claude to the wet nurse to suck,
but the child refused. She had had enough and was now on her
way to oblivion, either temporarily or forever. Nicole stared at
Philippe as she took Claude back from the nurse.

"Is there anything else we can do?" she asked, trying to
ignore the lump forming in the back of her throat.

Philippe looked at her. "There's something you can do."

"What's that?"

"Sing to her the way you once sang to Petard. Do you
remember?"

"That was nonsense." How could he mention such a light-hearted memory at such a grave moment?

"You got the horse to come to you," he pointed out. "Get the child to come back to us now. She is wandering in her sleep. Make her wander back to you before she wanders away for good."

Nicole nodded. They had nothing to lose, so why not try?

She began to hum. Soft and low she hummed. As she did, she put her mouth up to the little one's ear and tickled it with the vibrations of her lips. She blew around the rim of Claude's ear, then behind it. As she rocked the little girl, she sang to her, and soon enough the deep resonant hum of Philippe's voice joined hers. She felt cocooned in love; she hoped the little one in her arms did, too.

As the king and queen quietly slipped into the room, Nicole put up her finger to her mouth, indicating to the queen to join in.

The queen's hum was surprisingly melodious. She came up next to Nicole and put her hand on her daughter's head. Then King Louis himself moved closer and reached out for his daughter, touching her back. Together, the four of them clustered around the sleeping child, humming and stroking her.

Just as Nicole was beginning to think they were humming farewell to the sweet princess, Claude's mouth twitched.

"Come back to us, little one. Come back, sweet girl," Nicole crooned.

A sigh escaped the child's mouth. Nicole prayed it wasn't the soul escaping the body.

"Come back, *ma chère. Maman* has good treats for you," the queen sang.

Nicole motioned for the wet nurse to come. If anyone could stimulate the child, she could, with her familiar scent and touch.

The wet nurse took Claude into her arms, and the others gathered around them, each touching a different part of the little one's body, which was now unwrapped in order to cool the fever.

"Papa has a pony for his princess," King Louis crooned, surprisingly.

At the deep sound of her father's voice, the tiny child opened her eyes and stared up at the king. This time, her eyes shone brightly, no longer glazed over with fever. They remained locked on her father's eyes. At the sight, the queen let out a cry of joy.

"Bless God," she exclaimed, crossing herself.

"Bless God," Nicole sang out, continuing to stroke the child's back. It felt less hot, almost normal. Questioningly, she looked at Philippe.

Philippe stepped closer and put his hand on the princess's forehead. At the feel of his hand, Claude began to cry—a loud, vigorous, wail of protest. It was the best sound Nicole had heard in ages. Inside she laughed to think it had taken mention of a horse to bring back the girl.

"The fever has broken," Philippe exclaimed.

"Dear God, be thanked," the queen said.

King Louis continued to gaze at his daughter, whose eyes remained on his. The love between them was like a lifeline from father to daughter, reeling the princess back to Earth.

"In the name of the Father, the Son, and the Holy Ghost," the priest intoned, making the sign of the cross over the child's forehead. He continued to pray, not with last rites, but for the princess's recovery.

"Wrap her in clean, dry cloths and allow no draft in the room," Nicole ordered. "We will see in the morning if she sucks."

The little one closed her eyes and drifted off to sleep. This time, Nicole wasn't worried that she would never again awake.

"She will be fine in the morning," she assured the queen.

"How could you know that?" the queen asked, her eyes searching Nicole's.

"Madame, I saw it myself with other living creatures." She referred to Petard, but the queen might not take kindly to hearing her daughter compared to a horse. "Once the fever is broken, if conditions are not harsh, health returns."

"I will stay here while she sleeps," Queen Anne said.

"Very good, Your Majesty." Nicole smiled at her sovereign. The child would sense her mother next to her and draw strength from her presence.

And so it was that the queen lay down on the bed with her little princess next to her and the wet nurse in attendance, as Nicole slipped out of the room behind Philippe.

"Praise God," she said to him softly.

"Praise God for you," he answered her then took her into his arms. "And in the morning we shall see if we praise God for the princess's life as well."

Hidden in an alcove of the room next to the nursery, and ready to jump up fully-clothed should the child's condition worsen, Nicole slept in Philippe's arms. Neither wished to stray far from the babe, until the next feeding time arrived and they found out if Claude would either suck or take a cup of thin porridge.

It was close to mid-morning when Nicole awoke again, her head on Philippe's chest. She rose and slipped into the nursery. The queen was gone, the princess asleep with the wet nurse next to her in the large bed. Madame de Laval stood nearby, her face serene. "Madame—is she—did she?"

"She nursed just an hour ago. Sucked as if her life depended on it," Madame de Laval said with a smile.

"And so it did," Nicole breathed out. "Thank God she is alive."

"She wore out the wet nurse, as you can see," the noblewoman gestured to the hardy woman sleeping next to Claude on the large bed. "Then we gave her some gruel, and she finished that off too."

"Bless God."

"Bless God," Madame de Laval echoed, her smile widening. Her courtier's mask had dropped, revealing a ravishing smile only a select few were honored to see. Nicole understood why the Duke d'Agincourt continued to visit.

"Bless God and bless you, my lady," a male voice added behind them. There stood Philippe, his blondish-brown hair tousled, the morning sunlight from behind streaming over him. His green eyes were shot through with gold. They moved from Madame de Laval to Nicole. She knew it was her for whom his words were meant. She would do anything to keep him in her life forever.

CHAPTER FIFTEEN

Nicole's Desire

That night, Nicole left the door to her bedchamber unlocked. She was dizzy with anticipation. Would he be the same? Would their feelings for each other be the same? What would she do if they weren't? And if they weren't, then why had she felt exactly the same way he had always made her feel when he was next to her? Thoughts swirled in her head; it was as if she were fifteen years old again. But before long the tumult of the past few days overtook her, and she slid into sleep.

The sound of the door softly opening awakened her. From her warm bed, she watched as the tall shadow slipping into her room materialized into a man. Who else could it be but the one who occupied the innermost chamber of her heart?

"Hello," Philippe greeted her.

"Hello," she replied. She couldn't see his eyes, but she knew it was him. She would know him anywhere, in her dreams, in real life. She hovered between both worlds, praying that what she was waking to was as real to him as it was to her.

"Am I welcome, my lady?"

"Have you ever not been, my lord?" The words escaped her lips before she weighed their full import. She had addressed him as her husband. Just as it had been in the past, when Philippe was near, she couldn't think clearly. Lighting the candle on the table beside her bed, she lay back and watched as he moved toward her. At her side, he knelt and raised her dangling hand to his lips.

Breathing in, her lungs filled with the bracing fresh smell of him. Could it be possible that nothing had changed in over two years' time?

"Philippe, is it you?" she whispered, reaching for him.

"You know already," he answered, taking her into his arms.

His embrace crushed her; his scent overwhelmed her. It had been ages since she had felt such a dizzying blend of emotion with sensation. She had experienced strong sensations with Gerard, but the gentler emotion that accompanied it had been one of affection. She felt overwhelming love for her daughter, but the ineffable duet of sensation with emotion she had felt with Philippe alone had been something she thought she would never know again.

"Nicole," he whispered as he rocked her in his arms. They were larger, his wrists broader, his hands now with hair on the back of them.

"I can't believe it's you," she said, although she could. Everything about him was familiar: his voice, his scent, his

eyes. Hidden depths of her that had lain dormant were spring-
ing back to life.

"I will prove it to you then," he answered, his hands shift-
ing down to each side of her waist.

The muscles of his arms grew taut. Underneath them, she
quivered. She looked up to see the gold flecks in his green eyes
that last she had seen in the late summer moonlight on a hillside
in Amboise. *Nothing has changed. Nothing.*

"Will you?" she challenged, teasingly. She caught his eyes
with hers and returned the gleam he gave her. God knew she
was gleaming inside. Every part of her being, hidden and vis-
ible, had sprung to attention and was waving wildly, awaiting
direction from the maestro of her heart.

"Will you let me, my lady?" he asked.

Of course I will. How can you ask? "I'll decide one step at a time,"
she said as carefully as she felt the opposite inside. Reckless abandon to pleasure was something she hadn't experienced in over two
years. She ached to move to its insistent drumbeat again.

Philippe drew back from her, his look holding both admiration and desire.

"Where do we begin?" he asked, his gleaming golden eyes
squinting into slits.

"Here," she told him, as she circled the base of her throat
with her right index finger.

He replaced her hand with his and under his touch, she
quivered again. Then with the 'V' of his thumb and index finger, he slid his hand up the front of her throat and stroked it
under her jaw.

"And then?"

"Where do you think?" she teased.

"My lady, two years have sculpted your subtlety," he
remarked as his hand slid to the back of her neck, reaching up
under her hair.

Without words, he had known where she wanted him to touch her next, just as he always had. He had always known the path of her desire. Indeed, he had shown it to her for the first time.

"Two years haven't changed you at all," she sighed, leaning back into his muscular fingers as they worked their way into her scalp.

"You're right. Nothing has changed. Nothing," he breathed, echoing her thoughts.

She shivered. The only man who had ever known how to read her mind was back. How to keep him there was for the next day's list of problems. For the moment, all that mattered was that he was there.

Slowly she put her hands over his and pulled them to the top of her head. As she did, Philippe's head slid down to her throat and below. With his tongue, he traced her neckline above her sleeping shift.

"And next?" This time it was her turn to ask.

"And next is my decision," he replied, his voice low.

"Oh, is it?" she asked cheekily.

"What kind of game is it if only one player sets the rules?" he asked, not unreasonably.

"My lord, I have told you I'll decide one step at a time," she rebuffed him. He had a point. Was it a game if two people didn't play by the same rules? But what rules were there anywhere that were the same for men as they were for women? Nowhere in any world she had ever known.

His warm, muscular tongue slide over her skin, and her thoughts dissolved into a place with no rules and no boundaries.

⚜

The following morning they woke as pink dawn streaked the sky, wrapped in each other's arms. It was Philippe who spoke first.

"Let me leave before the house stirs and we are found out."

"Philippe, we are not youths anymore," Nicole protested. "Neither of us is married. Who cares if anyone finds out?"

"You do," he gently reproved her. "For the sake of your future and your daughter's future."

Nicole stared at him. The youth she had loved with wild abandon had grown into a man who knew how to face responsibilities, whether they were his own or those of one he loved. His sober maturity gave her the security she needed to feel as carefree as a young girl. Fresh and rested, refreshed by love, her mind danced with inspiration. Was there not a way for them to be together?

"Philippe?"

"Yes, my love?" He stroked a strand of hair from her cheek with one sure, muscular forefinger, exactly as he had done two years earlier.

"What if a way presents itself for you to stay here?" It was as if time had stopped, as if it had only been a week or two they had been apart.

"What if the sun turns blue?" He made a wry face at her.

"Be serious!"

"My love, it is not I who has trouble being serious. That is rather your challenge." His hand moved up her face and tousled her hair.

"Be still then! I'm thinking."

"You are good at that. Almost as good as you are at not being serious."

"Shush." She closed her eyes and concentrated as her fingers drew circles on his chest. There was plentiful hair on it now, a downy field of golden brown. Grasping a handful, she pulled.

"Ouch!"

"I am working on an idea," she announced.

"You always are," he remarked dryly. "Just like the queen."

Nicole smiled. "I learned that from her."

"Such things no one learns. It is who you are." He gazed at her. "You are like her."

Nicole thought for a moment. He was right. She was like her queen. She always had been. She went after what she wanted, and she tried to get it. Sometimes she succeeded, sometimes not. But she was not a passive woman, waiting in the shadows for life to come and grab her. She went out and reached for what she wanted. And what she wanted more than anything else was this man in her life forever.

"When must you leave for Carcassonne?" she asked.

"Early in December." His face fell.

"Then give me until then to work on it."

"What will you do?" he asked.

"I have a plan."

"My lady, you always do," he observed.

"Do you love me, Philippe?" she teased him.

"I do, my lady. More than life itself." His tone was anything but teasing.

"And what weight would your love hold if you should find yourself equally titled as me and—" she caught herself "—and Blanche?"

"Then my love would weigh heavily upon you with the burdens and duties of looking after a husband." He looked at her soberly, but the twinkle in his eyes belied his serious tone.

"Well stated, my lord." Her heart danced to think of Philippe as her husband.

"I am no lord."

"You are lord of my heart, and I will see if you might become lord of something else as well." With a firm shove, she pushed him from her bed. Time was short, and the plan forming in her mind needed refining. She would get to work on it that day.

CHAPTER SIXTEEN

The Spectacle of Us

In the weeks that followed, the queen's joy rippled through the court like a spring breeze. Never before had Nicole witnessed Anne of Brittany so happy. With the birth of Charles Orland, the queen had taken more care to recover her figure and relations with the king than with her newborn's daily routine.

But with her daughter Claude it was different. Queen Anne lavished attention on the princess, attending to every detail. Until her recent fever, the child had thrived. With Claude's return to health, it would seem that the queen had given herself permission to relax; with her, so did the entire court.

Nicole watched as the queen fussed and cooed over her daughter. Something told her this princess would be the child of her queen's heart; a link to her Breton bloodline running through future rulers of France. Perhaps it was because she had almost lost her, and the queen knew childbirth loss only too well, especially the loss of infant sons. The alchemy of Queen Anne's body and live sons hadn't worked. It was unlikely it ever would.

What had worked was Anne of Brittany's ability to hold the eyes and hearts of her husbands. She held King Louis XII's esteem even more so than she had held Charles's, who had also loved her. But Louis had given her sovereign control over her ancestral lands of Brittany, something Charles had not been entirely willing to do. Nicole speculated it was because King Louis had known Queen Anne as a seven-year-old duchess being groomed and educated to take over the throne of Brittany one day. He had seen with his own eyes that his wife had been raised to rule. With a temperament suited to leadership, he had known she would wish to carry out the mandate with which she had been charged from birth. A wise husband, he had not tried to interfere with what she had been born to do.

"How is my sweet beauty?" Nicole overheard the king ask as he offered a finger to the princess one mild day in late November. The month had been unseasonably warm, as if Claude's recovery had prolonged the harvest season. It wasn't just the queen who appeared besotted with her child. The king himself couldn't stay away from the nursery, popping in several times a day to visit his daughter, and even more surprisingly, to take her from the wet nurse and allow her to gurgle and drool on his shoulder. He seemed not in the slightest perturbed that Claude had not been a son. Plans had already been laid for his daughter's betrothal to Francis, Duke de Valois, his cousin Louise de Savoy's son, who stood next in line to the throne, should he and Anne produce no sons. Whether a son came to them or not, he would see a child of his on the throne of France.

Peeking out from behind the curtain that separated the alcove from the main room, Nicole's heart warmed at the sight of the queen giving the king a radiant smile.

As she took in the sweet scene, Nicole felt arms steal around her; a hard familiar body pinned her from behind.

"She is the spectacle of us," Philippe's voice whispered into her ear. "New tunes of joy and a mighty love."

Nicole melted back into him then turned, brushing noses with the man she had loved since womanhood had first awakened in her. Philippe de Bois's eyes bored into hers, and she knew the mighty love he spoke of was not just Queen Anne's alone.

Together they peered around the curtain at the king and queen. It was as if the love they both felt for their child deepened the love between them. Nicole could sense further that the regard that the king held for the queen was based not just on the love born of their married years, but of the feelings they had held for each other in their youth.

Philippe motioned to Nicole to follow him outside. As she did, she thought of the unshakeable bond between her monarchs. She could guess at its depth and its unassailability, because she felt it herself with the one who was now leading her out into the garden. He needed a moment. She needed a lifetime. Did he as well?

The air outside was surprisingly mild. They strolled to the end of the rectangular garden then turned the corner. As they passed behind a bush, Philippe took her hand.

She giggled, just as she had two years earlier when they had escaped time and again to the hill behind the stables in Amboise. Feeling as light as Petard's breath when the horse had nuzzled her, she turned to Philippe.

Surprising her, his face was serious, his eyes only one color for once, the color of steel.

"I am due to take up my post in Carcassonne before Advent," he said shortly. With the toe of his pointed shoe, he kicked the dry dirt of the ground.

"You cannot leave! We've only just found each other," she cried.

He pulled her toward him, crushing her to his chest. "What can I do, my love? What can any of us do but obey the orders of those who rule over us?"

"We are no longer children to obey the dictates of our parents," Nicole protested. "Just follow your heart. What do you wish for, Philippe?"

His eyes swept hers, looking less grave. "Spoken like my one true love." Then his tone turned serious again. "You know I wish us to be together. But how?" he murmured, stroking her hair as she clung to him.

"Can you not find a way?" she cried. The vital, bracing scent he had had two years earlier was still there. She wanted him now, before their racing blood cooled with age. God knew her own blood had not. Not one jot.

"My lady, there is your position to think of." He paused, looking at her sternly. "I am no longer a horse-trainer, but neither am I a nobleman."

Nicole stepped back, peering up at him in the golden afternoon sun. "What do I care if you are a nobleman or not? What do you mean?" she demanded.

"I mean that you must care about your position. You are noble by birth on your mother's side, and now by marriage," he reminded her. "You must not step down from the position fortune has put you in."

"A fig for my position," she remonstrated, ripping a solitary leaf clinging to a nearby tree and crushing it in her fingers. "We are free to be with each other at last. What are you worried about?"

"I worry about you and I worry about your daughter. One day she will come of age, and you will wish to find a suitable man for her. One of noble birth." His words bit into her; she couldn't deny their wisdom. Even she herself couldn't think anything otherwise.

"Why are you talking of such things so far off in the future?" she asked. Yet he was right. As much as it meant nothing to her what rank her next husband held, as long as it was Philippe, it meant a great deal to her to see her daughter married well one day, at a level appropriate to her station in life. Blanche bore Gerard d'Orléans' noble name. If she was to bear any other name, Nicole wished it to be noble, too. Anything less would be a disservice to her child, something no good mother would willingly allow. How could she pretend to be an exception?

"My love, listen." Philippe took both of her hands in his. "Blanche is almost eighteen months old."

Nicole trembled to hear Philippe pronounce the name she had given her daughter. It was the first time she had heard Blanche's name come from his mouth. He said it so well, so measuredly, as if it was important to him.

"In another dozen years you will wish to make a match for her," he continued. "A good match." He gazed at her, his eyes shining but serious.

"How is it you know all this?" she asked. He had remembered their carefree conversations on the hillside those summers before. He knew exactly how old Blanche was. Her stomach tightened. What else did he remember?

Philippe grabbed her wrist and pulled her to him, looking down at her, the green of his eyes shot through with gold. "I know you well, *ma chère.* I remember everything. How could I forget?"

Nicole's throat tightened. "Then, my love, what is to be done?"

"My darling, if only you could make me into a nobleman, I would marry you in an instant. There is nothing more I desire. But I don't want you to lower your daughter's social station because of me. That would not be what—what—"

"What good mothers do?" she asked, silently agreeing with him.

"What good parents do," he breathed back, then crushed her to him in an embrace that told her all she needed to know.

"My lady Nicole!" a voice rang from the other side of the garden.

Quickly they separated, and Nicole moved from behind the bushes to see Cook gesturing to her.

"Yes, Cook?" *The princess. Please, God, let the princess be alright.*

"They need you back there." Cook pointed behind her with one thumb.

Nicole's heart leapt into her throat. "The babe?" She couldn't bear one more infant loss for her queen. It was as Philippe had said; Anne of Brittany represented all of them. *She is the spectacle of us.* Her joys, her losses, belonged to every one of them who served her.

"The princess is fine, my lady. 'Tis the queen who wants you. She sent one of her ladies, who found me instead."

"I'm coming." Thank God it was the queen who needed her, and not the little one. If anything happened to Princess Claude after she and Philippe had worked so hard to save her, Nicole would never feel comfortable moving ahead with plans to be with him. Her joy would be at the expense of the queen's loss; it would be unthinkable. The queen's happiness was hers, and her own happiness belonged to the queen. That was the way of it and Nicole knew there could be no other way. In her heart of hearts, she didn't want it any other way. Her life was one small thread of a tapestry, in exactly the right place to support its design. She just needed to figure out how to sew in Philippe's thread next to hers.

Nicole bent her head as she picked up her skirts to glide back to the queen's quarters. She didn't wish to share her thoughts with Cook, knowing what a mind-reader her dear old friend was.

"You can tell the doctor to come out, too," Cook commented as Nicole brushed past her. With a chuckle, the older woman reached out and gave Nicole a playful pinch on the arm.

Despite herself, Nicole broke into a giggle. Nothing could be kept secret at court for long. Apparently nothing between her and the visiting assistant physician from the South could be either. She was glad the queen had asked for her. She needed to speak with Anne of Brittany, Queen of France, as much as the queen needed to speak with her.

⚜

"What can I give you for saving my little one?" the queen asked, greeting Nicole with a warm smile. Usually Anne of Brittany maintained a certain hauteur with her ladies of honor, but after the battle they had waged together to save the princess's life, her reserve with Nicole had relaxed. The queen's eyes shone as she looked directly at Nicole. Unmistakably, gratitude lay in them.

Nicole stared back at her. There was something her sovereign could do for her, but was it too much to ask? Philippe had been clear. He would not marry her if by doing so he would reduce her social station or that of her daughter. As much as she wanted Philippe far more than she cared about maintaining her rank as the widow of a nobleman, she agreed with him that Blanche's future was at stake.

Nicole was still her parents' daughter and her queen's lady of honor. Neither her father, her long-dead mother, nor her queen would be pleased with Nicole reducing her family's social rank by marrying a commoner. Her daughter's marriage possibilities would be diminished. Nicole couldn't pretend that such an action wouldn't matter, because it would. No matter how in love she was with Philippe, her duty was to her daughter.

Something else was at stake too: Philippe's pride. Nicole knew that Philippe would not wish to present himself to her as a partner unless he could be her peer.

Nicole's mother had told her more than once that it was unwise to neglect the pride of a man. She hadn't fully understood what her mother had meant, but now she did. If she were to be Philippe's wife, her job would be to nurture and tend it. As well as she knew him, she sensed he would not rest comfortably year after year with the thought that he had brought to the marriage table a reduced status in life for his wife. As much as she might say to him it meant nothing to her, it meant something to him. And because it meant something to him, she needed to consider his feelings carefully.

Above all, both of them needed to consider Blanche. Apparently, Philippe already did. Nicole loved him even more, to see how seriously he took the future of the young girl who had arrived on Earth just three quarters of a year after he and she had parted and she had married Gerard d'Orléans. As Cook had observed countless times, women were great mysteries to everyone, most of all to themselves. It appeared that Philippe de Bois respected the mystery.

"A ruby necklace? Or a bolt of silk for a new gown ?" the queen asked, breaking into her thoughts.

"Your Majesty, it is not jewels or gowns that I desire," Nicole said slowly, hardly daring to hope she could be within reach of her heart's desire.

"Then tell me what it is. I can see by your face that there's something, so out with it." The queen looked at Nicole expectantly.

"It's not something. It is someone," Nicole began. She must tread carefully, but quickly. The queen was receptive; she wouldn't be for long. Nicole knew her sovereign liked tying up loose ends; soon enough she would have Nicole's future tied to a new husband. She needed to make her appeal now for the only one she wanted, but the risk was great. If the queen declined her direct request, that would be the end of it.

"Ohhh. And who may that someone be?" Queen Anne fingered the braided belt at her waist. It was knotted together in the style of the Order of the Cord she had founded, in which she had enlisted the young ladies she had chosen to bring to her court as maids of honor. Nicole, with her half-noble, half-common background, had been lucky to be one of them. Her father's discreet financial assistance with the queen's tapestry commission had further tipped the balance in favor of the noble side of Nicole's equation. Who was she to tilt it the other way? She was nothing if not her parents' only living child, her mother's daughter, and her queen's subject. Her identity itself would be in question if she took steps to lower it. Every shred of reason she possessed told her she mustn't willfully move down in the social order. Yet every fiber of her being told her she was meant to be with the man who owned her heart.

She took a deep breath. "Your Majesty, it's Philippe de Bois."
"Who?"

"The assistant physician, my queen. The one who worked with me to save the princess's life."

"Is he unmarried?" As always, Anne of Brittany cut to the chase.

"He is."

"Is he or has he just told you he is?" the queen probed, looking at her skeptically. She took a direct interest in the marriages of all her ladies of honor, be they maids or widows. She knew the right questions to ask and she didn't hesitate to ask them.

"He has told me he is unmarried, and I believe him," Nicole cried. How could her queen question such a thing? Then she realized her sovereign was using her head, while she had lost hers the minute Philippe had re-entered her life.

"I shall make inquiries," the queen replied. "Meanwhile, do not get too hopeful. We shall see."

"Yes, Your Majesty. I can hardly wait to find out myself," she breathed out, taking the queen's cue. It was what a good courtier did.

"Nicole, you are like a young filly these days. Do you not remember how unwilling you were the last time the king and I married you off?"

"Do you remember, Your Majesty, that I told you once that my heart was with another?"

"I remember you mooning after some youth a few years' back." The queen looked at her questioningly. Hers was not a mind that focused on small details such as the sentimental lives of her courtiers. Hers was a big-picture intellect, as large as the tapestries on the wall behind her; the ones she had commissioned but hadn't thought out how to pay for. Such details were for others, not for born rulers such as her.

"He is a man now, back from Milan where he studied medicine," Nicole continued.

"Was he not a horse-trainer sent up from Agen?" the queen asked, her back to her. She straightened a corner of the tapestry on the wall of the large receiving room then turned to Nicole with a frown that indicated she thought her suit dismissible.

"Yes, Your Majesty." Nicole's heart raced as she struggled to formulate the words that would soften the queen's heart. "He has risen in position since that time, and is free to marry. And now I am free to marry, too." Nicole loved her sovereign queen, but she knew her weak points as well as her strong ones. Anne of Brittany, Queen of France, was born to rule, not to fuss over details. Sensitivity wasn't her strong suit. Knowing how to make a decision then seeing that it got done was where she excelled. Nicole prayed she'd make the one she also wanted this time: not to marry her to a man she would grow to love, but to one she already did.

"But is this man of noble rank, *ma chère?*" the queen pressed, one eyebrow rising.

"Your Majesty, I do not care. The ones who did were my father and uncle, and they are now dead." Both Michel and Benoit St. Sylvain had succumbed to an outbreak of pestilence that had raged through Paris the winter before, the same one that had visited Blois the summer before Princess Claude had been born.

"It is not just whether *you* care," the queen chided. "You must think of your children, present and future." Her words echoed Philippe's, making Nicole's stomach churn. To be opposed by enemies was difficult but expected; to be opposed by two of the three people she loved most was unbearable.

"My daughter is already noble, and future children—" Nicole blushed. Her resolve strengthened at the thought of a future with Philippe. Now was her moment. She must seize it before the queen married her off to yet another nobleman she didn't love, or Philippe disappeared to Carcassonne, far to the South. "My sovereign, I would give my soul to have children with the man I love," she blurted out. *Or at least try to create them as frequently as possible.*

"Get a hold of yourself, Nicole. You talk like a lovesick girl. You must think with your head, not your womb," the queen replied, waving her hand in a gesture of impatience.

"You are right, Your Majesty." Nicole peered intently at her queen, her mind racing to formulate the words to argue her case. "This man has risen far from keeper of horses to assistant court physician at Carcassonne. You have the power to make him rise farther." She willed her queen to take the bait. Anne of Brittany was not hugely receptive to romantic appeals. But she was a deft master at the game of upward mobility, and Philippe de Bois had already exhibited skill in that area.

"But—" the queen hedged. She looked impatient, as if she thought her courtier had lost her mind to be besotted over a man of such lowly rank.

Quickly, Nicole made her move. "Your Majesty, did you not say when you were expecting the princess that if any one of your ladies save your coming babe from harm or death, you would grant her one request, no matter what she asks?" It was the moment to pin the queen to her promise of the spring of 1499, when she had visited Amboise with her new husband, Louis. She had been in the first blush of newly-married love, with a babe on the way. Now Nicole had just saved the child Anne had borne of that love. Perhaps never again would there be such a time when the queen was so heavily in her debt.

"My darling, I cannot make water into wine. Neither can I make one of common birth into a nobleman." The queen's rosebud mouth formed into a moue of disapproval. Her expression was disdainful, as if she thought Nicole had very bad taste.

Summoning her courage, Nicole gave her a level look. Of course, she could. It was done all the time. Anne of Brittany,

Queen of France, had a healthy ego. It was time to appeal to it. Nicole prayed for inspiration, her eyes straying from the queen's face to the wall behind her.

"Your Majesty, I see your tapestry behind you," she said, referring to the massive lady and unicorn tapestry she had posed for years earlier. It had been her father and uncle who had paid the balance on the set of tapestries the queen had commissioned after the cost had gone far over the amount King Charles had authorized her to spend. Queen Anne had been in debt to Nicole's family more than once.

The queen glanced at the massive tapestry.

"And so?" she asked brusquely. Perhaps she was a trifle embarrassed, reminded that she had needed financial assistance from Nicole's family. "I know that's you in the design. So does everyone. Your father was trying to attract the eye of a good suitor by using you as the model, and I gave him permission to do so."

"My lady, the banner next to my image bears the device of my uncle, Benoit St. Sylvain."

"Your point?" The queen looked sharply at Nicole.

Nicole raised an eyebrow. "My lady, you know even better than I how he came by our device." For once, she had succeeded in gaining her sovereign's total attention.

Benoit St. Sylvain had bought it. It wasn't the first time it had been done. Nicole was putting her own family's reputation on the line, but she would wager all to win permission to marry Philippe. She had done her duty, and married to please her family members and her queen. This time, she wished to marry to please herself if she had any chance to do so. Now was her moment to convince the queen while her sovereign's thoughts briefly lingered on her debt to Nicole's family, as well as her long ago promise to her ladies of honor.

"Your uncle was a smart man, Nicole. He knew how to get what he wanted," the queen noted.

And so do I, with you as my example. "So does Philippe de Bois," Nicole said aloud. "He looked after the king's horses in Milan. Then because of the king's notice of him, became learned in healing arts. Then, he gained a court appointment. Now he has helped save your daughter's life."

"We have recognized both him and you for doing so. What else do you want?" The queen cocked her head and narrowed her eyes at Nicole. Philippe de Bois, assistant physician to the court of Carcassonne, and Nicole St. Sylvain had been jointly awarded the honor of saving Princess Claude of France's life in a ceremony conducted the week before by the king and queen. The queen herself had been grateful beyond words to Nicole for saving the life of her daughter with her unorthodox methods.

Nicole summoned every bit of courage she possessed. She would reach beyond what was reasonable, for her heart's desire. The queen had asked her what she wanted. She would tell her.

"Can you not use your great power and influence as our queen and queen of the king's heart to find a drop of noble blood somewhere in this man's bloodline?" Nicole asked, with a confidence inspired by the woman who stood before her. Inside, she felt anything but calm, but she needed to use her head to appeal to the queen's healthy ego.

Anne of Brittany, Queen of France, scrutinized her. Nicole sensed she was finally talking her sovereign's language. The queen was businesslike in her approach to life, including love. The business of raising Philippe de Bois yet another step in the social order was a project she could sink her teeth into. And she owed Nicole. She had just said so herself.

"Your Majesty, you, above all others, know how to get things done," Nicole continued, dropping her voice. She knew her sovereign. The queen took pride in her management skills, both over Brittany and in overseeing all manner of building and artistic projects, using Italian workmen and techniques that her first husband and then her second one had brought back from each of their Milanese and Neapolitan campaigns.

The queen also took pride in having won the hearts of both her husbands. Nicole knew how satisfying it was to feel that sort of power, even more exhilarating to occasionally exercise it. It was like flexing a muscle, or washing a man's hair, feeling him helpless and vulnerable beneath one's hands.

She trembled, thinking of Philippe.

"Above all others? Even the king?" The queen looked disapproving, but also slightly pleased. Perhaps more than slightly. The way she straightened her back told Nicole she felt at ease standing above all others, despite her diminutive size, as a woman born to rule should feel.

"Especially the king, Your Majesty. The king is king of us all, but you are the queen of the king." Nicole looked directly into her queen's eyes, willing her pride to swell at such a compliment. Anne of Brittany had practiced her charms on Charles VIII, and had fully succeeded in their effect on Louis XII. Everyone knew King Louis was besotted with his wife, even more so than the former king had been.

A moment passed. Then two. The queen's eyes lifted to the magnificent tapestry on the wall of the woman with the unicorn then down again to Nicole.

"What do you see in this tapestry here?" she asked, surprising Nicole with her question. A smile played on her lips.

Nicole studied the tapestry before answering. She sensed her answer would decide whether the queen would help her or not.

The design showed a young noblewoman with flowing fair hair, holding a long blue pole with a banner attached in one hand and the horn of an elegant unicorn in the other. The unicorn looked up at the woman admiringly.

A thought flashed into Nicole's head. The woman in the tapestry wasn't her at all. It was the queen. Nicole had been the model who posed for the design. But it was the queen for whom the artist had created the tapestry, per her commission. For the first time, Nicole realized the inspiration for the scene depicted was the queen herself.

"Your Majesty, I see a woman who holds her kingdom in one hand and her king in the other," Nicole answered boldly, hoping she was not overstepping herself by suggesting the queen held power over the king. All of France knew she did, but the queen might not wish to have this pointed out to her. Then again, she might. *Have courage and be bold.* Nichole stood tall and waited, holding fast to the phrase she had often heard her father use when toasting a new business venture with his brother.

The queen studied the tapestry, unspeaking. Then she turned, her face a smooth, marble mask. Finally, she broke into a smile, as if pleased with herself.

"Tell me, how is it that this Philippe de Bois has a name with a particle in it?" She referred to the 'de' that preceded 'Bois.' "Is it that he comes from a long line of woodsmen?" Anne of Brittany's laugh trilled clear and high. It sounded like a silver bell, the sort that rang at the conclusion of a marriage ceremony.

Nicole thought quickly. The queen had cast her a line. She had no idea which of his ancestors had added the 'de' but undoubtedly it gave Philippe's surname a noble ring. Adding a 'de' was a trick used by many a merchant family that aspired to the ranks of the nobility. It meant nothing except when the 'de' was there to indicate land ownership, the basis of anyone's claim to noble roots.

"Your Majesty, it is possible that he comes from a line of landowners of some forests down South," Nicole ad-libbed.

"Landed blood, perhaps?" The queen's mouth twitched. She was either mocking her or deep in thought.

"Quite possibly, Your Majesty." Nicole held her breath.

"If he was of noble stock, his parents would have made sure the world knew of it," the queen observed.

"His parents are dead. He's been orphaned since boyhood, looked after by Jeannot of Agen, who ran the stables down there."

"Ahh, Jeannot of Agen, and, before that, of Nantes." The queen's face lit up. "He ran the stables for my father when I was a girl. He, too, was an orphan."

"An orphan, Your Majesty. Think of it!" Nicole cried from her heart. How well the queen knew what it meant to be an orphan, she who had lost her mother at age nine, her father at age eleven, and her sister and only sibling, Isabeau, one year later.

"He was good with the horses, so my father favored him. After his parents died, he took him on as his ward," the queen remarked, fingering the lower border of the tapestry.

"My queen, you know then what a good man Jeannot was. He looked out for Philippe, but there was only so much he could do." *Thank God he sent him to Amboise in his place so that we might meet.*

"So there was no one to see to his interests when he was young, other than the stable-manager." The queen looked thoughtful.

"Your Majesty, there was no one at all, other than your husband, good King Louis, who noticed Philippe's talents in Milan and sent him to study medicine." Nicole's blood raced to think that the queen knew of Jeannot from childhood. It would warm her heart to protect the interests of his ward, just as Jeannot had been a ward of her own father, Duke Francis of Brittany.

"So my husband set him up for a profession," the queen mused. A puzzle had been handed her; she loved puzzles, but only ones worth working on. Had Nicole convinced her that this one was?

"As you can set him up for a social position," Nicole added.

"I told you before, I cannot change water into wine," the queen parried. The crease in her forehead told Nicole she was deep in thought.

Nicole took a long breath. This was her last chance. "Your Majesty, in this case, you may find wine in the flask already," she said, keeping her voice low but clear. As a good courtier, she would suggest, then let her sovereign lead.

"Might I?" The queen fingered the knotted cord of her belt. Nicole knew that gesture. It meant Anne of Brittany was working something out in her formidable brain.

"Your Majesty, with your talents, you might discover noble roots for Philippe's family name." The queen respected strength. Anything less she would see as weakness, to be tossed away.

Holding herself tall, Nicole closed her eyes and saw her queen's image as the petite but proud fourteen-year-old ruler of Brittany, defending her besieged city of Rennes from the king of France while she charmed him into handing over his heart to her.

"Wait for what I find out, and we shall see," the queen finally said.

"Yes, Your Majesty." Nicole knelt and took her sovereign's hand, laying it on her forehead. The queen was the type of person who got things done. Nicole didn't doubt she wouldn't wait long for whatever outcome was decided. "And thank you."

"Don't thank me. Thank my babe for putting your stableboy on the map." With a wave of her hand, Anne of Brittany, Queen of France, indicated their conversation was over.

CHAPTER SEVENTEEN

Love's Tapestry

"She knew Jeannot?" Philippe's voice caught in his throat as he uttered the name of the man who had been like a father to him. They stood just inside the door of Nicole's bedchamber, facing each other in the candlelight. Philippe had slipped in without a sound, but Nicole had been waiting. She had known he would come. The start of Advent was less than a fortnight away. Their remaining time together was short. Unless something was done.

"Yes," she breathed. "Her face lit up when I mentioned him. You should have seen her!"

"I hope we will have occasion to speak of him before I go back," Philippe mused.

"Don't talk of going back! Your life is here with me!" she cried, pummeling his chest. *And Blanche.*

"A man's life is where his appointment takes him," he corrected her, gently taking her wrist and kissing it.

"Then let us find you an appointment here," she argued.

"That is easier said than done," he observed.

"So let us work on the doing!" she cried.

"My love," he reached out and squeezed her shoulder, steadying her. His eyes were opaque, veiled. Did a trace of sadness shadow them? "Tell me more of what she said about my master."

"She said he was a favorite of her own father's in Nantes."

"You mean the good Duke Francis?" he asked, referring to the queen's long-dead father, Francis II, Duke of Brittany.

"Yes! She said he liked your Jeannot, and when his parents died, he took him on as ward because he handled the horses so well."

"Jeannot told me that Duke Francis had a love of horses," Philippe said, his face wistful.

"And so does his daughter, our queen. Think of how much she loved Petard!" The stallion was no longer alive, but he had been among the queen's favorites of all the horses in both of her husbands' stables.

"Aye. She must have gotten it from her father," Philippe agreed, breaking into a smile at mention of Petard.

"If it wasn't for your Jeannot sending you to Amboise in his place, I would never have met you," Nicole cried.

"'Tis strange, because Jeannot hadn't wanted me to go. It was I who convinced him."

"Why did you want to leave home?" she asked, one finger tracing the line of his collarbone. It was unbearable to think she would no longer be able to touch him in just a few short weeks.

Twice before, he had been yanked from her life. It couldn't happen again.

"I was ready for something—for something different." His muscles rippled under her touch.

"What do you mean?"

"I mean I wanted to not be treated like a boy anymore. With Jeannot master of the stables in Agen, there was no chance for me to become master there myself."

"A boy has to leave home to become a man, doesn't he?" Nicole remarked. She knew so little of boys. But she could imagine if they were to turn into men, they would need to set out on their own.

"Maybe he does." He paused. "There was something else, too."

"What was it?" she asked, remembering her own feelings of that summer. At age fifteen, something new had fluttered inside her, with no clear direction; until she spotted Philippe and her feelings had flown toward the youth with mutable eyes.

"I felt new things. But I didn't know what they were." He looked at her. "You know."

"I know! Oh yes, I know exactly." How well she remembered the excitement of that spring. She had yearned for something, but had had no idea what. Then Philippe had come along, and all of her unmoored longings had merged into a single quivering focus.

"So I wanted to learn more, but how could I, with Jeannot and all the men around watching me, making jokes and putting the kitchen girls in my path, watching to see what a fool I would make of myself?" he said wryly.

"We all make fools of ourselves at that age! I could barely talk when I first met you," she exclaimed.

"Your memory serves wrong, my lady. You did most of the talking, while I was doing the looking." His eyes glinted in the candlelight.

"I was looking, too, Philippe." All the fire and energy she'd felt at age fifteen was back, racing through her veins. She laced her hands around her true love's neck and drew his face down to hers.

CHAPTER EIGHTEEN

The Queen's Decision

After mass the following Sunday, Nicole trailed the royal retinue out of the chapel. The early December day was mild, the sun warm on her face. Marie de Volonté walked at her side, serene and content. Her son had been born a few months earlier. Nicole was grateful to God that He had spared the life of her friend's husband, Guillaume de Montforet, who had suffered a broken leg but nothing more the day of Gerard's death. She was also grateful for whatever part she had played in convincing Marie to keep her babe when she had thought to thwart its journey to the world the winter before.

If only Nicole could feel as happy for herself as she felt for Marie. But Philippe was due to take up his post in Carcassonne within the week. It hung heavy over her, like a looming specter waiting to whisk away her happiness, as it had been whisked away from her before.

"*A ma vie,*" she whispered under her breath. "To my life" wasn't just her queen's motto. Nicole had taken it as her own. Now she clung to it in hopes that the queen would understand and respond.

"Nicole, come walk with me," Queen Anne commanded.

"Yes, Your Majesty," Nicole exclaimed, hastening her step to join her. Her heart panged as she saw the queen limp, then catch herself.

Nicole was one of the few who knew of the queen's hip deformity. She had assisted with her sovereign's wardrobe and toilette for years and had seen with her own eyes that one of Anne of Brittany's hipbones rested higher at the base of her torso than the other. The petite queen's slightest of limps was only evident when she was tired or thought no one watched. Whenever Nicole saw it, love for her sovereign squeezed her heart.

"Your physician friend . . ." the queen began.

My love. "Yes. Philippe." Nicole trembled. Whatever her sovereign decided, she would be hard-pressed to challenge. She was under obligation to her queen for her position at court and her good marriage. But beyond duty, Nicole loved and respected her. She would have no choice but to submit if the woman she most admired dismissed her petition.

"Philippe de Bois," the queen continued.

"Your Majesty!" Nicole's heart flopped like a fish to think of the queen's words to come. "Did you find out something about him?"

The queen frowned, and looked at Nicole thoughtfully. "It is not entirely good."

"What do you mean, my lady?" She was taken aback. Whatever it was, Philippe was the love of her life. That she knew already and was powerless to change, whatever the news might be.

"I mean he has lived a strange life," the queen remarked.

"How so, Your Majesty?" Alarm quickened her blood.

"He was in Milan for almost two years, is what I heard."

"Yes. He studied medicine there at the bidding of your good husband, King Louis."

"Yes, my lord is a good husband." The queen smoothed her hands down over her hips, looking fresh and fully in love. Perhaps the king had been an especially good husband the night before. "But that is what your stable-hand-turned doctor has not been," she mused.

"Your Majesty, I don't understand." Cold beads of sweat broke out on Nicole's forehead. Foreboding clawed at her.

"He has not been a good husband," the queen replied.

"My lady, what do you mean?" Nicole's heart froze. She would die if she found out he was married. He had told her the widow had wed another. Was there another woman to whom he had bound himself? To be so near yet unable to finally come together would be too cruel. Yet the woman before her had borne more, and she was Nicole's role model. Squeezing her hands together as if to crush any bad news, she prayed she would not be asked by God to follow in her sovereign's footsteps.

The queen's face was stern. "He has not been a husband at all," she spelled out.

"My lady, that is good news, is it not?" Nicole's knees wobbled from relief.

"A man of no experience is hardly a fit partner for a widowed mother." The queen pursed her lips.

"Your Majesty, he told me this history himself, and he had his reasons."

"What were they?" The queen's eyes searched hers.

Nicole blushed. Heat crawled over her face.

"Ahhh. I gather there was one in particular," the queen observed.

"Yes, my lady." Nicole looked at the ground. "He was devastated when I married Gerard."

"You must think carefully, my dear. Marriage is not romance. Marriage is a contract that only works well when partners are equally yoked," the queen counseled her.

"Yes, Your Majesty." With a sinking heart, Nicole realized the queen had made the same point that Philippe had. It was true. Marriage between her and Philippe wouldn't work unless they came together as equals. If Philippe remained a commoner, he would feel less of a man at Nicole's side, with endless stares and whispers from those at court judging him a nobody. And Nicole would feel a certain sting each time a candidate for her daughter's hand slipped away, once Blanche's stepfather's social background was examined and found wanting. She prayed the queen had hit upon a way to raise Philippe in rank.

"I question trusting a man who has studied to become a doctor. It is such a useless profession," the queen continued.

"Your Majesty, his skills were formed from healing horses." Well Nicole knew the queen's loathing of physicians. She blamed them for not saving Charles Orland or knowing what to do when her newborns had died, one after the other.

"Now, handling horses is a practical skill." The queen's eyes lit up at the mention of one of her favorite subjects.

"He is a man who learned the healing arts from living creatures, not from books," Nicole exclaimed. The queen loved books, but when it came to arranging marriages, she looked for practical skills along with assets.

"He may now be ruined from all that adventure abroad and medical book-learning. It will take a patient mistress to harness him to the ways of married life."

"Your Majesty, I am such a one. Truly!" Nicole pleaded.

"You are not patient at all," the queen scoffed, "but I remember how good you were with Petard." Her eyes softened at mention of the black stallion.

"I loved him. He was a fine horse," Nicole recalled. The queen was right. She wasn't the patient type. She was the get-it-done type, just like her sovereign queen. Now was the moment to reach for her goal.

"He was not easy to handle. You were one of the only ones who knew how to manage him. How did you do it?"

"I used a few tricks, Your Majesty."

"Playful ones, I'd wager."

"Exactly so, Your Majesty." She smiled inside to think of the made-up songs she had sung to Petard. Would she ever feel so light-hearted again?

"Because that is exactly you. I know you, Nicole," the queen remarked. She extended a gold-bejeweled hand and smoothed down the cloth of Nicole's headdress. "No one can be what they are not. You are not patient, but playful and full of imagination. You would need your full set of skills to tame a man who has seen the world, yet never felt the bridle of marriage laid on him."

"My lady, I am the one for the job. Please say you would bless our match if he, if we—"

"You want a stable-hand for your second husband?" the queen's eyes grew wide, boring into hers. It looked as if she was trying to determine whether Nicole really meant her words, or was just acting on romantic impulse.

"I want Philippe de Bois for my husband. No one else." Nicole kept her voice clear and strong. She was as sure of what she wanted as she was unsure of whether she would get it. *Have courage and be bold.* Her father's words steadied her as she tried to remain calm. Michel St. Sylvain had applied those principles to his business dealings. Her mother had applied them to her healing methods as well as her personal life, the one that had begun before meeting Nicole's father. Blanche St. Sylvain had seized the reins of her own happiness, and so would Nicole. *A ma vie,* she intoned silently as Philippe's image sprang into her mind. He was her life. She wanted him in it forever.

The queen took a deep breath, and let it out. "I have discovered one other thing," she continued.

"What is it, Your Majesty?" She steeled herself for the queen's response.

"It seems that your Philippe de Bois is the son of Marguerite de Gascon, whose natural father was a chevalier at the court of Gascoigne."

"Madame, do you mean Philippe is of noble lineage?" A tingle shot up Nicole's back.

"On the wrong side of the sheets, *ma chère.* You know what I mean, do you not?" The queen gave her a level look.

Nicole tried to match her gaze. "Yes, Your Majesty, I do." How well she knew.

But the king has studied the situation," the queen continued, "and . . ."

"And?" Nicole grasped the knotted cord of the belt she wore, as if it were a lifeline. Was Anne of Brittany, Queen of France, now tossing her one?

"And, due to the great love he feels for the princess and the physician's help in saving her life, he has decided . . ." The queen paused and looked at Nicole gravely. Despite her severity, the twinkle in her eye made Nicole's heart leap.

"Your Majesty, tell me!"

". . . to award your Philippe the title of Chevalier de Bois, and offer him a position here as assistant court physician."

"My queen!" Her sovereign had worked on her behalf. When Anne of Brittany, Queen of France, threw her weight to a project, it got done.

"I can't stand the one we already have, so it would be good to bring on someone we trust. A man who has worked with horses will be far more valuable than any of those quacks with their heads stuck in books," the queen went on.

"Your Majesty, does this mean you give your permission for us to marry if he is so inclined?"

"He helped you save my child. You may have him." The queen's smile was warm, melting Nicole's heart.

"Your Majesty, thank you!" She held out both hands to her sovereign, palms up.

"Don't thank me; thank my daughter for bringing him to you." The queen took Nicole's hands in hers and squeezed.

"I do, Your Majesty. I do! And if ever we have another daughter, we shall name her after you," Nicole burst out. She was beside herself with happiness.

The queen stared at Nicole a moment, a curious expression on her face. Finally, she released her hands and spoke. "Are you not thinking of having a son one of these days?"

"I shall have daughters as long as you have them, Your Majesty." *I shall have whatever comes with my one true love.*

"Fine. You already have a grown-up boy to train, and that should be quite enough. Now go and let him know you have our blessing."

"Your Majesty, I shall wait to see what his offer is before I give him such good news," Nicole said, overjoyed, but remembering her dignity.

The queen put her hand on Nicole's shoulder and squeezed it tenderly. "My dear, his offer is already in. Our king gave him the news of his knighthood last night. After thanking him, the Chevalier de Bois asked for permission to seek your hand. I told him if you were willing to take on an untrained man at your age, you could have him. He is waiting to hear from you now."

"My lady, I will go to him and hear his words. None will pass my lips until he proposes."

"You are a clever one, *ma chère*. No wonder your stableboy could not forget you. You played coy with him, as you did Petard, and made him come to you, did you not?"

"Perhaps I did, my lady." It hadn't been intentional. It had been as spontaneous and genuine as first love always was. And now love's never-quenched embers had sparked into flame again.

"One other thing," the queen added.

"Yes, Your Majesty?"

"You neglected to tell me that you had already begun work on a family with your Philippe."

"I neglected—I did—how did you . . ." Nicole felt her face flushing red, as red as it had ever flushed before.

The queen's eyes twinkled. *"If ever we have another daughter* . . ." she intoned, repeating Nicole's words.

"Did I say that?" Nicole stammered, helpless in the face of her queen's penetrating gaze. "What was I thinking?"

The queen's laugh trilled through the December air, warming all around her. She put her hand up to Nicole's face and stroked her cheek.

"You were not thinking at all, my dear. You were feeling your heart's desire coming true."

"I —you—but—"

The queen placed one slim finger on Nicole's lips, silencing her. Her smile told Nicole nothing more needed to be said.

"Go find your stallion and make him behave." Anne of Brittany, Queen of France, dismissed her with a regal hand then walked away. This time, with no limp.

.

BIBLIOGRAPHY

Brock, Emma L, *Little Duchess*. Eau Claire, Wisconsin: E.M. Hale and Company, 1948.

Butler, Mildred Allen, *Twice Queen of France: Anne of Brittany*. New York: Funk & Wagnalls, 1967.

Chevalier, Tracy, *The Lady and the Unicorn*. New York: Plume, 2005.

Cushman, Karen, *Matilda Bone*. New York: Dell Yearling, 2000.

Davis, William Stearns, *Life on a Mediaeval Barony*. New York: Harper & Brothers, 1923.

De la Warr, Countess, Constance, *A Twice Crowned Queen*. London: Eveleigh Nash, 1906.

Eco, Umberto, *The Name of the Rose*. New York: Harcourt, 1994.

Greco, Gina L. & Rose, Christine M., translated by, *The Good Wife's Guide: Le Ménagier de Paris, A Medieval Household Book*. Ithaca and London: Cornell University Press, 2009.

Gregory, Philippa, *The Lady of the Rivers*. New York: Simon & Schuster, 2011.

Jogournel, Thierry, *Anne de Bretagne: Du Duché au Royaume*. Rennes: Éditions OUEST-FRANCE, 2014.

Michael, of Kent, Princess, Her Royal Highness, *The Serpent and the Moon*. New York: Touchstone, 2004.

Morison, Samuel Eliot, *Admiral of the Ocean Sea: A Life of Christopher Columbus*. New York: Little, Brown and Company, 1942.

Reed, Joseph J., *Anne of Brittany: A Historical Sketch*. New York: Graham's American Monthly Magazine of Literature, Art, and Fashion, June 1858.

Sanborn, Helen Josephine, *Anne of Brittany, The Story of a Duchess and Twice-Crowned Queen*. Memphis: General Books, 2012.

Siraisi, Nancy G., *Medieval and Early Renaissance Medicine: An Introduction to Knowledge and Practice*. Chicago: University of Chicago Press, 1990.

Tanguy, Geneviève-Morgane, *Sur les pas de Anne de Bretagne*. Rennes: Éditions OUEST-FRANCE, 2015.

Tourault, Philippe, *Anne de Bretagne*. Paris: Perrin, 2014.

Tuchman, Barbara W., *A Distant Mirror*. New York: Alfred A. Knopf, 1978.

Vieil-Castel, Alex., *Je Suis . . . Anne de Bretagne*. Paris: Hoche Communication S.A.S., 2015.

BOOK CLUB DISCUSSION QUESTIONS

1. Which relationship shapes Nicole's life more: her love for Philippe or her love for Anne of Brittany, Queen of France?

2. What do you think was the property in the moldy bread that helped heal first the queen's stallion and then her infant daughter, Princess Claude?

3. How is the tug between love and duty managed by the ladies of honor of the court of Anne of Brittany, Queen of France? How do they support each other in managing their private lives versus public ones?

4. What do you think contributed to the queen's repeated pregnancy failures and childbirth losses?

5. How was the first year of life handled differently in the 1490s than it is today?

6. What qualities did Anne of Brittany, Queen of France, possess to renew her hopes each time one of her children died?

7. What role does Marie de Volonté play in Nicole's life? How are the two women alike? How are they dissimilar?

8. *A ma vie*, "to my life," is Anne of Brittany, Queen of France's, motto. What is its meaning?

9. Do we ultimately know who the father of Blanche is: Gerard d'Orléans or Philippe de Bois? Does it matter?

ACKNOWLEDGMENTS

Deepest thanks to Atessa Helm, Annette and Alexa Jackson, Maddie Graham, Leslie Prentice Henry, Kim Huther, Beverley Piturro, and Allison Roesser for their critical feedback, and unflagging passion for *Sense of Touch*. And to Leslie M. Ficcaglia, talented portraitist and Catherine Delloue for their artistic eyes. Without you this tale would not have reached readers. Thanks also to Jamie Abruzzo, Yewande Akintelu-Omoniyi, Pat Andres, Jina Bacarr, Dawn R. Bacso, Yvonne Muciek Baker, Zsuzsanna Ballai, Gloria Balogh, Jan Bandura, Rick Bannerot, Devra Barrett, Karina Bravo, Magdi Bukovec, Brandon Bluhm, Alma Caparas, Rachel Carr, David Cascino, Renee Victoria Corl, Margi Aranyos Coles, Elizabeth Csordas, Emilie Davis, Melissa Thomas DiPlacido, Gregory and Paula Nagy, Ilona Kimberley Nagy, Ramona Calin, Remy Cook, Barbara Crawford, William Daley, Catherine Delloue, Gabriela Donescu, Andrea Eckerle, Elizabeth Fisher, Donna Ford, Linda Fuller, Candy Fryer, Sofia Gabor, Dennis Gagomiros, David Gibbs, Eshe Gimbya, Barbara Goldberg, Judy Green, Cynthia Gyurgic, Heidi Hadwick, Carolyn Hahn, Heidi Hamilton, Judy Kekes Harden, Ashley Harris, Linda Hanf Higgens, Craig Hart, Amora Nigella Hawthorne, Cricket Iceblade, Karen Jablonsky, Shannon Hall Jones, Matt Kachur, Ariana Csonka Kaleta, Susan Karpati, Fran Kimberley-Ironside, Elizabeth Kiraly, Gordon Little, Rebecca Lowry, Clarissa Marie, Anne Martine, Argelie Ponce, Thomas Pozsgay, Mary Wirth, Paula Crewe, Maria Urban, Jena Rose Johnson, Meg Kaicher, Tony Kayoumi, Vera King, Ilona Kiss, Istvan Kolnhofer, Rita la Rosa, Karen

Leger, Dominic Lombardo, Debra Olivera Lopes, Farie Makuto, Angela Manassy McGraham, Dana Mattson, Kathleen McBrien, Sean Moore, Ilona Kimberley Nagy, Romy Nordlinger, David Quinn, Toby Oliver, Gretchen Pingel, Susie Piturro, Erica de Pool, Andrea Rafael, Marilyn Roos, Ashlyn Ross, Kellie Rush, Laurence Siegel, Kevin Shelton-Smith, Wendy Sigurdson, Monica Bella Slonaker, Nan Smith, Joy Stocke, Mandi Sussman, Emma Szalay, Catherine Thomas, Dorothy Thompson, Edith Annette Torres, Nicole Tuck, Shon Tyler, Susan Unger, Maria M. Varga, Antonio Varrenti, Margaret Vitrano, Peggy Wager, Liz Weidlich, Diane Whitmore, Victoria Winter, Barbara Wisdom, Allison Wolf, Amy Wolf, Easter Yi, Magda Zentai, Kata Zwiefel.

ABOUT THE AUTHOR

Rozsa Gaston writes playful books on serious matters, including the struggles women face to get what they want out of life. In addition to *Sense of Touch* she is the author of *Paris Adieu, Black is Not a Color, Running from Love, Dog Sitters*, and *Lyric*.

Gaston studied European intellectual history at Yale and received her masters in international affairs from Columbia.

Gaston has worked as a singer and pianist all over the world. After leaving the entertainment industry she worked at *Institutional Investor*, then as a hedge funds marketer. She lives in Bronxville, New York, with her family and is currently working on *Anne of Brittany: Girl Who Ruled a Country*, the sequel to *Sense of Touch*.

Gaston can be found online on Facebook at https://www.
facebook.com/rozsagastonauthor, or at her website, http://
www.rozsagaston.com/. Her motto? Stay playful.

CHAPTER ONE

Duchess of Brittany, Age 11

"THE DUKE IS dead; long live the Duchess," rang from the courtyard below as the two girls watched from the balcony of the castle of Coiron. They looked at each other, the older one grave, the younger offering a wan smile to her sister.

"You are the Duchess now, Anne. What will you do?" Isabeau asked, her pale face tight with worry. A tear inched down her cheek.

"I will rule, of course. As Papa would have wanted. And *Maman* too." The older girl brushed away her sister's tear then straightened herself as she turned to face the group gathering below. Her pointed chin jutted out as she held herself high.

Raising a small white hand, she stepped forward and acknowledged the men, women, and children below, craning their necks to catch sight of their new ruler.

The roar of allegiance that went up pleased her, despite her grief. She nodded to the crowd, acutely aware that however she presented herself to the people of Brittany in these first days after her father's death would be pivotal to ensure their support.

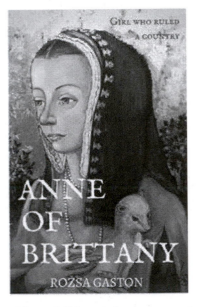

ANNE OF BRITTANY

ROZSA GASTON

It wasn't hard to ask for it. She loved the Breton people, their hardy, indomitable and honest spirit. Gladly, she would guide them as their leader. If only the nobles in between her and her people could curb their fighting and unite to repel the French invaders.

Her father's position had not been particularly strong in the last years of his reign; neither had that of any of the other nobles jockeying for position to challenge him. But Anne, as Duke Francis's eldest child was the only one legally invested with the succession of Brittany; therein lay her advantage. She would make sure the common people were reminded again and again of her legal claim to rule the land so that they would support her. Her tools would be her royal bearing as well as her love for them. Her arms would be her ability to enlist the nobles loyal to Brittany to bear arms for her. Otherwise, her Duchy would be swallowed up by its larger, more powerful neighbor France.

To begin, she would stand tall and show her people their new ruler: no tears, no sad face. She would work out the rest step by step.

Her expression regal, Anne slowly backed into the room, careful to tiptoe on her right foot. No one must see her limp; no one would. Her father had taught her to carefully conceal the limp caused by one of her hipbones resting higher than the other. She had spent enough time accompanying him to meetings with his advisors to know that those just a step removed from power would be the first to pounce at the slightest indication of weakness. There would be none from her.

Cover image of painting by Anca Visdei, 2013

ALSO BY ROZSA GASTON

"With vivid detail and humor, *Paris Adieu* takes readers straight into the heart of Paris."
—*Wild River Review*

"A compelling, entertaining, and deftly crafted read from first page to last."
—*Midwest Book Review*

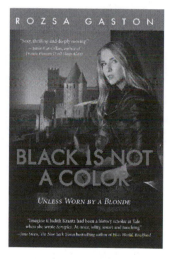

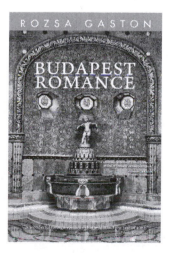

A "thoughtful romance."
—*Publishers Weekly*

39781539R00181